PRAISE
AND THE SAV

"This long-running ~~~~~~~~~ ~~~~~~~~ ~~~~~~~~~ nty
of humor into the mystery and heightens interest
with the frame story concerning rare genetic
diseases. And, of course, the larger-than-life
Savannah continues to delight."
—*Booklist*

"Clever banter adds levity to an emotionally
taxing mystery, and Savannah's Granny Reid
offers her earthy wisdom and a shoulder to cry
on. Fans of darker cozies will be well satisfied."
—*Publishers Weekly*

BURIED IN BUTTERCREAM
"A wonderful edition to the series."
—*Suspense Magazine*

CORPSE SUZETTE
"Savannah's as feisty as ever."
—*Kirkus Reviews*

MURDER À LA MODE
"Added to a well-plotted mystery, the very funny
depiction of a different side of reality television
makes *Murder á la Mode* a delight."
—*Mystery Scene*

PEACHES AND SCREAMS
"A luscious heroine, humor, and down-home
characters."
—*Library Journal*

Books by G.A. McKevett

SAVANNAH REID MYSTERIES

GRANNY REID MYSTERIES

Published by Kensington Publishing Corporation

G.A. McKevett

Bitter BREW

A SAVANNAH REID MYSTERY

KENSINGTON BOOKS
www.kensingtonbooks.com

To the extent that the image or images on the cover of this book depict a person or persons, such person or persons are merely models, and are not intended to portray any character or characters featured in the book.

KENSINGTON BOOKS are published by

Kensington Publishing Corp.
119 West 40th Street
New York, NY 10018

Copyright © 2018 by G.A. McKevett and Kensington Publishing Corporation

All rights reserved. No part of this book may be reproduced in any form or by any means without the prior written consent of the Publisher, excepting brief quotes used in reviews.

If you purchased this book without a cover, you should be aware that this book is stolen property. It was reported as "unsold and destroyed" to the Publisher and neither the Author nor the Publisher has received any payment for this "stripped book."

All Kensington titles, imprints and distributed lines are available at special quantity discounts for bulk purchases for sales promotion, premiums, fund-raising, educational or institutional use. Special book excerpts or customized printings can also be created to fit specific needs. For details, write or phone the office of the Kensington Special Sales Manager: Kensington Publishing Corp., 119 West 40th Street, New York, NY, 10018. Attn. Special Sales Department. Phone: 1-800-221-2647.

Kensington and the K logo Reg. U.S. Pat. & TM Off.

ISBN-13: 978-1-4967-2011-5
ISBN-10: 1-4967-2011-3
First Kensington Hardcover Edition: May 2019
First Kensington Mass Market Edition: April 2020

ISBN-13: 978-1-4967-2012-2 (ebook)
ISBN-10: 1-4967-2012-1 (e-book)

10 9 8 7 6 5 4 3 2 1

Printed in the United States of America

*Although Halstead's and Novak's are fictitious diseases,
other fatal, genetic disorders are all too real.*

*This book is dedicated to the people, and their families,
who battle these terrible illnesses.*

*With weakening bodies, but mighty spirits, and
inspiring courage,
they do what we all should. . . .*
They live every day as though it was their last.

Thank you, Leslie Connell, for everything, always. I wish I could clone you and give a copy of you to every author and person who needs a loving friend.

I also wish to thank all the fans who write to me, sharing their thoughts and offering endless encouragement. Your stories touch my heart, and I enjoy your letters more than you know. I can be reached at:

sonja@sonjamassie.com
and
facebook.com/gwendolynnarden.mckevett

Chapter 1

Savannah Reid wasn't sure how she had pictured this wedding anniversary, the sacred celebration that would mark a year of wedded bliss to the love of her life, her soul mate, her blessed helpmate. But this certainly wasn't it.

True, Dirk wasn't the most romantic husband in the world—or even on the block. On their side of the street. Among the white, stucco houses with red tiled roofs. With a magnolia tree in the front yard.

When it came to planning a date night or buying a present, he tended to do the absolute minimum. Just enough to avoid matrimonial strife. Barely.

Their first Christmas gift-giving effort as a married couple had proven disastrous. For some reason, which he couldn't imagine, she had been less than thrilled with her new lawnmower. Pointing out the bonus trash bag-grade cover and the fact that it was a manual, push-reel model and didn't use "all that expensive gas" hadn't sweetened the package. Go figure.

Dirk was overjoyed with his beer-making kit, until he read the directions and realized that it was a bit more complicated than stirring a Kool-Aid packet into a jug of water.

Savannah had wound up making the brew herself—a major nuisance that took eight weeks. When it was finally ready, he sampled it and pronounced it, "Flat and tastes like cat piss."

In the interest of giving and receiving something that they actually wanted, and to avoid arguments about who might or might not have actually tasted feline urine over the course of their lifetime, he and she had decided that, rather than give each other one large thing, they would give each other several little things.

Hopefully, this would improve the odds of getting something one actually wanted, since "It's the thought that counts" didn't seem to account for much in the Reid/Coulter household.

At his insistence, she had shopped for him *and* herself online. It took a three-day weekend for her to read all the reviews of possible products, consider how many stars it had been given by how many users, and, after figuring in the various shipping costs, calculate the best bargain bangs for their bucks.

Once the research was finished, she had ordered the merchandise with her personal credit card, then collapsed into her comfy chair and consumed most of a box of chocolate truffles with some strong coffee, trying to recoup her normally cheerful spirit—the state of mind that did not include fantasies of strangling husbands.

When the boxes containing her things arrived, she placed them into his outstretched hand.

With a mighty sigh of soul-deep exhaustion, he shoved some cash into her bra and asked, "Am I gonna have to suffer through all this rigamarole again on Valentine's Day? Whatcha say we skip the presents crap and just fool around a little longer than usual?"

So much for domestic tranquility.

Considering their history and his memory lapses concerning romantic milestones, she had drawn an enormous red heart on the calendar on the kitchen wall, marking their anniversary. That way, a guy who could remember the month, day, and time of the next Light Heavyweight championship fight and the winning numbers of last Wednesday's Powerball, would have no excuse. As the day approached and the "Whaddaya want?" question hadn't been asked, she'd gone online, once again, picked out a book, some chocolate, and a stress-reducing meditation download for herself, along with his things.

Then she told him that his shopping was finished, the stuff was on its way, and she gave him the total owed. He'd been so grateful that she could've sworn she'd seen tears in his eyes, as he'd shoved the money down her blouse.

Someday, she would mention that she'd much prefer to have the cash placed in her hand rather than poked into her bra, Barbary Coast hooker-style. But it could wait. She hated to spoil a tender moment between a husband and his wife.

Now, sitting in her favorite chair, her two black cats on the footstool, curled warmly around her feet, she waited for Detective Sergeant Dirk Coulter to come home, so they could begin their anniversary festivities, whatever those might be.

A rooftop stakeout of a suspected drug house had kept him far longer than he had estimated. Having been a police officer herself at one time, Savannah knew all too well that part of carrying a detective's gold shield included the "joy" of never knowing when one's tour would end.

"You knew what you were getting into, Savannah girl," she whispered. They were words usually spoken by her sage grandmother.

The cats at her feet looked up at her, their pale green eyes glowing with anticipation.

When Mom spoke, there was always a chance that some sort of food treat might be forthcoming.

"Gluttons," she told them. "Always thinking about food. You'd eat treats for breakfast, lunch, and dinner, if I'd let you."

She recalled one of the packages the UPS man had delivered—a cardboard box with dark chocolate truffles inside. The container that, along with its sister package, was not-very-secretly stashed behind the recliner upstairs in the guest bedroom, otherwise known as Dirk's "man cave." That was where he tossed the parcels containing her gifts, once she handed them to him. There they would stay, gathering dust, until the day arrived, when he would dig them out and proudly present them to her.

She looked at the grandfather clock in the corner. "It's almost eight, and I'm about to pass out from hunger," she told the cats. "If that boy doesn't show up soon, I'm gonna go find that box of chocolates and have them for supper."

At that moment, she heard the jingling of keys and the front door lock turning. One of the kitties, Cleopatra, sprang off the stool and headed for the foyer, tail twitching.

Savannah looked down at Cleo's sister, Diamante, who was watching her sibling's departure, black nose lifted with an air of contempt.

"I know," Savannah told Di. "She's plumb pitiful, a real daddy's girl, a sucker for a deep voice."

"Hey, how's my pretty girl?" came a male voice from the foyer as Cleo greeted her master by the door.

A warm, pleasant sensation trickled through Savannah. Cleo wasn't the only female in the house who was a sucker for a rough, tough guy with a bass tone and a soft spot for kitties.

She rose from her cushy chair, smoothed her blouse, fluffed her hair, and walked to the foot of the stairs and the guest closet, where force of habit predicted that her husband would be hanging his coat and stowing his Smith & Wesson and holster on the back corner of the uppermost shelf.

She found him in front of the closet door, holding and stroking Cleo. Instead of a smile at seeing her, he was wearing a disgruntled frown, not to mention his coat, holster, and weapon.

"Oh, no," she said, her heart, not to mention her hungry tummy, sinking. "You're going back out again?"

He nodded. "I'm sorry, babe. The captain caught me on my way out the door and told me that

McMurtry called in sick. I'm supposed to babysit that burned-out shoe store on Lester. The front window's broke."

"What's to babysit? The place is a goner."

"Apparently, the owner's second cousin to the mayor or some such crap. Gotta make sure there's no looting."

"Yeah, there's a big demand for melted sneakers and scorched loafers that reek of smoke."

Savannah thought of the reservations they'd made at their friends' gourmet restaurant. She could practically see that delicious dinner sprout wings and fly south.

Apparently, Dirk was thinking the same thing. A look of abject grief, usually observed in funeral parlors and the weigh-in area of diet clinics, appeared on his face. "I'll bet John's making me that beef Wellington stuff that he's so good at."

Savannah nodded. "There goes my salmon soufflé. I'll call Ryan before he gets too far along with the preparations."

"I'm sorry, darlin'," he said, setting Cleo on the floor, then folding his unhappy wife into a bear hug. "My tour's over at midnight. I'll make it up to you when I get home."

"When you get home, my butt." She looked up at him with a twinkle in her eye. "I'm going with you. You can make it up to me in the back seat of that patrol car."

Okay. That was kinda nice, considering the cramped quarters, Savannah told herself, as she wriggled back into her recently discarded knickers. Very recently. Three minutes before, as a matter of fact.

Married sex, even anniversary sex, didn't last as long as newlywed sex, she had discovered.

Not even close.

Apparently, the back seats of patrol cars, like airliner seats, got smaller and less comfortable with every passing year, strangely enough, in direct proportion to the increasing size of her backside.

It wasn't a mystery Savannah cared to solve.

Her new, lacy, "for the occasion" drawers back in place, she glanced at her watch. All right, she told herself, only three more hours and fifty-seven minutes left until "dinner," whatever that might be.

As though reading her mind, Dirk said, "If all else fails, there's that all-night diner by the highway. They make a good burger, and the fries aren't bad." He grunted with frustration as he fiddled with his Harley-Davidson belt buckle in the dark car interior, parked in a dimly lit alley behind the shoe store he was to guard.

Remembering the greasy, cold burgers and limp fries she had been served in that less-than-stellar establishment on previous occasions, Savannah had a hard time summoning any enthusiasm when she replied, "I'm sure we won't starve. One of your presents to me is a box of truffles."

"Really?"

"Yeah." She decided to change the subject before a gift-giving argument ensued and dimmed the afterglow. "Exactly why did the captain stick you with this wonderful assignment? Since when is a detective given the dubious honor of guarding a burned-out shoe store?"

He coughed and cleared his throat. Reaching through the rolled-down window, he pulled the exterior handle, opening the door. Once outside the vehicle, he offered his hand and helped her exit with a tad more chivalrous decorum than usual.

Anniversary manners? she wondered. *Or something a bit more diabolical?*

Once they were settled into the front seat, and he had started the car and rolled up the back window without answering her question, she ventured a guess. "Did you do something in particular to get on his bad side?"

"Doesn't take much," was the curt reply.

Okay, that was a "yes," she decided. "What did you do?"

Dirk drove the patrol car out of the alley and around the side of the building to the front of the store, where the large plate glass display window was broken. A string of bright yellow police tape threatened anyone crossing the line with death and dismemberment.

Another cruiser was parked in front of the shop, and when the driver noticed them approaching, he waved and took off, obviously eager to leave his post.

"What did I do?" Dirk asked with one of the worst "fake innocent" tones she'd heard in ages. "Why would you assume I did something?"

Having been a police officer herself, Savannah was all too familiar with the old tactic of "Ask a Question While Trying to Come Up with an Answer." Whatever his offense, it must have been a doozy.

"Come on, spill it," she said, poking him in the ribs with a forefinger.

He grumbled something unintelligible under his breath as he pulled into the vacated spot and parked.

"Did he know it was your anniversary?" she asked.

He turned off the ignition, sighed, and ran his fingers through his hair. "Yeah. He knew. He had the date circled in red on his calendar, so's he wouldn't forget."

Savannah thought of the calendar in their kitchen with its red heart, but decided that, since the captain despised them both, he wasn't likely to have marked their special day just to remind Dirk to buy her a present.

"Are you telling me that he deliberately ruined our anniversary?" she asked.

"Something kinda like that." He gave her a quick, sideways, haunted look. "Okay, something *exactly* like that."

"Why?"

"Maybe because I ruined his."

"You ruined the captain's anniversary?"

"So he says."

She took a deep breath, but regretted it, as the interior of the vehicle reeked of Dirk's discarded fast-food wrappers on the floorboards. She rolled down the window to get some fresh air and asked, "How the heck did you manage that?"

"It wasn't easy."

"I can only imagine. Do tell." She filled her lungs with the cool night air, expecting it to be scented, in typical Southern California style, with eucalyptus, wild sage, orange and lemon groves. But instead, all she smelled was burnt leather and assorted scorched plastics from the store. Not a nice scent at all. She quickly rolled the window back up, opting for stale tacos and old tuna sandwiches.

Dirk slid down in his seat and rested his forearms on the wheel. In the dim light of the street lamp, he looked tired, and Savannah felt sorry for him. Her husband wasn't above making a dumb mistake or two from time to time, but he had a good heart, and she was sure that whatever malfeasance he might have committed, it was done with good intentions.

Semi-good anyway.

"Last month, Cap forgot his own anniversary," Dirk began, "until he went home, kicked off his shoes, and settled down with a beer to watch TV. His wife walked in, dressed up and ready to go out for dinner and . . . well, she saw him and got all pissed off."

"Can you imagine such a thing?"

"Yeah, well . . . so he snuck away to the bathroom and called me. He told me to leave the station house and go get him a dozen roses."

"Probably not enough to get him out of the doghouse."

"That's what he figured, so he wanted me to go by a jewelry store and pick up a ring for her, too. One she'd had her eye on. Said he'd already called the jeweler and set everything up. Then he told me to text him once I had the stuff, and he'd meet me at the corner on his block."

"Wow. I'm surprised he didn't tell you to pick up his dry cleaning while you were at it."

"I'm sure if he'd thought of it, he would've."

In the middle of their commiseration, a couple of teenage boys strolled by the front of the store, paused, and appeared to be having a conversation about some high-priced, if somewhat smoky, sneakers just inside the broken window. The shoes were well within their reach.

Dirk tooted the horn and, when they turned to look, he waved them along.

"Well, what did you do, pick up the wrong ring?" Savannah asked.

"Worse than that. Way worse."

Reaching across her, he opened the glove box and took out a baggy filled with cinnamon sticks. He removed one, stuck it in his mouth, replaced the rest inside the compartment, and slammed it closed.

"After I got the ring at the jewelry store, I was on my way to his house, but that's when I saw Loco Roco running outta that liquor store there on the corner of Main and Seaview with a pillowcase in his hand."

"Oh, I remember. That's the day you came home covered in Loco's blood."

"Yeah, I chased him down, found a bunch of cash and a ton of those little, travel-size bottles of booze in the pillowcase, and started to cuff him."

"He resisted?"

"They don't call him Loco for nothin'. He fought me. He lost and bled. A lot. I tossed him into the back seat—"

"—on top of the roses."

"How'd you know?"

"I know you. Go on. And . . . ?"

"He mashed 'em flat."

"And bled all over them?"

"That, too."

"I had to take him to the station house and book him before I got a chance to tell the captain."

"Who'd been waiting all that time on the corner?"

"So he informed me." He took a deep drag on the cinnamon stick. "After I had Loco all locked down and the report written, I went back out to the car and that's when I saw the mashed flowers and"—he gulped—"the empty ring box."

"You'd left the jewelry on the back seat?"

"With the roses."

"Oh, no."

"Yeah."

"But didn't you search Loco? Didn't Booking search him?"

"Of course, we did. After I figured out he'd taken the ring, Charlie and me did everything but turn him upside down and shake him. Which means . . ."

"He had 'secreted' it."

Dirk just nodded. One small, totally disheartened nod that told Savannah far more than she wanted to know.

"Gross," she said.

"Yeah."

"Did the captain find out?"

"Charlie told him."

"Did it ever . . . um . . . show up?"

"Nope. Captain said, even if it did, he wasn't going to give his wife a ring that had spent time—"

"Secreted."

"Exactly."

Savannah thought it over. She considered how much she disliked the captain and his rigid, dictator style of bossing his underlings. She recalled seeing his wife strut around the station house from time to time, flashing her jewelry—not to mention various body parts—as she flirted quite openly with some of the younger, better looking cops, despite the fact that she was old enough to be their mother.

No, neither the captain nor his dirty ol' lady of a wife would have wanted that ring after Loco Roco had "disposed" of it.

"No wonder we're here tonight, instead of dining at ReJuvene," she said. "It's a wonder you're alive."

But Dirk didn't answer. He was eyeing a vehicle that was coming down the street toward them. When it got a bit closer, Savannah realized it was another patrol car.

"What's Vince Muller doing here?" Dirk grumbled, as the driver—one of his least favorite brothers in blue—pulled over to the curb in front of him, parked, and got out.

Savannah said nothing. She just gave Muller a scowl that was only slightly less cranky than the one her husband was wearing as the patrolman sauntered past them.

Having joined the SCPD after Savannah had left, Muller hadn't offended her personally, their paths having seldom crossed. But Dirk had told her a few tales about Muller's bullying tactics and less-than-honest dealings with shadier members of the public. Not to mention the fact that, in a short period of time, he had managed to become the captain's pet.

But the deciding factor, as far as Savannah was concerned, was that Dirk didn't like him. If her husband said Vince Muller was a dirt clod, Savannah was convinced he was.

She figured loyalty was important in a marriage, so she made a point of not smiling at anybody Dirk loathed. At least not in his presence.

It wasn't easy. She was fairly sure that it would lead to premature wrinkling of her forehead.

Dirk loathed a lot of people.

Vince walked by them without saying a word, offering nothing but a curt nod of his head. In his right hand he held an oversized duty flashlight.

Following suit, they withheld both spoken greetings and curt nods, simply deepening their scowls.

Vince didn't seem to notice or care. He strolled to the front of the store and poked his head through the massive hole in the display window.

"He'd better watch out," Savannah said. "A chunk of that broken glass at the top could break loose, fall, and chop his head off."

"If we're lucky," Dirk replied dryly. Then he smiled. A nasty, unpleasant smirk. "That'd make my day, getting to tell the captain that his number one flunky suddenly lost about ten pounds of unsightly fat."

They watched as Vince straddled the yellow caution tape, then gingerly stepped into the store.

"What the hell is he doing?" Dirk asked.

They watched as he flipped on his flashlight, producing a beam in the dark interior of the burned store.

"Maybe somebody died and made him head of the SCPD Arson Squad," Savannah suggested.

"He's acting like he owns the joint. He shouldn't be in there at all. That tape's there for a reason."

"Arson hasn't investigated yet?"

He gave a little snort. "More like Arson hasn't 'pretended' to investigate yet. Remember, the owner is a good friend of the mayor."

"Oh, that's right. I forgot. And storeowners with friends in high places never set a match to their own stores."

"Never. In the history of the world." He shrugged. "Well, at least not in San Carmelita, under the current administration."

"Quaint, seaside village with sparkling beaches, antique shops galore, palm trees swaying in the ocean breeze—"

"A city government as crooked as a snake with a bellyache. The travel websites don't mention that."

"Now, now. No place is perfect."

Savannah watched with mounting interest as the beam of light appeared to work its way through the store, up and down each aisle.

"Seriously," she said, "what *is* he doing? If I didn't know better, I'd say he's shopping."

At that moment, the light and Vince came toward them, and a few seconds later, he was stepping through the hole in the window and back onto the sidewalk.

Dirk sighed, a bit relieved. "Good. He's got no

business poking around in there. I don't appreciate him doing that. Especially when I'm supposed to be keeping everybody out."

Again, without a greeting or acknowledgment of any sort, Patrolman Vince Muller strolled past them as he returned to his cruiser.

Savannah happened to glance down at his feet. "Since when do SCPD personnel wear sneakers on patrol?"

"What?"

She nodded toward the retreating figure's feet. "Your buddy's wearing tennis shoes. Expensive ones. On duty."

"Why, that dirty, rotten—"

"What on earth?" Savannah said as, to their surprise, Vince opened the rear door of his cruiser and slid inside.

"I don't know. But he forgot to roll the window down. I hope he closes the door and gets locked in."

Savannah snickered. "How long would you wait before you let him out?"

"Since he greeted me and my wife so cordially when he arrived . . . I'd say, when Satan sets up house in an igloo."

A few moments later, the partially-closed rear door of the patrol car swung fully open once again, and Muller stepped out.

As before, he walked past them and to the front of the store, flashlight in hand. Savannah glanced down at his feet and couldn't believe what she saw.

"He's barefoot!"

"No way!"

"See for yourself. Hairy toes, ingrown toenails, the works."

"And broken glass everywhere. He's nuts. I knew he was annoying and a major kiss-up, but he's totally off his rocker."

"Scored himself some expensive sneakers though, didn't he?"

"He certainly did and right under my nose."

"Does he really think you're going to let him get away with that?"

"Apparently, bein' Captain's pet has gone to his head."

Once again, they watched as Vince Muller maneuvered over the police tape and, far more gingerly than the last time, stepped inside the store.

As before, the flashlight beam moved back and forth between the aisles, illuminating the shelves on one aisle, then the next.

"Looks like he's gonna get hisself some dancing shoes, while he's at it," Dirk said.

"Hey, a guy's gotta look sharp when he's doing the salsa." She pulled her phone from her purse and began to take a video of the proceedings.

This time it took a bit longer before Patrolman Muller exited the store. When he finally did, Savannah couldn't come to grips with what she was seeing. But once she had partially recovered her composure, she zoomed in on his feet, making sure she got the image clearly, because no one would have believed their story without seeing it for themselves.

"No," she heard Dirk mutter. "No. Just . . . no!"

She took one look at his face and knew that he was shattered. Brotherhood of the Boys in Blue, and all that.

"They're probably for his wife," she offered, trying to make her distraught husband feel better.

"He ain't married. No girlfriend. And those have gotta be a size eleven, at least."

"Yes. At least," she said. "Who'd have thought they even made those that big?"

"Okay, that's it." Dirk removed the cinnamon stick from the corner of his mouth and tossed it onto the floorboard. "This ain't happenin' on my watch. I don't care if the guy *is* the captain's favorite recess teeter-totter mate."

"Are you actually going to arrest him?"

"Depends on how much grief he gives me."

"I'll keep filming."

"Good idea." He reached for the door handle, then hesitated. "Um . . . you can edit out that 'teeter-totter' comment, right?"

"Tammy can."

"Then keep rollin'."

Chapter 2

"I don't allow my child to watch violent, X-rated films."

"It isn't X-rated," Savannah told Tammy, who was sitting on Savannah's couch, her child in her lap. She was shielding baby Vanna Rose's big blue eyes with her hand. "We didn't start filming until after the anniversary, back seat hanky-panky was over, and everybody was fully dressed."

Sitting next to Tammy was Savannah's younger brother, Waycross. His left leg was encased in a cast and resting atop a pillow on Savannah's coffee table.

"Whoa!" he said with a groan as he put his hands over Tammy's ears. "Way too much information for my wife's virgin ears to hear," he said in his slow, Southern drawl that was as soft and gentle as the young man himself.

Savannah laughed as she plugged her phone into the wide-screen television in her living room and punched the appropriate screen icons. "What are you guys, the See-No-Evil, Hear-No-Evil, Speak-

No-Evil monkeys? If you're going to hang out around *here,* you'll have to toughen up."

"I know. A toxic environment if ever there was one," Tammy replied with a grin on her pretty face. "Sex, violence, caffeinated coffee, not to mention saturated fats and gluten everywhere."

Dirk rose from his leather recliner—the newest addition to Savannah's otherwise girly-girl living room and former bachelorette pad. He stretched out his arms to the red-haired imp sitting on Tammy's lap. "Give me that kiddo. I'll keep her occupied so's she won't get scarred by all the on-screen violence and mayhem."

Vanna Rose gave Dirk a big grin, cooed, and eagerly lifted her chubby, baby hands to him.

He scooped her into his burly arms and hugged her to his chest as he settled back into his recliner. "We're going to play us a game of patty-cake, while your mommy and daddy watch Uncle Dirk knock the crap outta a bad guy."

Receiving a disapproving look from Tammy, he added, "Don't worry. Once she gets old enough to understand what I'm saying, I won't say it."

"He'll even stop quoting those charming bedtime limericks to her," Savannah said.

Tammy gasped, and Waycross gave her a playful nudge. "Don't worry, sugar," he said. "They're just yanking your chain. Even ol' Dirk wouldn't rattle off a dirty limerick to a baby."

Savannah cast a quick glance at Dirk, who was choosing to ignore the comment, while kissing the baby's tiny fists.

"Well," she mumbled under her breath, "at least not the one about the gal from Nantucket."

Waycross heard the comment and turned a brilliant shade of pink that only true redheads can achieve with such little provocation.

Savannah had a feeling that, as soon as his broken leg was healed, Poppa Waycross would be having an old-fashioned behind the barn—or garage, as the case might be—conversation with Uncle Dirk about what was and was not appropriate bedtime entertainment for a six-month-old baby girl. Especially a little lady of Southern heritage.

Dirk turned his niece to face him, her back to the TV, and engaged her in a no-holds-barred game of patty-cake.

Meanwhile, the questionable images appeared on the widescreen television.

The after-dark, street-lamp-only lighting was barely adequate to reveal the onstage action. But with a little effort the adults in the room had no problem discerning the major players.

There was Det. Sgt. Dirk Coulter in his Harley-Davidson T-shirt and jeans, doing what he had done hundreds of times before, wrestling with and attempting to subdue a suspect on the not particularly mean streets of picturesque San Carmelita. Only this time, the culprit was a police officer in full uniform.

Almost.

Mostly regulation, except for the footwear . . . which was all too obvious when Dirk grabbed the smaller man, who was fighting him like a felon going away for life, lifted him off his feet, and body slammed him onto his back on the sidewalk.

At that point, the perp's legs were sticking

straight up, his trouser legs sliding down, and his fashion-forward attire all too visible.

Tammy squealed. "Gladiator sandals!"

"Sparkly ones?" Waycross added, wide-eyed and incredulous.

"Yes," Savannah replied, giggling and freezing the action. "Rhinestone-studded. Assorted jewel-tone colors, guaranteed to match evening gowns of all shades and hues."

"And he's got really gnarly, calloused toes and heels, too," Tammy observed, cocking her head sideways to get a better view of the upturned, un-pedicured feet. "That's just . . . wrong."

"On so many levels," Savannah agreed.

"You're arresting him!" exclaimed Waycross as Savannah pushed "Play" to resume the action, and they saw Dirk flip the wildly flailing Vince Muller facedown and attempt to cuff him.

"Of course, I did. I told the sonofabitch . . . sorry, darlin'. . . ." He ruffled the baby's red curls. "I mean, I told the mean ol' bad man to put those stupid sandals and the runners he'd just stole right in front of me back where he got 'em. Or else."

Tammy gazed, fascinated by the twitching, jerking figure on the sidewalk, sandals kicking wildly. "I guess the taser was the 'or else.'"

"Yeah. Didn't wanna have to shoot a fellow cop for stealing a pair of hooker shoes."

"Men's size eleven," Savannah said.

"Okay," Dirk replied. "Male hooker."

Tammy shook her head, gave a *tsk-tsk* and a nod toward the baby. "We're really going to have to clean up our speech around here and keep it clean for the next twenty years or so."

Savannah thought for a moment and said, "Male entrepreneur specializing in the wholesale, free-lance marketing of society's unsanctioned salacious pleasures."

"Now see there." Tammy grinned. "Was that so hard?"

"What I wanna know," Waycross interjected, "was what that captain, the one y'all dislike so much, said when you told him you'd arrested his favorite cop."

Dirk grinned, as though recalling a memory warm and dear to his heart. "I thought it was best if I told him right away, so as soon as I had Muller booked, I went to the captain's house to inform him."

Savannah chuckled. "Tell them the best part."

"He had company. A party, in fact. Lots of guests. Even the mayor and his wife were there. Everybody wanted to hear all about it. Every sordid detail." Dirk breathed a sigh that bespoke soulful satisfaction. "Turns out . . . it was his mother-in-law's birthday party."

Chapter 3

Sleep didn't come quickly or easily to Savannah that night. But her insomnia had nothing to do with the rare Southern California rainstorm raging outside the bedroom window.

She actually enjoyed the sound of the rain, the wind, even the occasional rumble of thunder and lightning flash. One of the few things she missed about her childhood home in Georgia was the less-than-perfect weather.

She welcomed the occasional spring storm, mudslides and all, just to break the monotony of the perpetually blue sky and seventy-three-degree days.

Normally, she would be snuggled beneath her grandmother's quilt, enjoying Mother Nature's temper tantrum. But tonight, she could neither savor the drama nor fall asleep.

Being on the outs with one's husband tended to have that effect on a gal.

They usually got along quite well. Other than their routine snipping and sniping throughout the day—a habit formed years ago on boring stakeouts for the purpose of keeping them awake and entertained—they seldom had a serious disagreement.

Today's unpleasantries were no exception. They could hardly be classified as "serious." Not a harsh word had been exchanged, no voices raised, nary a household object hurled.

Savannah might have felt better if that had been the case. She would prefer to anger, annoy, or even infuriate her husband any day, rather than hurt his feelings.

Gruff, tough Dirk pretended he had no feelings, but she knew better. Today, she had hurt them quite seriously. She knew because he had been uncharacteristically quiet throughout the evening. Hardly any eye contact had been established, even over the dinner table.

His good-night kiss had been lackluster, at best.

Now, after taking much longer than usual to fall asleep, he was lying on his side, his back to her, and no physical contact whatsoever. Not even a friendly foot seeking hers and nuzzling comfortably against her arch.

She knew her man well, and she was all too aware that this time "making it up to him" was going to take considerable, creative effort on her part.

Wrapping her arm around Diamante, she pulled the cat against her tummy and snuggled her close. A warm, purring kitty wasn't as good as a warm, happy, and contented husband, but since one wasn't available at the moment, the feline substitute would have to do.

Just as the digital clock showed 2:00 A.M., Savannah

began to nod off, her plans on how to re-woo her estranged husband firmly in place and her peace of mind somewhat restored.

That was when she heard it. Some sort of disturbance downstairs.

At first, she thought it was storm-related, the wind having knocked over a flowerpot, another clap of thunder, or rain pelting the living room windows.

Then, as she became more fully awake, she realized someone was knocking on the front door.

Not just any knock. Hard and fast with a note of urgency.

Savannah sat up and glanced over at Dirk. He was still sleeping soundly, snoring even.

Rather than wake him, she slid out of bed and slipped her faithful old terry-cloth robe over her Minnie Mouse pajamas.

Diamante followed her out of the bedroom and down the staircase that led from the upstairs hallway down to the foyer.

"If it's a magazine salesman at this hour," Savannah told the cat, "I'm going to open the door so you can rush out and sink your toofers into his Achilles tendon. Okay?"

Diamante looked up at her with eager, green eyes.

Savannah wanted to think it was because the cat was excited about rushing to her defense. But she knew her mini-panthers all too well. Diamante thought she was offering treats.

What a glutton.

Since they were both up anyway, Savannah decided that, once they had dispensed with their nocturnal visitor, a cup of hot chocolate might be in order. Just the thing for settling the tummy and the spirit before going back to bed.

"Don't worry," she told Di, as though the cat was reading her mind. "I'll give you a squirt of whipped cream."

As Savannah passed the coat closet where both she and Dirk stowed their weapons, it occurred to her to grab hers from the top shelf. Just in case their visitor wasn't of the friendly persuasion.

But then, she wasn't about to open her door at 2:00 A.M. without looking out the peephole first. Once she knew who was on the other side, she could decide whether or not she needed the 9mm Beretta.

She flipped on the porch light, slid the hole's cover aside, and squinted through it.

At first, she wasn't sure what, let alone who, was standing there. They just looked like a dark, sodden mess.

Then a particularly nasty gust of wind blew the black, wet curtain of hair back from their face, and Savannah recognized her rain-drenched guest.

She threw the dead bolt and yanked the door open. "Dr. Liu! What in tarnation? Get in here right now, girl!"

A loud crash—one of Savannah's hanging flowerpots being blown off its hook and hitting the porch—caused the already traumatized Jennifer Liu to shudder, then rush inside the house.

Savannah struggled to grasp what she was seeing. This disheveled, shivering, obviously distraught woman bore no resemblance whatsoever to the cool, calm, frightfully intelligent medical examiner whom Savannah had known for years.

Savannah had never seen the good doctor with even a hair out of place or a wrinkle in her haute couture—if somewhat slutty, in an expensive call girl sort of way—apparel.

Instead of her usual silk blouse, leather miniskirt, and stilettos, Dr. Liu was wearing a baggy boyfriend shirt, yoga pants, and past-their-prime running shoes. All thoroughly drenched. She couldn't have been wetter if someone had tossed her into a swimming pool and left her there to dog paddle for half an hour.

"Good Lord, woman," Savannah said, "you look like a half-drowned swamp rat."

She expected some sort of smart aleck reply. Dr. Liu might have flunked out of Tact and Sensitivity School, but she had an honorary doctorate from the University of Savage and Sarcastic Repartee.

Instead of a sassy retort, Jennifer's eyes met Savannah's for the first time since entering her home, and the sadness and fear that Savannah saw registered there chilled her more than any cold rainstorm.

"You're in trouble," Savannah said.

It wasn't a question. She was just thinking aloud.

"I am. Big trouble." Jennifer started to softly cry, her tears mingling with the rain on her face. "I'm sorry, Savannah. I wouldn't bring my problems to your doorstep if I could think of any other way out. I've been walking for hours, trying to come up with a solution on my own. I can't. I need help.

Please——" Her voice broke, and she began to sob in earnest.

Savannah put her arms around her trembling, cold, wet friend and pulled her close. "Of course, I'll help you, Jen. Whatever's going on, I'll do everything I can for you. You know that."

"You don't mind me coming here in the middle of the night like this, getting you out of bed and——?"

"Oh, hush, darlin'. Do you reckon this is the first time that Trouble has ever knocked on my door in the middle of the night?"

Jennifer gave a derisive sniff and half a smirk, and for a moment, she looked like her old self. "No. I suppose not. After all, you're married to Dirk Coulter." Her expression quickly defaulted back to fearful as she glanced up the staircase. "Is he here?"

"He's upstairs asleep. Out cold. He wouldn't wake up if a bulldozer crashed through the front door."

Savannah took the doctor by the arm and led her through the living room and kitchen toward the back of the house and the downstairs bathroom. Jennifer was unsteady on her feet and, in spite of Savannah's support, she stumbled along the way.

"The first thing we have to do," Savannah told her, "is get you warm and dry."

"Yes. Loss of coordination, difficulty thinking, shivering, and irregular heartbeat," Jennifer replied, as though by rote, in a clinical, flat monotone. "I suspect I'm in the initial stages of hypothermia."

"I don't know about that. But you're cold as a frog on a mountain, if that's what you mean."

Savannah took off her robe and shoved it into the doctor's hands. "Get in that bathroom and peel off those wet things. Toss them out the door, then take a hot shower and thaw out a bit. I'll throw them in the dryer, and they can run while we're talking about this awful problem of yours."

Jennifer said nothing, just gave Savannah a weak smile and disappeared into the bathroom.

Savannah walked back into the kitchen and put the kettle on. Her overly active imagination started churning out scenarios, one after the other, as she tried to picture what might have gone so wrong in the M.E.'s life.

Just judging from Jennifer Liu's risqué wardrobe, her frequent use of the double entendre, and her references to the wild parties she attended, Savannah suspected that the doctor had an unconventional sex life. Beyond that, Savannah knew next to nothing about her personally. The two women had bonded over chocolate, while assisting each other with numerous difficult cases, but they had never truly socialized.

Only a few days earlier, Savannah had dropped by the morgue with Dirk, when he had needed to identify the body of one of his informants. Dr. Liu had seemed okay, though perhaps a bit preoccupied. Even then it had occurred to Savannah that she hadn't seemed quite herself.

Perhaps this problem of hers had been brewing for a while.

Savannah took a lemon from a bowl of fruit on the counter, cut a few slices from it, and studded them with some whole cloves.

When she opened the cupboard, looking for a

mug, she automatically reached for the bright pink Minnie Mouse one, then reconsidered. This was for Dr. Jennifer Liu. Something told her that a woman who dissected dead bodies for a living might require something a bit less cheerful on a dark and stormy night when she was beset with personal problems.

Savannah picked the cup she had scored on her last trip to the "Happiest Place on Earth," adorned with the black and purple wallpaper of the Haunted Mansion. It seemed more Dr. Liu's speed.

She tossed the clove-adorned slices inside, added a squirt of lemon juice, spooned in some honey, poured in boiling water from the teakettle, then stirred the whole thing with one of Dirk's cinnamon sticks, until the honey dissolved.

There's nothing quite like an Irish hot toddy to cure what ails you, she thought as she added a generous amount of whiskey. *Or, at least make you not mind so much.*

She heard the shower start in the bathroom, so she hurried to scoop up the wet clothes off the floor where Jennifer had left them and shove them into the dryer.

As she did so, the former police detective and present private detective in Savannah couldn't help examining each garment for anything untoward—rips, scuffs, dirt . . . blood.

Nothing appeared amiss.

No sooner had Savannah adjusted the settings on the dryer and started it spinning than the bathroom door opened and Jennifer emerged. Her hair was still wet, but she was wrapped snuggly in Savannah's thick terry-cloth robe. While it looked

Chapter 4

Savannah sat in her comfy chair with its colorful, rose-print chintz, her feet on the equally cushy footstool, and Diamante curled into a purring ball of ebony silkiness in her lap.

Seated on the sofa to her left, Dr. Liu clutched the black and purple mug, wrapping her fingers around it tightly, as though welcoming its warmth.

"You caught quite a chill out there, sugar," Savannah told her as she scanned her friend from her damp head to her bare toes. She had never seen this natural, no-frills version of the sexy M.E. Her otherwise carefully and generously applied makeup was only a few dark smudges under her eyes and her hair, normally as glossy as Diamante's coat and tied back with a brightly colored, silk scarf, was now hanging in limp strands around her shoulders. The only reminder of her former flamboyant self was her scarlet toenails, peeking out from under the hem of Savannah's robe.

Savannah took a sip of hot cocoa from her own

Minnie mug. She had opted for a non-alcoholic warmer, figuring she might need all of her mental faculties to deal with whatever she was about to be told.

When she saw Jennifer take the last sip of her toddy, Savannah decided it was time to find out the reason for this impromptu midnight visit.

"Are you ready to talk about it?" she asked in as gentle a tone as her rabid curiosity would allow.

Jennifer set her mug on the coffee table. "Not really. When this all started, I never dreamed I'd have to tell anybody about it. I figured I would just do what had to be done, then wash my hands of the whole thing, and try my best to forget it. As if I ever could."

Savannah resisted the urge to ask another question. Dr. Jennifer Liu was a fiercely private person. Something told her that probing too hard and too fast might prove counterproductive.

So, she stroked Diamante's soft ears, and listened.

"In the beginning, I just thought I was helping a friend," Jennifer said. "My best friend in the world."

Tears filled her eyes as she stared down at her hands. "To be honest," she continued, "Brianne was my *only* friend. We were closer than most sisters."

Savannah thought of Tammy, so very dear to her heart. Then she thought of Marietta, the oldest of her many sisters, whom she fervently wanted to bludgeon with a decorative sofa pillow at least once a week.

She nodded. "I understand."

Jennifer's tears started to flow again. "Brianne

was a giver, not a taker. We knew each other since we were children, and she never asked me for a single thing. Until the end. Then she pleaded with me to do her one favor, something she desperately needed. Something that only I could do for her. Now it seems I can't even give her that."

"What did she want, Jen?"

"She asked me to perform the autopsy on her body."

They sat in silence for a few moments, as Savannah contemplated the horror of doing such a thing to a beloved friend.

Finally, Savannah handed Jennifer a box of tissues and said, "I don't blame you. I think most people would find it terribly difficult to autopsy anyone they knew, let alone someone they loved."

Jennifer wiped her eyes and blew her nose. "Oh, I did the autopsy. Someone had to, and I certainly wouldn't have wanted Dixon to do it. I wouldn't let that old butcher within a mile of her body."

"Then why . . . ?"

"It was the second half of her request that presented the problem. A big problem."

"How? What else did she want?"

"She begged me to falsify the report."

Savannah suppressed a shudder. "But you couldn't bring yourself to do it, right? To falsify an autopsy report is a felony. You could lose your license, maybe your freedom."

Jen's fist tightened around the tissue in her hand until her fingers turned white. "I brought myself to do it."

Savannah heard herself gasp. All she could say was "Why?"

"I told you, she was my best friend. For a long time, she was the only person in the world who loved me."

"No, Jen, that can't be true."

"It *is* true. Savannah, I don't like to talk about it, but I had a . . . complicated . . . childhood."

She wrapped the robe tighter around her, as though the fabric could somehow protect her from the pain of memories recalled. "When I was four, my father was killed in a car accident. A year later, my mother died of cancer. I was adopted by an elderly couple who had more money than time or affection for the child they thought they wanted . . . then discovered they didn't."

Savannah felt her own throat tightening. "I'm so sorry."

"They were generous to me. Gave me anything I asked for. Raised me in a beautiful mansion. Sent me to the finest schools. Ignored me. Barely tolerated my presence. I was a very lonely kid, until I met the girl who lived on the estate next door to ours."

"Brianne?"

Jennifer nodded. "Yes. Brianne Marston. She was my playmate, sister, my whole family, rolled into one. We spent hours together, roaming around the two properties, exploring, getting into all sorts of wonderful trouble."

For a moment, a sweet smile softened Jennifer's face.

"What sort of mischief are we talking here?" Savannah asked.

"We put purple dye in the koi pond."

"Oh, no!"

"Non-toxic, of course."

"Of course."

"We took one of the ponies from her stable and put it upstairs in my adopted parents' bedroom suite."

"It must have been tough getting him up the stairs."

"We had an elevator."

"Doesn't everyone?"

"The worst was when we raided her mom's jewelry box for 'pirate loot' and buried it in the backyard."

"Sounds like fun."

"It was. Until we lost the treasure map and couldn't remember where we'd hid it."

"Uh-oh."

"Yeah. We got in huge trouble over that. We dug holes all over that yard for years, looking for it."

"Was it ever found?"

"No. As far as I know, there's still an old strawberry jelly jar with a glorious stash of custom pieces by Cartier, Tiffany, and Harry Winston there on the property, somewhere in the wooded area about four feet down."

"Four feet?"

"We took our piracy and booty burying very seriously."

"Apparently so."

Jennifer smiled again, and Savannah thought, not for the first time, how beautiful the woman was . . . when she wasn't crying and beside herself with grief.

"Those were the good times," Jennifer continued. "But they ended. When Brianne's mom came down with Halstead's disease."

Savannah searched her memory for the term, recalling very little. "That's a form of dementia, right?"

"A deadly form. Always fatal. Though it takes its victims slowly, robbing them of their identities, their dignity as human beings, long before it's finally finished with them."

"How sad."

"It is. And it was. Her whole family really suffered during that time. Her mom, obviously, but her dad and her brother, too. I tried to help them, especially Brianne, the best I could. She told me later that I made it easier for them. I doubt that's true, but I appreciated her saying it."

"You had walked a similar, difficult path with your mother's cancer," Savannah replied. "I'm sure you were a great comfort to Brianne and her family. That must have been a deeply bonding experience for you two girls."

"It was. And that bond held, even when we became women and went our separate ways. She became a corporate attorney and, as you know, I pursued forensic medicine. But I knew all I had to do was pick up the phone, and she'd drop whatever she was doing and run to me. That's why I couldn't say, 'No,' when she asked me to . . ."

"Falsify her autopsy report."

"Yes."

"I don't understand, Jen. Why would she ask you to do that?"

"Because she was beginning to manifest the symptoms of Halstead's herself. It's hereditary. If your parent had it, you have a fifty-fifty chance of manifesting it yourself. Unlike some other diseases that are similar, there's no definitive test for Halstead's. The diagnosis is based solely on symptoms, and hers were getting bad."

"That's so sad. I'm really sorry."

"Rather than suffer the way her mother did, Brianne decided to commit suicide."

Savannah cringed. "And she wanted that to remain secret because of insurance money or . . . ?"

"No. Nothing like insurance fraud. Brianne had no policies. She was never married and had no children. Just a boyfriend she was thinking of dumping, a brother and sister-in-law. But she didn't want them or her friends to find out. She didn't want to be known as the woman who had killed herself."

"I see."

They sat quietly for a few moments. Then Savannah said, "So, you did the autopsy and ruled her death as natural causes?"

"Yes. It wasn't difficult, considering her symptoms and family history. Her doctor had already diagnosed her condition as Halstead's."

"Then what's happened? Did someone discover what you'd done?"

"No. Well, not yet anyway."

Savannah studied the M.E.'s face, trying to see past the solemn expression that told her nothing. "Then, what's the problem?" she asked. "And how can I help you?"

"If you can find a way to do it discreetly—you can understand why I don't want anyone else to know about this, especially Dirk—could you come to the morgue tomorrow? Alone. I have something to show you."

Savannah thought about her husband, sound

asleep upstairs. No, she wouldn't want Dirk to know, and not just to protect Jennifer. If he found out what the M.E. had done and didn't report it, he would be in jeopardy himself. She couldn't put him in that position.

It was bad enough that she found herself in that difficult place.

"Can you tell me what it is?" Savannah asked.

Jennifer gave another furtive glance toward the foyer and its staircase. "I'd rather not go into the details," she whispered. "Not here."

"Okay. But can you give me *some* idea what we're up against? Why you came to me for help?"

Once again, Jennifer's eyes flooded with tears, and she began to shiver. Only this time, Savannah suspected it was from fear rather than cold. "I have reason to believe that Brianne didn't commit suicide after all. I need you to investigate and see if what I fear may have happened."

"What do you fear? What do you think happened?" Savannah asked, thinking that, from the look of deep sadness in her friend's eyes, she already knew the answer.

"I'm afraid that my best friend, my sister, was murdered."

Chapter 5

"What's the matter with Dirk? Got his bloomers on backward?"

Savannah looked across her breakfast table at her grandmother and thought, not for the first time, that Granny Reid was hardly a woman of mystery. Rather, the octogenarian was a clear mountain stream, totally transparent, who had nothing to hide and, therefore, concealed nothing.

You never had to ask where you stood with Gran.

Her honesty was a spiritual gift, born of a clear conscience. A blessing and life-enriching example to all around her.

And, occasionally, a pain in the rear.

Especially when combined with her acute powers of observation.

"He's just a bit grumpier than usual at the moment," Savannah told her, reaching for the basket of biscuits and the jar of peach preserves.

"He didn't eat breakfast," Gran replied. "That's

not 'grumpy.' For *your* husband, that's danged near suicidal."

"Both of our husbands are a bit gloomy at the moment," Tammy said as she sipped her seaweed smoothie and balanced Vanna Rose on her knee. It wasn't an easy task, as the baby was constantly reaching for the glass.

The precocious child had recently figured out that people larger than herself had culinary options besides breast milk, and she was determined to imbibe as well.

"I thought Waycross seemed a bit jumpy yesterday," Savannah observed, buttering her biscuit. "You'd think my sofa was infested with fire ants the way he was squirming and fidgeting around."

Tammy nodded. "The pain in his leg just won't let up, and it's getting to him, sitting around, hurting all the time, not able to do much."

"But he can drive now, right?" Gran asked.

"He can. But it's a hassle with the cast and all. He hates it. Plus, he's worried about missing so much work at the garage. He was in the middle of restoring a beautiful old Ford pickup, and the boss gave it to someone else to finish. Broke his heart." Tammy's big eyes filled with tears. "I feel so guilty. I shouldn't have asked him to clean those gutters. Or at least, I should have helped him."

"It's not your fault, sugar. Somebody had to keep both feet on the ground and take care of the baby," Granny said. "Accidents happen, and Waycross, sweet boy that he is, has always been prone to them. I can't recall the exact number of casts that child wore in his day. He was forever divin' *off* somethin' or *into* somethin' or gettin' in the way of an object that weighed a ton more than him."

"Like Farmer Haskell's prize bull?" Savannah said with a shudder.

"Oh, hush. I can't even bear to think about it. That boy, all bloody and broken, his clothes tore clean off him." Gran shook her head. "He was miserable for months and missed all that school. I swear, that mess took ten years off my life!"

Gran stood and carried her plate and silverware to the sink. Making herself at home in her granddaughter's kitchen, she washed and dried the dishes, then put them away in the cupboards.

The domestic chores finished, she walked over to Tammy and held out her arms to Vanna Rose. "Come to Granny, puddin', and let your mama drink that pitiful green guck of hers in peace," she told the child, who instantly brightened and began to hop up and down on her mother's lap, her own chubby baby arms extended to her great-grandmother.

Granny scooped her up and planted a kiss on each of her pink cheeks.

Once Gran and little Vanna were settled back in Granny's chair, the questioning continued. "What *is* wrong with your husband, Savannah girl? I've seen him grumpy for years. This ain't the case of his usual contrariness."

Savannah hesitated, then decided to share. More than once Granny's insight on husbands and marriage had helped her out of a predicament. Gran's advice on such matters tended to be golden.

"We had a little anniversary-gift-giving spat." Savannah shoved a bite of biscuit into her mouth and washed it down with a gulp of strong coffee.

"Seemed like maybe more than 'a little,' and worse than a 'spat,' " Granny observed.

Tammy dabbed the green froth off her lips with a paper napkin and said, "It couldn't have been any worse than the Christmas-gift-giving spat."

"Oh, that was a doozy," Savannah admitted. "But this beat it by a mile. A total debacle. Waterloo and Custer's Last Stand all rolled into one."

"Okay. Let's hear about it," Granny said, "and don't spare any of the gory details."

Savannah took a deep breath. "When we got home the other night, or should I say morning, we were in a pretty bad mood after all that malarkey with Vince What's-His-Name and his rhinestone gladiator sandals. So, we decided to exchange gifts."

"You probably should have gotten a good night's sleep first," Tammy offered. "Sleep is second only to nutrition when it comes to health maintenance."

"I know, Tamitha." Savannah sighed. "But it had been a pretty crappy anniversary up to that point. We figured the only way it could go was up."

Granny gave her a sad, sympathetic smile. "Little did you know—"

"Exactly. My first mistake was telling him that I was tired of opening my presents from him with a box cutter. If I went to all the trouble of choosing my gifts, ordering them, and literally placing them into his outstretched hand, I figured the least he could do was shove them into some gift bag, stick some tissue in the top, and present them to me properly. I even bought him the bags and tissue paper to make life as easy as possible for him."

"Let me guess," Gran said. "When you told him all that, he gave you the deer-in-the-headlights look. The one that men always use to try to fool us into thinking they're total imbeciles, so's we won't expect them to do stuff they don't wanna mess with."

Savannah nodded. "That's the look."

"Waycross gave me that look once," Tammy said, "when I asked him to help me bake a gluten-free soufflé."

Gran and Savannah stared at her blankly.

"Once?" Savannah asked. "He gave it to you *one* time? And it was about baking a *soufflé?*"

Tammy nodded.

"He's a poor country boy from Georgia, darlin'," Gran said. "He couldn't tell a soufflé from a skunk's rear end."

"No kidding, Tams," Savannah joined in. "You better hang on to that boy. He's a keeper if ever there was one."

Gran turned to Savannah. "So, did Dirk put your stuff in the bags, like you asked him to?"

"Surprisingly enough, he did. He took the bags and disappeared into his man cave upstairs. A minute later, he yelled down the stairs, 'Do I have to take them out of the boxes they came in?' I hollered up, 'Yes!'"

Tammy rolled her eyes. "How very Dirk-ish."

"He's a man," Granny offered. "They just don't think like women, and that's both their charm and their aggravation."

Savannah continued. "He was up there for a long time, messing around. Then he stuck his head out the door again and shouted down, 'You want to look at this junk before I wrap it all up? I don't remember buying all this stuff for you."

"How much was it?" Tammy asked.

"Just three things. That's what we'd agreed on. Three little things instead of one big thing. I hollered back up to him, 'No! It's bad enough that I already know what it is. I don't want to see it until I unwrap it!"

Granny nodded. "Okay. Go on."

"Then he started carting down the bags. Armloads of them."

"Armloads?" Tammy's eyes widened. "Really?"

"Tons. Seriously. I'd given him a big bunch of bags that I got on sale. There was a whole box of them in assorted sizes and colors. I'd only intended for him to use two or three. But here he came, carrying three bags to each hand. And he made several trips. Up and down. Up and down. By the time he was done, the living room floor was littered with gift bags, and he was a downright sweaty mess."

"Mercy," Granny said. "Now there's a mystery for you to solve."

Savannah nodded. "No kidding. I was feeling *so* guilty. All I'd got him was a Harley-Davidson keychain, a new Dodgers cap, and his main present— a 1980 mint condition poster of the Roberto Duran versus Sugar Ray Leonard fight. As he was toting all this stuff down the stairs, I heard him mumbling under his breath. He said something like, 'Well, she's a generous wife, so . . .' "

After pausing for another swig of coffee, Savannah came to the conclusion of her sad saga. "I

opened the first bag and it was my chocolate truffles, which I was expecting. Then I opened the second bag and found . . . of all things . . . that ugly
scarf that I tried to crochet a couple of years ago.
The third one had some white pants that made my
butt look a mile wide."

"What in tarnation?" Gran exclaimed.

"And the fourth had some mugs and glasses
from when I'd decluttered my kitchen cabinets.
That's when I remembered—"

"Remembered what?" Tammy leaned across the
table, eager for the answer.

"I recalled what happened last Christmas Eve."
She turned to Granny. "Remember, you had to
spend the night with us after you mistakenly drank
some of the spiked eggnog, instead of the nonal-
coholic stuff I made for you?"

Gran shook her head sadly. "I was a sorry sight to
behold. Drunk as a three-eyed goat and on the good
Lord's birthday, too."

"You were fine," Savannah told her. "A little flat
when we were singing Christmas carols, but as spif-
flicated as you might have been, you behaved like
a perfect lady. Anyway, when I went upstairs to tidy
up the guest room . . . um, Dirk's man cave . . . I
gathered up some boxes of stuff I'd laid out on the
futon. They were things I was intending to donate
to the local thrift store. I shoved them all there in
the corner behind Dirk's recliner, just to get the
mess out of sight. I forgot all about it, and that's
where Dirk was 'hiding' my presents."

Tammy gasped. "Oh, no!"

Granny began to laugh. Bouncing on her lap,
Vanna Rose giggled along with her.

"How'd you handle this knee-slappin' but mighty delicate situation?" Granny asked.

Savannah gulped. "Not with grace or compassion. I laughed myself plumb stupid. I couldn't stop. It was the funniest thing I'd seen in ages. But the look on his face when I told him . . ."

"I can only imagine." Granny paused to wipe her tears of laughter away and catch her breath. "But since he ain't talkin' to you now, I reckon he didn't find it so funny, huh?"

"He seemed to take it okay, at least at first. He laughed along with me, and I finished unwrapping my gifts and gave him his, which he was happy with. Especially the poster. We talked a little while and went to bed. The next morning, y'all dropped by, and we showed you the video. He seemed okay then."

"He did," Tammy agreed. "I didn't pick up any negative vibes from him. No more than usual anyway."

"I know," Savannah continued, "and then he went off to work as usual. But when he got back home, I could tell he'd been thinking about it or something, because he wasn't saying much."

"The silent treatment isn't exactly your man's style," Granny said. "He ain't the sort to suffer in silence."

"He never was, but apparently, he is now. I apologized for putting him through that whole wrapping ordeal and then laughing at him, adding insult to injury. But he just gave me the brush-off and went outside and mowed the lawn."

"He did yard work without you finagling him

into it?" Granny scowled. "Are you sure that boy's not sick with something? Reckon he might be comin' down with a cold?"

"No, he's just mad at me. Or worse yet, he's got his feelings hurt something fierce. And I feel lower than a limbo stick at a Hawaiian luau."

Gran reached across the table and patted Savannah's hand. "It was an honest mistake, sweetheart. You just keep showering him with kindness and affection, and he'll get past it when he has a mind to."

Savannah glanced at her watch and jumped up from the table. "I don't mean to eat and run, but I have, uh, someplace I have to be in a few minutes. I've gotta go."

She could feel their eyes on her back as she carried her dishes to the sink. They were an open trio, who usually shared every detail of their days with each other. When some facts were withheld, curiosity levels were bound to rise and the inevitable questions asked.

"Where do you have to be, sugar?" Granny asked.

Savannah smiled to herself. Yes, clear as a mountain stream, that was her grandmother. Nosy to the point of being somewhat rude but endearing all the same for the loving concern her questions expressed.

Unfortunately, this wasn't Savannah's secret to share. "I told a friend I would meet her," Savannah said, hoping it would be enough.

"Anybody we know?" Granny's curiosity, like that of her private detective granddaughter, was insatiable—a family trait that was sometimes a virtue, other times a vice.

Savannah gave her grandmother a loving, sweet

look. "I wish I could tell you about it, Granny," she said. "But she's in a difficult situation, and it's confidential in nature."

Granny returned the same affectionate smile. "I understand, darlin'. If you've been entrusted with an important secret, it's your sacred duty to guard it. I'll say a prayer for your friend, that she finds a way out of her difficult situation. Tell her not to worry. All will be well."

Tammy nodded. "With you as a friend to help her, I'm sure she'll be okay in the end."

Savannah thanked them both, grabbed her purse, and left through the kitchen door. But as she got into her car and headed toward the county morgue, she wished that she could be even half as confident as her grandmother and best friend were. Well wishes and prayers helped, to be sure. And in the end, most things did turn out for the best.

But not all.

Experience had taught her that life, and the myriad problems it presented, didn't always resolve in a satisfactory manner. Not everything turned out the best in the end.

Not always.

Sadly, not everyone lived happily ever after.

Chapter 6

Savannah wasn't afraid of dead people. As a police officer and then a private detective, she had seen more than her share of them.

Usually, folks passed gently from natural causes. Sadly, accidents cost other people their lives. Under those two circumstances, the mourners left behind could sometimes find an ounce of comfort in the idea that their loved one's "time had come" or "it was meant to be."

And then there were the others, whose passings had nothing to do with illness or accidents. Rarely and tragically, someone left this earth at the hands of another.

Those who lost their loved ones in that horrific manner had no such platitudes to comfort them. All they had left were gaping holes in their hearts and the age-old questions: Who? How? Why?

Savannah harbored strong personal opinions about those events. She firmly believed that the act of murder was the purest form of evil on earth,

that it rocked both the physical and spiritual worlds
to their core.

Homicide could never qualify as "meant to be,"
as every victim was cheated out of whatever time
they had left to complete their life's work and
enjoy the earth's beauty, not to mention the love
afforded them by their friends and families.

While she couldn't restore anybody's loved one
or even begin to assuage their pain, occasionally,
Savannah had been able to answer a few of those
haunting questions and secure some degree of justice for the survivors.

She was fiercely proud of that.

She firmly believed that no one could understand the true value of justice until they had suffered a great wrong and then been denied it.

So, on her way to the morgue she felt a strong
sense of apprehension, mixed with a determination,
that if Brianne Marston had been robbed of her life,
she would do all she could to bring her killer to justice.

But this time it was a bit different, more complicated. She couldn't help wondering what price
her friend, the county's first and only female medical examiner, might have to pay before Lady Justice's scales would find a place of balance.

One day at a time, Savannah girl, her mind whispered with a quiet, gentle voice that, as always,
sounded a lot like Gran's. *One moment at a time, if
that's what it comes to.*

As Savannah pulled her bright red 1965 Mustang into the morgue's parking lot, she fought that

ever-increasing heavy, sinking feeling in her belly that usually accompanied visits to this place of death. She couldn't help dreading the prospect of adding to the burden she already carried—that of knowing the horrors one human being could perpetrate on another.

Also, there was Officer Kenneth Bates.

She and Kenny had a love/hate relationship.

He loved her. Although his feelings for her tended more toward hard-core pornographic lust than sweet soul mate adoration.

She loathed him, his too-tight, grease-stained uniform, his lopsided toupee . . . the scratched, faded linoleum he walked upon, the chili-cheese, nacho smelly air he breathed.

Unfortunately, the reception area of the building was his domain, and she had to sign the clipboard on his counter before she could enter the secure interior, where Dr. Jennifer Liu conducted her autopsies, supervised identifications, and wrote her reports.

As always when opening the front door, Savannah steeled herself for the upcoming onslaught of double entendres, insulting propositions, indecent proposals, and elevator glances that took in every "floor" of her body edifice, lingering on his favorite locations.

Society at large might have finally begun to shine a light into the darkness of sexual harassment, but not even a penlight had illuminated the murky cave that was the heart of Kenny Bates. Savannah truly doubted it ever would. She suspected that Enlightenment was low on Ken's priority list, well below female body parts that would fit beneath a string bikini, beer, and a pastrami and limburger cheese hero sandwich.

But today, Savannah was shocked to see that things were different in the reception area of the county morgue.

Instead of finding Officer Kenny sitting alone behind his desk, playing video games, looking at porn, and munching on spicy chips—yes, for a nitwit, he was remarkably good at multitasking— he had company. And he didn't look particularly happy about it.

Dr. Jennifer Liu stood beside his desk, her hands on her hips, a stern look on her face, as he pretended to work by shuffling stacks of papers on his desktop from one spot to another.

The moment Savannah opened the door and stepped into the reception area, Jennifer turned to Kenny, jabbed a warning finger at his nose, and said, "Not a word, jackass. You speak to her, you die. Badly. Got it?"

He looked up at her, an expression of sheer terror on his face, his orange, nacho-stained lips aquiver. He nodded.

Savannah saw him start to turn his head and glance her way, but in the last second, he seemed to think better of it and, instead, stared intently down at the newly-arranged papers on his desk.

Jennifer leaned over him and, since she was now dressed in her usual attire—a low-cut, silk blouse, black leather miniskirt, and stilettos—the move afforded him quite a view of feminine pulchritude.

Savannah was shocked to see that he didn't take

advantage of the opportunity. Instead, he ducked his head and averted his eyes.

Good Lord, she thought, *what's the world coming to?*

She heard Jennifer whisper in a menacing tone usually reserved for mustachioed cartoon villains wearing black capes as they tied helpless blondes to railroad tracks, "She does not have to sign in. She was never even here. You never saw her."

"Right," he mumbled. "Never here. Never saw nobody."

Jennifer turned to Savannah and crooked her finger, beckoning her to follow as she headed for the hallway.

Savannah hurried after her. When she caught up with her, they walked side by side down the grim corridor, the medical examiner's stilettos clicking on the worn tile and echoing off the gray walls.

"How the heck did you do that?" Savannah asked, still flabbergasted.

"How did I do what?"

"Tame a beast like Bates. Dirk has slugged that guy. I've beaten the tar out of him with his own porn magazine. And it didn't even make a dent in his stupidness. How did you manage it?"

"It's just a matter of having the proper equipment. The first day I arrived, he tried that crap on me. Suggested I come over to his house and watch a geisha girl-American G.I. porn movie with him."

"But geishas aren't hookers and, besides, your heritage is Chinese."

Jennifer shrugged. "He's an idiot. I dragged him to the back, took him into an autopsy suite, and showed him firsthand what I can do with a scalpel, a rib cutter, and a skull saw."

Savannah thought it over, then nodded solemnly. "That explains a lot. Thanks for sharing."

"Anytime. I'm an amazing source for life hacks. Bring me a box of your chocolate and macadamia cookies the next time you come in, and I'll tell you how to avoid clumpy mascara and split ends."

For a moment, Savannah thought her old friend was back—stilettos, miniskirt, sarcasm, and all. But one sideways glance was all Savannah needed to see that Dr. Jennifer Liu's jaw was still tight, her backbone a bit too straight, and her arms tight to her sides.

She looked like she was heading off to war.

One she expected to lose.

As they approached the stainless-steel double doors that led to the autopsy suite, Jennifer seemed to grow more tense by the moment.

She glanced up and down the hallway and seeing no one, she swung one of the doors open and told Savannah, "Come on. The first thing I have to show you is in here."

Savannah braced herself for what she might find inside the autopsy suite. She hated to add to the growing list of waking nightmares in her head.

Dr. Jen would do it for you, she told herself as she stepped inside. *Just get it over with.*

"There's someone I'd like you to meet," Jennifer told her as she led her through the main room with its dissecting tables, steel sinks, bright lights, counters covered with trays of equipment, and cabinets, toward a heavy metal door on the back wall.

As soon as the M.E. began to open that door, Savannah understood that the person she was about to "meet" would not be among the living. Inside was the cooling unit, where bodies were stored before and after autopsies.

She was pretty sure that no one in their right mind would want to hang out inside what amounted to an enormous refrigerator full of dead folks, not even if they were wearing thermal long johns and an Alaskan parka.

Jennifer flipped on the light switch, revealing a simple, straightforward storage system that consisted of sturdy metal shelving that looked like a series of uncomfortable bunk beds, lining three of the walls.

On those shelves, Savannah saw four bodies. One was in a black, zippered, and locked bag. The kind used for suspected homicide victims. The other three were wrapped in heavy, clear plastic.

With an officious look on her face and a determined stride, the medical examiner walked over to the body in the black bag, pulled a key from a chain around her neck, and opened the lock. Then she unzipped it and peeled back the sides, exposing the head, face, and upper chest.

She stepped back to give Savannah a clear view. "This is Nels Farrow, a successful, local real estate broker. Yesterday, his wife, Candy, found his body lying in their backyard, in the middle of his rose garden that he was so proud of. She said he'd been sick for some time, but Candy was shocked and devastated to find him dead."

Savannah moved closer to the deceased and took a good look at him. Even in death, she could tell he had been a handsome man and in the prime of his life. He had thick blond hair, a strong jaw, and a dark tan, which Savannah surmised was from all the hours he had spent in his rose garden.

Her heart ached for him. Thanks to her Granny Reid, Savannah had a soft spot for those who spent their time and love nurturing roses.

"He looks about thirty-five," she said. "And in good health."

"Good guess. Thirty-seven and in excellent health. Except for the Halstead's. His father died of it. His physician recently diagnosed him."

Savannah turned to Jennifer, surprised. "Really? He had it, too? I thought it was a rare disease."

"Yes, fairly rare. With people of European descent, approximately one point five per one hundred thousand. Among other populations, like those with Japanese, Chinese, Hispanic, and African heritage, it's even less common."

"San Carmelita's population is about one hundred thousand," Savannah observed. "That would mean, on the average, about one and a half people in town would have it. Even less if you factor in the thirty-three percent Hispanic population."

"Low odds. And what are the chances that two of them would die from it less than hours apart?"

"That defies credibility. On the average, how long does it take for somebody to die from Halstead's?"

"From the time people began to manifest the symptoms, especially the seizures, they're usually gone in about five years."

"Was your friend, Brianne, sick that long?"

"Not even close. A few months. That's all."

Savannah nodded toward the body in the black bag. "And how long did Mr. Farrow's wife say he'd been sick?"

"He's been exhibiting symptoms of confusion, irritation, and paranoia for the last two months. He had a seizure last week."

Savannah was starting to feel the queasiness in her stomach that had nothing to do with the fact that she was in a morgue.

Jennifer leaned down and pulled the zipper of the bag closed. Then she proceeded to replace the lock.

"I can see why you're concerned," Savannah admitted.

"I'm not concerned." Her job finished, Jennifer led Savannah from the room and turned out the light. As she closed the door and fastened it securely she said, "I'm scared to death."

Jennifer Liu sank into the chair behind her office desk and sighed. "If I wanted to lie to myself . . . If I wanted to get a few hours of uninterrupted sleep without having to jump out of bed and run to the bathroom to throw up from sheer terror, I'd try to believe that Brianne and Farrow died at practically the same time of a rare disease. Two people who, from what I can tell, didn't know each other. And it was just a sad coincidence."

Sitting in the chair beside the doctor's desk, Savannah watched her friend with concern. Having dealt with people in crisis too many times to recall, Savannah knew the look of a person on the edge.

Jennifer Liu was definitely teetering.

"Is it possible that they died of something other than Halstead's or suicide?" Savannah asked.

"It most certainly *is* possible. In fact, I'm afraid it's highly probable. That's why I'm so upset."

Jennifer took a set of keys from her purse. Savannah noticed they were her personal keys—car, house, and several others.

She used one to unlock the bottom drawer of her desk. Taking out a manila envelope, she said, "This wasn't simple coincidence. This was death by design. Whether suicides or homicides, I'm not sure."

Opening the folder, she shoved it into Savannah's hands. "Have a look at Nels Farrow's tox report."

"You got his toxicology report back from the lab already?"

Jennifer shrugged and gave her a weak smile. "I have friends in high places. I was worried, so I had it fast-tracked."

"I'll say you did. Dirk waits days, weeks, sometimes months for this."

"He doesn't have friends in high places. Not that many in medium or low places either."

When Savannah shot her a quick, warning look, she added, "Sorry. Now that he's your husband, I guess I can't insult him anymore. Too bad. It was so much fun."

"Well, now, you don't have to go that far, but at least not as often."

"He's dressing better now that he's married to you."

"I try. God knows, I try." Savannah glanced over

the medical report, looking for anything that appeared to be plain English that she could understand and not finding a single word.

Laying the folder on the desk, she said, "I have no idea what those test results mean. You'll have to translate for me."

Jennifer pulled a second envelope from the bottom drawer, only this one was sealed. She reached into her purse and surprised Savannah by producing what appeared to be an antique, ivory-handled switchblade.

Savannah couldn't help thinking that Dr. Jennifer Liu had always been and continued to be an ongoing source of wonder.

In one practiced swipe, she had cut the envelope open.

After placing the deadly weapon back in her purse, she pulled a paper from inside the envelope and handed it to Savannah.

"This is Brianne's tox report. The real one." She lowered her voice. "Not the one I submitted with my final ruling."

Savannah started to ask whose blood she had sent to the lab to get the fake report but seeing the small bruise and pinpoint red spot in the crook of her elbow, she decided not to.

"See the list of chemicals entered on line five?" Jennifer asked.

Savannah found the spot she was referring to and read the first entry. "The list that starts with pri..mi..barbital?"

"Yes. Primibarbital is the primary ingredient in an extremely rare and highly efficient suicide cocktail.

Mixed with the others listed below it and taken in a large enough dosage, death would be quick, sure, and relatively painless—at least, as painless as dying ever gets."

"Then Brianne took the cocktail and committed suicide, like she told you she intended to do?"

"So we would be led to believe." She tapped a fingernail on Farrow's folder on her desk. "Now look at his report. Line five."

Savannah did as she was told. "Primibarbital." She checked the remainder of the list, then compared them with Brianne's. "And the others, too. All the same."

"That's right."

Savannah's brain whirred, trying to take in the information she'd been given and make sense of it.

"Apparently, they both took the same rare cocktail and committed suicide. I'm sorry, Dr. Jen. That's very sad. But I'm not sure why you're so concerned that you're going to be exposed, or why you suspect they were murdered."

Jennifer sighed, leaned back in her chair and, for a moment, massaged the back of her neck.

Savannah could only imagine how tight and sore it must be.

"I did a bit more testing," Jennifer said. "I used a sample of Farrow's hair. And fortunately, although Brianne was cremated, I had saved a strand of her hair for sentimental reasons. Thought I'd put it in a locket or something."

At first, Savannah thought that sounded a little creepy, then she recalled reading that the Victorians often did that. They had commonly worn hair jewelry, designed to hold those precious locks, so that they could keep a bit of their loved one with them at all times.

Although it was no longer a common practice, this was Dr. Liu, so "common" hardly applied.

"You ran a test on their hair?" Savannah asked.

"I did a segmental analysis."

"What's that?"

"I cut off sections of the hair, then tested each piece individually for drugs and other toxins."

"If they took the cocktail and then died right away, the drugs would have only been in the hair closest to the scalp, right?"

Jennifer nodded. "If at all, yes. But I found it in both of their samples, in the one centimeter and two centimeters segments. Hair grows approximately one centimeter per month, so . . ."

"They were ingesting those chemicals as long as two months before they died?"

"Exactly."

Savannah sat, silent, as a sinking feeling swept through her.

Finally, she said, "Who would take poison over a period of sixty days, feeling horrible and killing themselves gradually and miserably?"

"No one. And certainly not two people."

"Someone was slipping it to them."

"That's what I think."

"What would be the symptoms of this sort of poisoning . . . using those drugs in that combination?"

"Loss of motor control, irritability, confusion, paranoia, difficulty swallowing, and finally seizures. According to their doctors, both manifested those symptoms in their last two months, intensifying in the days before their deaths."

The two women sat and looked at each other, absorbing each other's thoughts, fears, and anger.

Tears glistened in Jennifer's eyes, and Savannah knew they were indicative of the grief and rage she felt for the young man lying in her cooling room, and even more for her childhood friend.

"The sickest, most evil part of this," Jennifer said, her voice breaking, "is that those are also the symptoms of late-stage Halstead's."

"So, whoever killed them, did so in such a way that they thought they were dying of a horrible disease."

"The same debilitating, dehumanizing disease that took their parents."

Jennifer wiped her eyes with the cuff of her shirt with a quick, angry movement and squared her shoulders. "You asked why I'm worried about being exposed. I'm not worried about being found out. 'Exposed' be damned. I covered my tracks well. I'm upset because I know I'm going to have to come forward and admit what I did."

Savannah said nothing, just shook her head solemnly.

"Because if I don't," Jennifer continued, "they'll get away with it. That monster made my best friend, my heart's sister, think that she was dying of the same disease that destroyed her mom. And the whole time, Brianne was perfectly healthy."

Jennifer grabbed the reports off the desktop,

crammed them into the drawer, and slammed it closed. "Then, as if that wasn't enough, they killed her! I don't care if I lose my license and spend the rest of my life in prison, they're not going to get away with doing that to the person I loved most in this world!"

Chapter 7

As Savannah drove back to her home, she could hardly concentrate on her driving for all the thoughts racing through her head. This wasn't going to be easy.

No case was. But this would be trickier than usual.

Normally, she would assemble the members of her Moonlight Magnolia Detective Agency. They would sit down to her dining table with a plate of chocolate chip and macadamia nut cookies, discuss what had to be done, then distribute the various tasks among themselves, according to their skill sets.

At the very least, she would have hurried home to share the news with Dirk. She and her husband would kick it around over a cup of coffee and a slice of pie and come up with a game plan.

However, not only had Jennifer sworn her to secrecy, but Savannah couldn't compromise her law-enforcement husband in such a way. It was bad enough that she, a civilian, was failing to report a felony. But to expect Dirk to put his job on the line, possibly even face imprisonment, to keep Dr. Liu's secret . . . no, she couldn't. She wouldn't.

As she approached the town pier, she found herself pulling into the parking lot. She had always found the act of gazing at the ocean therapeutic, not to mention enlightening and restorative.

With the grandeur of nature spread before her, the salt sea air filling her lungs, the sound of the surf rolling in and the palm trees dancing in the breeze, it was far easier for her to still the frenetic, yelping hyenas in her brain and listen to the calm whisper of her spirit.

So, you're on your own. What are you gonna do, kid? she heard herself ask.

Obviously, she thought, *the first step would be to do some research on Brianne Marston and Nels Farrow.*

Yeah, that would be great, wouldn't it? yelled a nasty little voice in her head. *Now, don't we wish we had taken a few of those computer lessons that Tammy offered us? Then we wouldn't be so dependent on others to do the simple things that any six-year-old can do.*

"Oh, shush," she told her inner accuser. "If you don't have anything constructive to say, keep your trap closed."

Savannah had no problem differentiating between that ugly, bossy voice's rantings and the calm whisper of her spirit. Her spirit was, well, calm . . . and it whispered. The witchy gal had an abrasive, nasal tone, barked out her judgmental opinions with wild and reckless abandon, and seldom had anything of value to add to the situation.

Yeah, you just hate it when I'm right, don't cha? her

internal nemesis interjected once again. *If you'd put out any effort at all to learn that researching crap, we wouldn't be in this predicament, unable to sneeze without Tammy telling you how and in which direction. You'd be able to check out Brianne and Nels yourself, not to mention find a good recipe for pecan fudge pie.*

Savannah waited. She knew it was coming.

But then, we don't really need another recipe for pecan fudge pie. The last thing we need is more pie on our butt because, as it is now, we can't even squeeze into—

"Aww! Shut! Up! Ugggh!"

She lifted her fist to pound the steering wheel, then reminded herself how much she'd paid for it when the red pony had been totally refurbished a few years ago.

Even when losing one's temper, a gal had to be practical.

So she just gripped it. Really hard.

Eventually, having recovered a bit of her dignity and composure, she rolled down the window, inhaled the pungent, salty air, and breathed out her frustration, along with at least some of the fear that was churning through her insides.

After the third repetition of this familiar ritual, the yelping hyenas quieted down a little. The sharp-tongued shrew seemed to find something else to do and someplace other than inside her head to do it. Thankfully.

That was when she heard it. The quiet, gentle whisper of her spirit.

You've got this, Savannah girl. You were called into this sad situation for a reason. You'll fulfill your purpose, whatever it may be. Just take it one step at a time.

Savannah studied the face of the woman in her

rearview mirror. She saw her fear, sadness, and concern.

But that wasn't all she saw.

The eyes of the woman looking back at her were filled with wisdom born of tough living, of myriad hardships overcome, and wounds that had healed . . . or at least not gone fatally septic.

"What are we going to do next?" she asked the woman with the wise eyes and kind smile.

That's easy, she heard her softly reply. *We're going to trust our friends to be friends.*

"Good idea."

Savannah turned the key in the ignition, sat there for a moment, then spoke to her car phone. "Call Tammy."

A moment later, a cheerful voice answered, "Hi, Savannah. What's going on?" She sounded a bit breathless, as though she might have rushed to the phone.

"If you're not too busy," Savannah began, "if my little namesake isn't driving you nuts with that try-ing-to-learn-how-to-crawl business, I could really use your help."

"Absolutely! No problem. I can be at your house in ten minutes. Is that soon enough?"

"That's perfect, darlin'. Thanks a bunch."

But Tammy had already hung up the phone.

Savannah smiled, loving her friend. All it took was a whiff of mystery in the air to get Ms. Tammy Hart-Reid in gear.

By the time Savannah had driven home and en-tered her house, Tammy was already on the job. Sit-

ting at the rolltop desk in the corner, computer on,
an eager smile brightening her pretty face, the San
Carmelita version of Nancy Drew was raring to go.

Tammy was the only person Savannah had ever
known who actually carried a magnifying glass in
her purse.

Seeing how handy that particular tool could be,
Savannah was determined to buy one someday,
when she was in the store that sold such items.

Unfortunately, until the grocery store began
stocking detection tools in the Ben & Jerry's freezer
between the Chunky Monkey and Chubby Hubby
selections, Savannah wasn't likely to remember how
much she needed a magnifying glass, a deerstalker
cap, and a Meerschaum pipe.

"Did you actually drive over here?" Savannah
asked, plopping down on her comfy chair and
gathering the two cats onto her lap. "Or do you
have some sort of space-age transporter that you
haven't told me about?"

Tammy giggled and turned her chair around to
face Savannah. "I ran."

"You did *not*. Don't even tell me that. You live six
minutes from my house. And I was only three minutes away when I called you. You couldn't possibly
have—"

"I was up on Hillside Road, halfway through my
run. I was only a block away when you phoned me."

Savannah sighed with relief. It wasn't easy living
with a superwoman who was a size zero and had
boundless energy.

"Oh, right," she said. "I remember, your car wasn't
out front."

"Your powers of observation less than optimal today?"

"My pretty much everything is less than optimal today. Thank you very much for reminding me."

Savannah looked around the room for the usual lightweight, portable baby stroller with a sleeping infant inside. "You didn't bring the munchkin?"

"Not this time."

"I thought you were taking her running with you every day now."

"She enjoys it, and so do I. But today, Waycross was feeling a little better, and he offered to take care of her while I was out. It's getting a bit easier for him to get around with his leg now than before."

"I'm glad to hear that. I know he was in a lot of pain there at first."

"Oh, he's still hurting. The doctor says it's the damaged tendons. He told us they can take longer to heal than broken bones. Sometimes, he hurts so much he can hardly stand it. His pain's been so bad that it even caused him to throw up."

Savannah felt a momentary, sympathetic ache in her own leg. A twinge that only a mother could feel, or perhaps, an older sister who had helped to raise her eight siblings.

"Poor Waycross," she said, shaking her head. "My brother is such a good man. There are so many other people I'd rather see tumble off a roof than a sweetheart like Waycross."

Mentally, she added, *Some I wouldn't mind giving a bit of a nudge just to make sure they did.* But she kept it to herself.

Being a far better person, Tammy wouldn't approve.

Sniffing the air, Tammy said, "So, you went to see your mysterious, troubled friend, eh?"

"Um . . . yes."

"And how *is* Dr. Jen these days?"

Savannah caught her breath. "What the heck? Why would you even say it was Dr. Liu? I didn't—"

"You smell of formaldehyde. Unless you've been hanging out in some museum of natural history or olde curiosity shop with marinating organic oddities, you went to the morgue."

"You are far too good at this, girl."

"I learned from the best."

"Well, that's true." She patted the cats for a little while. When she looked up again at Tammy, she saw her assistant watching her with such a keen eye that it made her uncomfortable.

On the job, when she absolutely had to, she could spin as convincing a lie as the best of them. But with loved ones, she had never developed a taste for it nor the skill.

"What's wrong with Dr. Liu?" Tammy asked. "And why is it such a secret?"

"You don't want me to break a confidence, do you?"

For a half a second, Tammy looked truly repentant. Her head even hung down a bit, hiding her face with the silky, golden curtain of her hair. But when she lifted her head and looked at Savannah, there was a definite twinkle in her eyes as she said, "Is it breaking a confidence if the other person swears not to pass it along any further?"

"Yes! It would be. Dang, Tams. I haven't decided how much to tell you about what I'm not supposed to tell you yet. You're like a bulldog sometimes."

"A cute little French one?"

"Stop."

"Does it have anything to do with her friend Brianne Marston dying?"

"What?!" Savannah inhaled too abruptly and choked on her own spit.

She truly hated it when that happened. It made a gal feel so stupid to be suddenly gagging to death on her own saliva. So far from the cool, chic, and collected image she tried to portray. Most of the time.

"I read about that friend of hers online. Her name was Brianne Marston. She died a few days ago of this horrible disease that killed her mother. I think it's called Halston's."

"Halstead's."

"Yeah, that's it. Aha! Gotcha!" The young woman looked far too pleased with herself to please Savannah. Apparently, there was such a thing as teaching someone too well. "Halstead's is a very rare disease," Tammy continued triumphantly, "and I don't think you'd have known that if you hadn't just—"

"Shh," Savannah said, eager to end the conversation for more reasons than one. "Drop it right now. Dirk just pulled in."

Chapter 8

Sure enough, through the window, Savannah could see the cruiser was parking in the driveway beside the Mustang. She watched her husband get out of the vehicle and trudge up the sidewalk to the front door.

Yes, she decided, there was a definite slogging quality to his walk—slower and even less energetic than his usual saunter.

Unless he was chasing a fleeing felon. Then, for a big guy, Detective Sergeant Dirk could really move.

"What's wrong with him, seriously?" Tammy asked. "He's really droopy lately, even for him, and it can't just be the anniversary presents-fiasco." She paused a moment, mulling over the possibilities. "His iron shouldn't be deficient. It's ridiculous how much red meat he eats. Maybe his potassium is low. Does he eat bananas? He's seriously dragging buns."

It occurred to Savannah that Tammy was the only adult she knew who was so pure of heart that they actually used the phrase, "dragging buns." But she didn't have time to contemplate the possible nutrient deficiencies of a man who ate doughnuts for breakfast, fast food for lunch, and pure Southern culinary genius at the hands of his wife every night at the dinner table.

The door had opened.

With a finger to her lips, Savannah motioned for Tammy to hush.

Savannah heard him moving about just inside the door, as Cleo jumped off her lap and flew into the foyer to greet him. Dirk could come through that door fifty times a day, and every event was Kitty Christmas Morning for Cleopatra.

Placing a pouty Diamante on the floor, Savannah rose and hurried toward the door to meet him. Not quite as eagerly as Cleo, who didn't know the word *dignity* when it came to "Dad," but spritely enough to score a few badly needed Wifey Points.

When she entered the foyer, she saw he had picked up Cleo and was petting her as she rubbed her whiskers on the front of his bomber jacket. That was when Savannah noticed he was still wearing his coat. No doubt, his holster, too.

Not a good sign.

She expected him to turn and give her a hearty hug and a significant lip kiss, as was their routine. But, although it was a subtle difference, he gave her a simple, curt nod, only fleeting eye contact, and a peck on her forehead when she leaned in for the kiss.

Her heart sank.

Small gestures, broken rituals, sometimes spoke volumes.

"You're home early, darlin'," she told him, trying not to look or sound disappointed. "I haven't made lunch yet."

"That's okay. It's just a pit stop," he said. "Gotta pick up something I forgot and go right out again."

"What did you forget?"

"That camera. The one with the really good zoom lens."

Her heart sank. "The captain's got you surveilling that drug house again tonight?"

"Yeah," was the barely-there reply.

"Darn. He's really got it out for you. I mean, the overtime's nice once in a while, but I've hardly seen you all week."

"Sorry. Can't be helped."

"Okay."

"Do you know where it is? The camera."

She nodded. "Have a seat. Put your feet up a couple of minutes at least. I'll get it for you."

He followed her into the living room and sank onto the sofa, while she went to one of the bookshelves on either side of the desk, and took the expensive, department-issued camera from the top.

Tammy spun her desk chair around to face Dirk. "You look tired," she told him.

He fixed her with a blank, noncommittal look that Savannah recognized as the one he used when forced to exchange pleasantries with someone he considered incapable of intelligent and meaningful conversation.

He drew a breath, released it slowly, and then said, "That's because I'm dead tired. You work two eight-hour tours, and then we'll see how peppy you look."

Savannah winced. Frequently, Dirk bantered with Tammy, but his words were almost always seasoned with humor and softened with affection.

This little speech had been delivered without a trace of humor, softness, or affection.

One glance at Tammy told her that the barb had found its mark and stung. But it didn't appear to have gone too deeply, because Tammy rolled her eyes in Savannah's direction, gave a nod, and said, "Yeah, I'm still thinking bananas. A nice banana purée with some seaweed and blackstrap molasses."

Savannah tried not to gag at the thought. In a world where biscuits, cream gravy, and Granny's peach preserves were available, why would anyone want to pour gunk like that down their throat?

Dirk glanced around the room, obviously searching for something, and Savannah saw his already-low mood-o-meter drop a few more degrees.

"Where's the little redhead?" he asked Tammy. "She usually comes over here with you."

"She's with her dad," Tammy replied.

"Her dad?"

Nodding, Tammy said, "Yes, he's watching her now. He's doing better and better with that cast . . . most of the time anyway."

The look of disappointment on Dirk's face went straight to Savannah's heart. It touched her, how much her rough and gruff, grizzly bear husband loved that baby. The child and Kitty Cleo were the stars in his nighttime sky.

A few days ago, Savannah would have said that she was his sunlight. Though these days, the weather forecast seemed to be trending toward, "Cloudy with a threat of occasional thunderstorms."

"Bring her with you next time, wouldja?" he asked. "I miss her when she's not around."

Tammy smiled, any former bad feelings disappearing in an instant. "I will," she said. "She loves you, too."

Just for a moment, Savannah saw her husband's face soften and a light of happiness glimmer in his eyes.

But then he glanced her way and, once again, his troubled look returned.

Oh, no! Savannah thought. *It is me he's mad at,* she thought. *Not the world. Not the captain. Not Tammy. Me.*

It was a deeply upsetting thing to realize. For the first time since she had said, "I do," Savannah wondered if there might be something seriously wrong with her marriage.

Like any couple, they'd always had their share of squabbles. Maybe even more than their fair share, considering his basic lack of good manners and her low tolerance level.

But this was a whole new and worrisome situation. She wasn't sure how to handle it.

She walked over to the sofa, dusted the top of the camera with her sleeve, and placed it on the coffee table in front of him. "There you go, sugar."

Having lived alone for most of his adult life without anyone to fetch him a cold beer, offer a spontaneous back rub, or deliver a spare roll of toilet paper to the powder room at an opportune moment, Dirk was usually most grateful for these small niceties that communal-living people often took for granted.

That heartfelt gratitude, warmly expressed, was one of the pleasures of living with him . . . along with the fact that he was quick to offer such favors himself.

But today, all she received in return for her efforts was an unintelligible grumble.

One more try, she thought, her own irritation triumphing for a moment over her concerns for their relationship. *And if that doesn't work, I'm going to leave him and that grouchy face of his alone. He can either wallow in his grumpiness or decide to get happy in the same pants he got cranky in.*

Her plan of action formulated, she tried again. "I've got some of that leftover smoked turkey in the refrigerator," she told him. "There's a fresh avocado, a nice, big tomato from the garden, some Dijon mustard. I could make you some sandwiches to eat on your stakeout tonight. If you ask nice, I might throw in some cookies, too."

He considered it long and hard. Then he gave her a quick, troubled look and said, "Naw. That's all right. I'll grab some tacos or somethin' at Juanita's stand."

Oh, howdy! This is serious, she told herself.

In all the years she'd known him, Dirk had never chosen tacos from a stand, not even Juanita's, over her smoked turkey sandwiches. Not to mention freshly baked chocolate chip cookies.

She looked over at Tammy and saw that her young friend's mouth was literally hanging open.

Surely, this would make the network evening news. The lead story! It was one of those moments in history when, later, you would look back and say, "I remember exactly where I was, the precise moment when I heard . . ."

Savannah had a feeling it was going to take a lot more than one of Tammy's infamous banana and seaweed smoothies to set her husband right again.

Even more troubling, there was another element to his mood that bothered her. It concerned her more than his surliness.

Since their anniversary squabble, he had been avoiding her eyes. On the rare occasion when he had sneaked a peek at her, she'd seen something that would bother any wife.

Guilt.

Not being a man who was given to a great deal of self-examination, Dirk wasn't someone who suffered a great deal from guilt. Since he didn't give half a hoot what his fellow humans thought of him, he seldom lied. If someone didn't agree with his actions or like his words, too bad. He didn't feel the need to cover any perceived wrongdoings with falsehoods.

Contrary to popular opinion, Dirk Coulter held himself to a relatively high standard of conduct. If tempted to do something that he was likely to feel guilty about later, he simply didn't do it.

But there had been that time when he had accidentally broken her favorite Beauty and the Beast mug. Not only had he neglected to mention the catastrophe when it happened, but he had unabashedly lied his butt off about having no idea what might have happened to it.

She distinctly remembered the look on his face when he had fake-hunted for it with her on the top shelves of the cupboards. His eyes had the same furtive, anxious look that Waycross had worn when he came home from school on report card day.

Dirk had that look now.

Unexplained guilt.

It was certainly enough to raise any wife's hackles and set her on a truth-finding mission.

She sat down in her chair and propped her feet on the footstool. "Did you mention to the captain that you had done four double tours this week? Seems like he'd want to avoid that for budgetary reasons, if nothing else."

Dirk waited, a moment too long, before answering. "You know the captain. Nobody can tell him nothin'."

Hardly an answer to her question.

She donned the most casual of her pseudo-casual voices. "Where is this drug house he's got you sitting on? A rough area?"

"Rough enough."

Again, not exactly full disclosure.

She laid her final card on the table. "I could go with you tonight, keep you company. Help you stay awake."

He gave her a look of alarm, then quickly recovered himself and put on his own poker face. "Naw. That's not necessary. There's no point in both of us losing sleep."

Rather quickly, for a guy who had been "dragging buns" only minutes before, he jumped to his feet, snatched up the camera, and draped the strap around his neck. "I gotta get back to the station house. Got stuff to do. A lot of stuff."

Before Savannah could even give him a proper good-bye kiss, he was gone, slamming the front door behind him. Even Cleo sat on the floor, staring at the closed door and looking confused.

Savannah walked over to the front window and watched as he moped oh-so-slowly to the cruiser, his head down, his hands deep in the pockets of his bomber jacket.

For a guy who had just roared out the door as though somebody had set fire to his coattails, he seemed to be in no hurry at all to get to the vehicle.

See? He's not rushing around now, that nasty voice in Savannah's head said. *He doesn't have to be anywhere quick. He just wanted to be away from you! He doesn't love you anymore, and he can't bring himself to tell you. Not yet anyway. He will. Soon.*

Tears flooded Savannah's eyes until she could barely see him pulling out of the driveway and heading down the street . . . in the opposite direction from the one he would take to the station house.

You don't know that he's fallen out of love with you, her calm, wise voice countered. *Something is wrong, but you have no idea what it is. Many things could be bothering him. There is no reason to assume it's you.*

Finally, with those comforting words in mind, she managed to halfway collect herself. She dabbed at her wet eyes with her shirt cuffs and turned her back to the window.

That was when she realized that Tammy was watching her. To her horror, she saw that Tammy's eyes were filled with tears, too.

See? You aren't imagining it after all, her fears told her, as though mocking any trace of optimism she had managed to conjure. *Even Tammy knows there's something wrong. Really, badly wrong. It's over. And not just the honeymoon. The marriage. The whole kit and caboodle . . . down the toilet. Ker-flush!*

Tammy shook her head solemnly. "I'm telling you," she said, "potassium. Make up a big batch of that banana pudding he likes so much. It'll turn him right around."

"Since when does Miss Health Food Tammy recommend a sugary food like banana pudding?" Savannah asked. "You know, as well as I do, that whatever's wrong with him, it isn't going to be fixed with a big helping of dessert."

Tammy looked down at the floor, blinked, and the tears ran down her cheeks. "I'm just trying to help."

"I know you are, darlin'. That's all you've ever tried to do, and I love you for it. But I think this time it's serious."

Tammy rose from her chair and hurried across the room. Wrapping her arms around Savannah, she pulled her into a tight hug.

Savannah wanted to melt into her friend's embrace, but she knew that if she allowed herself that luxury, she would dissolve into a hot, sobbing mess. And she couldn't let that happen. Tammy wasn't just her friend, she was her employee, her assistant.

Somewhere in the manual, *Gaining and Maintaining Your Employees' Respect 101*, Savannah was pretty sure there had to be a chapter warning bosses not to blubber all over the help.

It just didn't look good.

Chapter 9

Putting her own marital troubles and concerns aside for the moment, Savannah left Tammy at the computer in the living room and exited the house by way of the rear door.

No sooner had she stepped off the porch and into her backyard than she began to feel a bit better. Along with a generous amount of help from Granny Reid, Savannah had created a virtual fairyland garden of flowers including roses, hollyhocks, geraniums, jasmine, and hydrangea. Then there were the edibles: strawberries, tomatoes, cucumbers, grape vines, raspberry bushes, and myriad herbs. Of course, a Southern cook couldn't be without a few food-producing trees. Years ago, she had planted a peach and apricot tree. Both produced a generous amount every spring, along with the ongoing supply of lemons, oranges, and avocados.

No one went hungry in Savannah's presence, and certainly not in her backyard.

The floral and fruit scents alone were enough to satiate the soul.

But today, Savannah didn't enjoy her corner of Eden quite as much as she usually did when entering it. She had other things on her mind, things more important and urgent than propping up peonies or thinning the lettuce.

She walked over to one of her favorite spots on earth, her wisteria arbor, sat down in one of the comfortable lawn chairs beneath it, and pushed some buttons on her phone.

Dr. Liu answered it almost instantly. "Yes, Savannah?" She sounded anxious.

"Hi." Savannah drew a slow, full breath. The perfume of the garden soothed her spirit and helped her to arrange her thoughts. "I've been thinking," she said.

"Good" was the quick reply.

"I know I swore to you that I'd keep this problem of yours to myself. And I'll keep my promise for as long as you hold me to it. But it's not going to be easy."

"Okay. Go on. . . ."

"My granny and Tammy were both aware that I went out to see a friend this morning."

"No harm in that."

"You wouldn't think so, would you? But Tammy's too bright for *my* own good. The minute I walked through the front door, Miss Smarty Pants asked me how Dr. Liu was doing."

"No way!"

"She did. I'm not kidding! She said I smelled like formaldehyde and the only person I ever visit and come home from smelling like a natural history museum is you."

Savannah heard Jennifer chuckle a bit on the other end of the line. "That's a new one," the doctor said. "Usually, I'm accused of making people smell like week-old corpses. I guess that's an improvement."

"True," Savannah said. "But it presents a problem. As it turns out, my friends and family are some of the brightest people you're ever going to meet. Keeping a secret from them, especially a big one that I'm going to be working on day and night . . . I'm not sure I can pull it off."

"I see your point."

"Worse yet, I have to be honest with you, Jen. Without their help, I don't know where to start. I haven't worked alone on anything for a long time. Until this minute, I didn't realize how spoiled I've become. I depend on Tammy for research, Ryan and John for surveillance and technology, Dirk for his law enforcement connections and know-how."

"Not to mention his brawn. He may not be my favorite person on the planet, but he's a good bodyguard, I'm sure."

Savannah smiled, a bit sadly. "Having a big bloke alongside you, one who loves you to pieces and would die for you, it does come in handy once in a while."

Yeah, but you don't know for sure that he still loves you, whispered her inner tormenter.

Oh, stick it up your left nostril, she replied.

She returned her attention to the external conversation at hand. "With your blessing, Jen," she began, "and *only* with your permission, I would like to at least share the situation with Tammy. I can't tell Dirk about it and put him in a compromised position, and I don't need to bring Ryan and John in at this point. We can keep Waycross out of it. His leg renders him pretty useless anyway. But Tammy's research abilities are invaluable to me. Especially with your problem, because we're trying to keep everything under wraps. It's a lot easier to spy on people using the Internet."

"Unfortunate, but true."

"I just can't do without Tammy. She's like my right arm. My left arm, too."

Jennifer was silent for a moment, and Savannah could tell she was mulling it over.

"You can depend on Tammy," Savannah added for good measure. "I would trust her with my life. Heck, I *have* trusted her with my life, and she's never let me down."

Finally, Jennifer reached her decision. Savannah heard her sigh and clear her throat. "Okay," she said. "I trust you, Savannah, and you trust Tammy. That's enough for me. Go for it."

"Thank you, Jen. I appreciate it. You won't be sorry. I promise."

Savannah made sure she had ended the call and put the phone into her pocket before she whispered a little prayer. "Now, Lord . . . don't make me out a liar. Okay?"

As she stood and made her way back through the garden toward the house, toward Tammy, Savannah felt a wash of relief sweep over her. At the thought of bringing her best friend into the investigation, she instantly felt less alone in the world.

She also experienced a bit of an epiphany. In that moment, Savannah realized how much her relationship with Tammy had changed.

The giddy, nosy little wanna-be detective, who was pretty good with computers and endearingly eager to improve her craft, had learned a lot and grown into a woman with powerful investigation skills.

Skills that Savannah could hardly function without.

She had also become a dear friend that Savannah never, ever wanted to be without.

"I'm thinking it was some sort of suicide pact," Tammy said, after Savannah had filled her in on the scant details of the case that had been gathered so far.

"That's what I was thinking, too, considering those lab reports showed the exact same cocktail of drugs," Savannah agreed. "What are the odds that both of them would have the same recipe otherwise? Dr. Liu said it's a rare concoction. One that would be particularly lethal."

"Maybe someone's posted instructions on how to mix it on the Internet."

Tammy left the sofa, where the two women had been sitting as they discussed the case and possible avenues of investigation. She walked over to the desk and perched herself on Savannah's old, leather, diamond-tucked chair. "Let me see if I can find any reference to it online."

Savannah picked up the copies of Brianne's and Nels's toxicology reports, that Jennifer had made for her, from the coffee table and thumbed through them. "The main ingredient is primibarbital, if that helps."

"It might," Tammy said as she signed on. "Unless that's the major ingredient in all suicide cocktails. I can't say as I stay on top of that sort of thing."

Savannah thought of all the joy that Tammy had in her world . . . a husband who adored her and the cutest baby on earth . . . at least in the Reid-Coulter family's estimation. No wonder she wasn't well-versed on how to end a life.

Not everyone was so blessed. Or, if they were, not all were capable of realizing it.

As Tammy worked, Savannah sat patiently, happy to have her computer genius at work on her behalf. When the pinnacle of one's Internet expertise consisted of checking one's email and saving recipes on Pinterest, it was good to have a techno-savvy, whiz kid on the job.

"Okay," Tammy said at last, "I've used numerous search engines, and I see only a few references to that drug. None of them include any sort of recipe. From what I can tell, some specialized anesthesiologists administer it to patients during surgeries, but it isn't widely used. There have been some problems with it."

"Then we'll certainly check to see if either Brianne or Nels had any former lovers or family members who are anesthesiologists."

"Or vets. Apparently, it's used to euthanize animals, as well."

"Okay, would you please check out some of these other drugs, too?" Savannah started to read the list, then decided against it. After even a few of the ten-syllable words, her tongue started to tie in knots.

She took the papers to Tammy and spread them out on the desk next to the computer, all the while making a mental note to be sure to pick them up and hide them before Dirk returned home after his late shift.

It wasn't easy hiding things from a good cop. He wasn't carrying a gold detective badge for nothing.

Savannah walked into the kitchen and got herself a glass of iced tea and a filtered water for Tammy.

By the time she returned, Tammy had given up the search. "I found references to all of these other drugs individually, but I don't see any mention of this combination anywhere," she told Savannah, taking the glass with its decorative celery stick. "If I can't find it, I don't believe Brianne or Nels could have either."

Savannah pulled up a side chair and sat next to her, watching as she zipped through several websites, scanning their information.

"I've checked these pro-suicide websites," Tammy said, "and there's no mention of using this combination of—"

"*Pro*-suicide?" Savannah was shocked. "Are you telling me there are websites that support that sort of thing?"

Tammy nodded. "If you search 'suicide,' mostly you'll find sites that try to talk you out of it. Others inform the public about how to help a loved one who's depressed or how to save someone's life who's overdosed. But there are plenty of other sites designed by people who fully support an individual's right to decide to end it all."

Savannah thought it over for a moment and said, "I think life is sacred, and I can't imagine ending mine or encouraging someone else to. Though I wouldn't judge someone who did if they had a painful, fatal illness."

"I agree. But not all of these people have a fatal illness. Many are suffering from depression."

"That's a terrible pain of its own, but there are treatments for it. There's hope."

"I know. But on some of these sites, they even encourage depressed people to go through with it. They tell them there's no other way out, that their loved ones would be better off without them."

"That's horrible! Those poor folks have enough demons in their own heads whispering lies like that. They need to be encouraged to seek help. They need to be told not to give up, that it's still possible to get help and live a happy and productive life, no matter what their depression's telling them."

"I agree. But some of these sites encourage individuals to form suicide pacts between two or more people, then discuss how they're going to go through with it. If someone tries to back out, the others lay a guilt trip on them, telling them they've let down their suicide partners."

"That's chilling."

"It gets worse. There have been instances where some sickos, who have no intention of killing themselves, have gone onto these sites pretending to be depressed and suicidal. They've talked desperate, vulnerable people into entering a pact with them, claiming that they, themselves, would do it at the same time and in the same way."

"I hate to even imagine why."

"Get this. . . . They encouraged them to film it, to send it out, live, on the web."

"No doubt because they wanted to watch someone die. They were probably aroused by it . . . like a serial killer when they take a life."

Savannah felt sick. It was yet another scar on her soul that would never heal. Something else to think about when the lights were off and sleep wouldn't come.

"I hope they were tried for first-degree murder and are serving a life sentence," she said.

"Not even close. One man was charged with assisting a suicide and got six months. Another guy pretended to be a depressed young woman in a chat room. He developed this warped mother/daughter relationship with a depressed, older lady, begging her to 'do it' with him, er, her. The woman finally agreed. Instead of offing himself, he watched the video. Over and over."

"And he got . . . ?"

"A year for counseling someone how to commit suicide in a state where it's still illegal. He was let out on probation after nine months and told not to use the Internet for a year. A month later, they caught him doing the exact same thing again."

"Maybe it was some psycho like that who talked these two into it," Savannah surmised. "Or maybe they found each other in one of those suicide chats and agreed to do it around the same time."

"Which brings us back to the idea of some sort of pact."

"Right."

Tammy flipped off the screen. "If I could get my hands on their personal electronics—phones, tablets, laptops, whatever they commonly used— I'd probably be able to find links to websites like that. If I'm lucky, maybe even a chat."

"That won't be easy under the circumstances, with everything being hush-hush. I'll see what I can do."

Savannah stood, drank the last sip of her tea, and took the glass to the kitchen. Tammy followed, nibbling on her celery stick.

As Savannah poured Kitty Vittles into the girls' bowls, she said, "I'm going to try to interview Brianne's fiancé, see what he has to say."

"What's your cover story going to be? You can't tell him the truth about who you are."

"I'll tell him the truth. But only part of it."

"Which is?"

"That I'm a private investigator who's looking into the passing of more than one person who was struggling with a fatal illness. I'll tell him my client is doing research about the depression people feel when confronting the end of life."

"If he asks who you're working for . . . ?"

"I'll tell him that I can't say. It's true. I can't."

"You aren't going to suggest that someone might have murdered her, are you? Or that maybe she wasn't even sick?"

"No." Savannah petted her cats' soft, glossy backs as they began to devour the food. Usually, it helped when she felt bad. But not at the moment. "I'm not going to tell a grieving man a thing like that unless I absolutely have to. If he didn't kill her himself, then he's drowning in grief right now. The last thing I'd want to do is hold the poor guy's head under water."

Chapter 10

Savannah tossed the last half of her turkey sandwich into the kitchen garbage can, then stood
there looking at it, trying to remember the last time
she had been too upset to eat and had thrown away
the better part of her meal.

It had been a long time. That was for sure.

Back then, her discarded lunch had probably
been a pterodactyl drumstick.

Having put off her next unpleasant chore for as
long as her conscience would allow, she decided
that, personal problems or not, it was time to get
back to work.

Scooping up her phone from the kitchen counter,
she gave Jennifer Liu another call.

"Okay," she said when the doctor answered,
again sounding anxious and a bit out of breath.
"I'm heading out to find Brianne's fiancé to see
what I can get out of him."

"Be careful. We don't want to raise his suspicions."

"That's a risk, I grant you," she admitted. "But it can't be helped. How do you conduct a proper investigation without interviewing at least the principal players? They don't get more 'principal' than the people your possible victims were sleeping with."

"I know. Go ahead. Do what you have to do."

Glad to have that behind her, Savannah said, "Where *is* Paul this time of day?"

"I assume he's still in Brianne's house up in Cañón Ventoso. They've lived together about a year. He's an artist, and his studio is there."

"Do you happen to know the exact address? A number?"

"You won't need a number. It's the house at the top. The only mansion in that canyon that looks like a massive barn."

Savannah tried to picture it. "A mansion-*barn*?"

"That's right," Jennifer replied. "Brianne's dad died a couple of years ago and left her a ton of money. I told you, we had a lot of fun playing in the stables there on her parents' estate. She wanted a place of her own that reminded her of better, simpler days, before her mom got sick."

"Okay. I'll look for a barn—"

"That you would be thrilled to live in. It's gorgeous."

Jennifer was quiet for a moment, then said, "There's someone else living there who might be worth talking to. Her name is Delilah, Dee for short, and she's the groom. She has her hands full tending the horses and livestock."

"Livestock?"

"Brianne's property covers ten acres."

"Wow! Ten acres in this area? Daddy sure *did* leave her a ton of money!"

"Yes, he did. And she loved animals. Talk to Dee and ask her to show you the miniature goats. This might be grim work you're doing for me, but that'll be the bright spot in your day. They're super cute."

I could use a bright spot, Savannah thought as she told her friend good-bye. *Because, sooner or later, this day's going to end with me back here at home.*

With a disgruntled husband.

Jennifer had been right. Savannah didn't need a street number.

At the top of Cañón Ventoso there was only one mansion that looked like a barn, and quite a mansion it was! Although it had the basic shape of a barn and was made of rustic materials, like stone and rough-hewn wood, it had the elegance of a Tudor manor house and the imposing presence of a Spanish citadel.

As impressed as she was, Savannah couldn't spend a lot of time admiring the place. She was too busy practicing the lies she might have to tell to cover the unpleasant truth of her mission.

Long ago, even back when she was a street cop, Savannah learned that telling the occasional fib was just part of the job, and she was particularly good at it.

How many times had she told a suspect that she had them dead to rights, when all she had was a sneaking suspicion of their guilt, just to gauge their reaction?

Good at it or not, lying certainly wasn't her favorite part of the job. Granny Reid's training has gone far too deep for Savannah to be comfortable with uttering an out-and-out falsehood.

But Gran had also taught her the necessity of being practical. Sometimes a body had to be shrewd when battling the forces of evil.

Or trying to get an artist to open up about the death of his fiancée.

The farther into the canyon she drove, the larger Brianne Marston's estate appeared and the more Savannah appreciated the grandeur of it. She could see various substantial outbuildings behind the main house. Farther up the hill she spotted a smaller, honest-to-goodness barn and a paddock that held several horses which, even to Savannah's unpracticed eye, appeared to be healthy, well cared for, and probably expensive.

On the other side of the barn was a smaller pen that contained a structure that looked like a storybook house—with about a zillion tiny goats standing on its steeply sloped roof.

It was certainly one of the more charming sights she had seen in her lifetime.

Savannah couldn't help smiling. As Dr. Jen had said, they *were* super cute as they jumped up and down off the house, jockeying for the highest position. She wondered what Diamante and Cleopatra would say if she managed to smuggle one of the kids home in her purse.

Pulling the Mustang into the driveway, she put

all thoughts of adorable, miniature goats aside and concentrated on the upcoming task. She had practiced her spiel so much that she would have to work at not sounding like a third grader reciting a poem in front of the class.

"Let Paul be home," she whispered as she took her purse from the passenger seat and got out of the car. "Him or at least Dee, the goat lady."

She walked to the door, rang the bell, and had to wait quite a while before someone answered.

A tall, thin man with blond hair, a smear of green paint on his cheek, and multicolored stains on his hands, forearms, and the front of his T-shirt gave her a quick, overall glance, and said, "Good afternoon. May I help you?"

"If you would be so kind," she said, daring to hope that this visit might go better than she had originally thought.

He seemed to be friendly and open, not suspicious or guarded. With any luck and all of the diplomacy she could muster, perhaps she could keep him that way.

Stretching out her hand to him, she said, "My name is Savannah Reid. I apologize for arriving on your doorstep unannounced like this. But I was wondering if you could give me a few minutes of your time."

"That depends," he said, still cordial. "Are you selling something I need?"

"Not at all. Actually, I'm a private investigator. At the moment, I'm conducting some research on behalf of a client who is trying to help people . . ." She paused, trying to remember the rest of her well-practiced speech. "People like, forgive me, like your fiancée who recently passed. I'm so sorry for your loss, Mr. Oxley, and for intruding on you at a time like this. Believe me, I wouldn't, if it wasn't important."

He looked away for a moment or two, then down at his stained hands.

She sensed he was about to tell her to leave or, worse yet, slam the door in her face. But to her surprise and relief, he did neither.

Instead, he opened the door a bit wider and said, "Okay. I was working, but I could use a break. Come on in."

Gratefully, Savannah hurried over the threshold, before he could change his mind.

She had made it to first base and without even telling a single lie.

Granny would have been proud.

A few minutes later, Savannah and Paul Oxley were sitting in the massive, post-and-beam living room of the mansion. She was settled comfortably, where he had directed her, on an oversized, leather chair that faced the two-story-high stone fireplace. Numerous wrought-iron lantern chandeliers cast a warm, golden glow on the dark beams and knotty pine, cathedral ceilings and walls.

At her feet, the glossy mahogany pegboard flooring was partially covered with a large Navajo rug, whose cheerful red background and geometric patterns of turquoise and gold lent an intimate, cozy feel to the enormous room.

Paul walked over to the kitchen area for a few moments, then returned carrying a steaming mug in each hand. He gave one to her and took a seat in the matching chair beside the one she was sitting in.

Even before she looked into the cup, she could smell the rich aroma of a fine blend of coffee.

"Sorry," he said. "I should've asked how you take it. That's one sugar and some milk. If you would prefer something else . . ."

"No, this is fine. It smells wonderful. Thank you."

He looked down into his mug with a sad, wistful expression on his paint-smeared face and said softly, "One sugar and milk. That's how *she* liked it. I'm really not thinking straight just yet."

"I understand," Savannah assured him.

"I also can't get used to speaking about her in the past tense."

"That happens a lot with people who are grieving."

He took a long drink from the mug, then said, "What is it in particular that you want to know about Brianne? For your research, that is."

"We're studying people who are struggling with these terrible, genetic diseases."

"The fatal ones . . . like Halstead's?"

"Exactly. Forgive me for my lack of sensitivity, but we're especially interested in how these disorders affect them in their final days. You were probably the closest person to Brianne, so your input would be the most helpful, if you can share your observations."

He quickly drained the rest of the mug—obviously a veteran coffee drinker, Savannah noted—then he set it on the table between them.

"They told us that Halstead's can manifest differently from person to person," he said. "But Brianne's was highly atypical. Usually, once the symptoms start showing, the person has years, not good years, but years, to live. She only had a couple of months, and they were very tough ones."

"I hate to even ask, but can you tell me in what ways?"

"In all the usual ways that Halstead's affects its victims. The loss of coordination. She had always been so graceful and agile. The change was pronounced. She fell and hurt herself several times. In the end, she didn't want to eat. She had a hard time swallowing. Then there were the awful seizures."

He gulped, and she could see he was steeling himself before continuing. "But it was the changes in her personality that were the hardest to watch. She became a different person."

"If I may ask, in what way?"

"She had always been so open and trusting and clear-minded. A very gentle lady."

"But that changed?"

"Quickly. Drastically. She was paranoid, confused, fearful. She claimed someone was trying to kill her."

"Did she mention whom or how?"

"No. Nothing that coherent. It was more like delusional ravings. She was irritable and angry." He paused and wiped his hands across his eyes as though trying to rid himself of the painful visions of the past. "By the time her body finally quit, my Brianne was gone. Do you know what I mean?"

"Yes. I certainly do." Savannah gave him a few moments to regroup, then she asked, "Were you her primary caregiver?"

"Yes, I was. Brianne was my world. The best thing that ever happened to me. She'd given me so much. It was the least I could do for her. I would've nursed her for years and been happy to do so, but—"

His voice broke and tears flooded his eyes.

"I'm sure you would have, given the chance." She took a sip of the delicious coffee, then set the mug beside his on the table.

"We were going to get married and start a family," he said. "She knew the risks of passing the Halstead's gene along to our future children, and we thought about it long and hard. Finally, we decided . . . actually, it was her decision, because I left it up to her . . . to go ahead and live our lives and face whatever came. But no sooner had we set a wedding date than her symptoms began."

"How very sad. I'm so sorry."

"Thank you. I asked her to marry me, she said, 'Yes,' and then our world fell apart."

Savannah reached for her purse and said, "Do you mind if I take a few notes as we talk? My memory isn't what it used to be."

"That's fine."

As she took out her notebook and pen, she said, "Truth be told, it never was."

"Mine either."

For a moment, they exchanged half smiles, and Savannah wished she could be more candid with this open, seemingly honest man. But then she reminded herself that sharing her suspicions with him would only drive his grief deeper.

If, indeed, his fiancée had been murdered, he would find out soon enough.

"You say her symptoms began rather suddenly?" Savannah said, getting ready to write.

"Yes. Supposedly, Halstead's comes on gradually. Brianne told me that her mother's did. She was hoping that if, God forbid, she came down with it, hers would take a while, too. Give her a chance to prepare for the worst, complete unfinished business and all that."

"Did you know that she had this disease from the beginning?"

"Absolutely. Very early in our relationship, on our second date in fact, she told me all about it. She thought I deserved to know that there was a fifty-fifty chance she would die young. I can't say I didn't know what I was getting into. I knew this could happen."

Again, his emotions overtook him, and he couldn't speak.

Savannah filled the awkward silence. "She must've been very special for you to take that chance."

He shrugged and choked back the tears. "I was in love. I fell for her the minute I met her. I didn't have a choice."

Savannah studied him, trying to be her usual

detective self—cynical, unemotional, appraising, and most of all, suspicious.

But this man certainly didn't appear to be the sort who could commit cold-blooded murder, someone who could kill the woman he had just asked to be his wife.

Savannah would admit that she had not always been a perfect judge of character, that she had been fooled more times than she could count. Bad guys, and gals for that matter, were frighteningly good at deceiving those around them. They lived for it and had highly-sharpened skills. Even the most seasoned professional could be fooled.

But if, indeed, Brianne Marston had died at the hands of another, Savannah couldn't believe it was the man sitting in front of her, tears running down his face as he spoke of the woman he loved.

"I would've married her anyway, even knowing she had it," he said. "I was totally prepared to stand up in front of God and everyone who was important to me and swear to love her in sickness and in health. I was looking forward to it. But I didn't get the chance. I didn't have time."

Savannah looked deeply into his eyes and tried to offer as much consolation as she could when she said, "But, whether you had the wedding or not, even if you never got a chance to speak those vows, that's what you did. You loved her, in sickness and in health. You supported her and nursed her and eased her from this life into the next. No husband could have done better than that."

He studied her face and seemed to drink in the compassion he found there. Then he gave her a weak smile and nodded. At least for a moment, he seemed a bit comforted.

Knowing that, Savannah was glad that she was there, that she had paid this visit to the mansion shaped like a barn on the hill.

Chapter 11

Before Savannah left the Marston property, she wanted to see the miniature goats a bit closer and talk to Dee, their keeper.

Experience had taught her that, whether it was a maid, gardener, personal secretary, or in this case a groom, service providers tended to know what was going on in the home where they worked. Sometimes more than the people living there who employed them.

It didn't take her long to find Dee, who was in the goat pen, bent over a wee black goat with long, floppy ears. She was performing some sort of task on one of its dainty hooves.

Savannah lifted the sturdy latch on the pen's gate and walked in, making sure to fasten it securely behind her.

A few people in her hometown of McGill, Georgia, had raised goats back when she was a child, living there. After seeing those people running down the streets in their pajamas, occasionally even their

underdrawers, trying in vain to recapture their escaped nannies, billies, and kids, she knew what little Houdinis goats could be.

Dee looked up from her work and appeared
puzzled and not particularly pleased to see Savannah.

The young woman was a natural beauty with
large, intelligent eyes, wearing no makeup or jewelry. Her long, auburn hair was pulled back into a
ponytail and held with a tortoiseshell clip. She was
dressed in well-loved jeans, well-worn cowboy
boots that were caked with mud and other organic
material that Savannah didn't want to think too
much about.

Dee's faded, blue T-shirt had a silhouette of a
horse and the words, *"My horse is smarter than most
people I know."*

As Savannah walked across the pen, several of
the tiny goats ran to her, their tails wagging happily, like a pack of puppies. They bleated a greeting to her as they surrounded her and began to
nudge her with their heads.

Enjoying the experience enormously, Savannah
decided, then and there, that when she died she
wanted her manner of death to be ruled as "Play-
fully Butted by a Hundred Overly-Affectionate,
Well-Meaning Pygmy Goats."

But then, one of the diminutive rascals grabbed
her shirt cuff in its mouth and began to chew on it
with surprising determination and vigor.

"Hey!" she said, pushing the offending kid away.
"Knock that off! Do I look like a tasty clump of al-
falfa to you?"

"They aren't that picky," Dee called out to her.

"You don't have to be tasty, just edible, and you'd be surprised what a goat considers edible."

She seemed a bit friendlier now. Savannah surmised it was because the groom had seen her "bond" with the animals she cared for.

It was hard for one animal lover not to like another one.

Savannah looked down at her now-sodden cuff and saw he had left a substantial amount of green saliva behind as a calling card and her cuff button was missing.

Oh, well, she thought. *A story to tell Dr. Jen.*

Followed by a herd of new friends, she walked over to the woman. "You're Dee, right?" Savannah asked when she reached her.

"I am." Dee continued her work on the hoof.

Since the groom obviously had her hands full, Savannah didn't offer hers to shake. "My name is Savannah Reid," she said. "I was just talking to your boss, Paul, down at the main house."

In an instant, the groom's face went from partly sunny to cloudy.

"Paul isn't my boss and never has been," she said, as she clipped at the little black goat's hoof with a pair of sharp cutters that reminded Savannah of Granny's heavy-duty rose pruning shears.

Savannah didn't have to see the glint of anger in Dee's eyes to know she heartily disliked Paul Oxley. Her abrupt tone had said it all.

Maybe this little journey up the hill to look at goats will prove more productive than just seeing some cute critters, she thought.

To hide her keen interest, Savannah bent down and stroked the soft, pink nose of one of the white ones with pale blue eyes. She was surprised to see that its reaction was similar to that of Granny's bloodhound, Colonel Beauregard, and her own cats. She could almost swear she could hear it purring.

"Then I suppose your employer was Ms. Marston," Savannah said. "And I'm sorry for your loss."

"Thank you."

Dee gave the little hoof a final clip, and she must have done something wrong because the animal bleated plaintively and gave her a swift kick in the shin.

Bending down, she rubbed its neck and said in a soft, soothing voice, "I'm sorry, little one. You don't like me raising your leg so high, do you? I won't do it again."

She reached for a bucket of feed and held it under the kid's nose. Instantly, the animal buried its face in the grain.

"There you go, some of the good stuff," Dee told it, scratching its back. "You get a little treat for being so patient."

She let the goat have a few more bites, then she held the bucket up out of its reach. In an instant, she was surrounded by the herd, rearing up on her and scraping her thighs with their front feet as they tried to get to the bucket.

She gave Savannah an eye roll and said, "Goat pedicures . . . not the easiest and most glamorous of my many chores."

"What *is* the most glamorous?" Savannah asked.

"Nothing. There's absolutely nothing elegant or flashy about my job," Dee admitted. "But I wouldn't want to do anything else in the world."

"Then you're a fortunate woman. I don't think most people would say that about the work they do."

Dee gave her a long, appraising look. "Something tells me *you* do. I'd even bet that you *love* your job."

Taken aback, Savannah said, "But you don't even know what I do for a living."

"I don't have to. I can just tell by looking at you that you're a strong-minded woman who wouldn't do anything she didn't find fulfilling. At least, not for very long."

Savannah chuckled. "You're right. I love what I do," she said. "Well . . . on the days that I don't hate it."

"Are you a cop? An investigator?"

Again, Savannah was surprised. "Kinda."

"Nobody is 'kinda' a cop. Either they are or they aren't. You must be some sort of investigator. I was wondering when someone like you was going to show up."

Savannah fought to keep her poker face in place and sound casual when she said, "Oh? Why is that?"

"Because there's something about the way that Brianne died that's just . . . wrong."

"What do you mean? 'Wrong' how?"

Dee shrugged. "I'm not sure. I just have a feeling."

Savannah glanced around and realized they were in full view of the house and anyone driving up the road to the estate. Not to mention Paul Oxley, whom Dee apparently didn't like for some reason.

Savannah very much wanted to know that reason.

"Is there somewhere we can go to talk?" she asked.

"Sure. My place. Let's go."

Savannah followed her eagerly out of the goat pen, past the barn, and up the hill.

Any woman whose instincts told her that a person she had just met was either a cop or 'some sort of investigator' . . . that was a gal Savannah couldn't wait to interview.

"We call this the 'bunkhouse,' " Dee told Savannah as she led her into a small, but charming, cottage a bit farther up the hill from the barn. Closing the door behind them, Dee looked quite sad and added, "I guess I mean, '*I*' call it that. '*We*' used to mean Brianne and me. Now it's just me."

"You two were friends," Savannah observed. "Not just employer and employee."

"We were all of the above. When your boss is as kind and easygoing as she was, it's easy to be both servant and friend."

Savannah thought of Tammy and hoped her young friend and now sister-in-law felt the same way about working for her.

"You two were close then?"

"We were. I can't tell you how much I miss her. Have a seat. Make yourself comfortable."

Dee waved a hand toward the futon, which was made up with a bunch of assorted pillows and a green and blue, batik bedspread with the signs of the zodiac on its borders and an astrological chart in the center.

"You believe in astrology?" Savannah asked as she sat down and studied the pattern on the spread.

"Of course. Don't you?"

Savannah grinned. "I've been known to read my daily horoscope in the newspaper every once in a while. I wouldn't say I consult it to see if it's a good day to go grocery shopping or whatever."

"What sign are you?"

"You're good at guessing. What would you say?"

"A fire sign, definitely. I'd say Aries or maybe a Leo."

Savannah was beginning to feel like the tables were turned, and she was the one on the hot seat. This gal was far too good at interrogation.

"I'm an Aries," Savannah admitted. "What are you?"

"A Scorpio. We're very intuitive, and we love a mystery."

"And you sense some sort of mystery having to do with Brianne's passing?" Savannah asked, eager to shift the conversation back to the business at hand and something less personal.

"I do." Dee sank onto a large, beanbag chair nearby. Once seated, she stretched out, her arms hanging at her sides, her booted ankles crossed. She looked tired, as though the rest was overdue and welcome.

"Would you care to elaborate?" Savannah asked.

"First tell me who you are."

Okay, here we go again, Savannah thought. She'd managed to tell Paul Oxley mostly truths, but something told her that Dee was far more astute and less likely to accept the pat answers she'd given him.

"Like you surmised, I'm an investigator and—"

"A private investigator?"

"Yes."

"Hm, I don't think I've ever met one of you before."

"We aren't as common as butchers, bakers, or even candlestick makers."

"True."

"But then . . . you're my first lady groom."

"I'll tell you what it's like to muck out a barn if you'll tell me what it's like to locate a missing person or solve a crime," Dee said teasingly.

"It's probably more fun than shoveling horse poo, but we don't find a missing person every day or solve a crime, for that matter. It's not a common occurrence."

"I wish the same could be said of mucking."

They shared a companionable laugh, then Dee suddenly became quite serious and said, "I think Brianne was murdered, and I think you do, too. I have a feeling you're here to investigate that possibility, whatever you might have told Paul."

Savannah felt her pulse quicken. This could be good news as far as finding justice for Brianne and Nels—if justice needed to be found—but possibly bad for Dr. Liu.

Savannah couldn't remember a time when she had experienced more mixed emotions about a case.

"I told Paul that I'm doing research," she said.

"O-kay. If that's what you want to call it. What exactly are you, um, researching?"

"The final days of people who suffer from Halstead's and other illnesses like it."

"He bought that?"

"He seemed to believe me."

"Paul's always been a bit thick. For the life of me, I don't know what Brianne saw in that guy."

"You don't like him?"

"What's to like? He's boring, a nerd. He lived off her and her money from the moment he met her. She thought that by supporting him she was somehow this great benefactor of the arts. He's a third-class painter, at best, with no ambition or talent, who took advantage of her."

Savannah grinned. "Don't hold back. Tell me how you really feel."

"He's a waste of space."

"Anything else?"

"I think that no-account bum might have hurt Brianne. Or worse."

Every cell in Savannah's brain snapped to attention. "Really? He and I talked for quite a while. He seemed to love her and be heartbroken that she's gone."

"I think those strong emotions that you picked up off him may have been guilt and remorse. He treated her very badly the last few months of her life."

Savannah thought of the man who had sat in the mansion's living room fifteen minutes ago, cried, and professed his undying love for his now-deceased soul mate. As interesting as this conversation was and as astute as the groom might appear, Savannah found her opinions hard to accept.

"I thought he was her primary caretaker," she said.

"He was . . . for the last couple of weeks. Once she was bedridden, he insisted on being the one to tend her. Made a huge show of it. Wouldn't accept help from a professional hospice team, although, heaven knows, he could have used it. He wouldn't let anyone but her brother and sister-in-law come near her. Not even me. But before that . . ."

"Before that . . . ?"

"I could hear him screaming at her there in the house, all the way up to the paddock. I don't mean your usual, run-of-the-mill arguing either. He was, like, out-of-control nuts. I considered calling the cops on him a few times."

"Could you understand what he was saying?"

"I'm sure the horses and goats could understand him. He was accusing her of being unfaithful to him. He was trying to make her tell him who the guy was that she was seeing. He was threatening to break the engagement and cancel the wedding if she didn't. Although at that point, I don't think it was much of a threat. She seemed pretty tired of him, too."

"Was she? Being unfaithful to him, that is."

She shrugged and glanced away. "Well, I can't really say for sure, but . . ."

"Come on, Dee. On an estate like this, the employees—especially those who live on the property—know pretty much everything."

Dee gave Savannah a small, enigmatic smile, but she didn't reply.

"Come on," Savannah coaxed her. "You want to tell me, or you wouldn't have brought it up."

Laughing, Dee said, "I guess that's true. I see I'm not the only clever detective in the room."

She reached back and pulled the tortoiseshell ponytail holder from her hair. She shook her hair loose and combed her fingers through it, then massaged her scalp with her fingertips for a moment.

Savannah chalked it up to "self-soothing." She had seen many people do such things when they felt stressed.

For all of her self-confidence and bravado, Savannah sensed that Dee was having a difficult time with this part of the conversation.

All the more reason to press her about it, Savannah reminded herself.

"*Was* Brianne seeing someone besides Paul?" she asked.

"She was seeing someone. A man. I'm sure of that much. She was sneaking out to meet him at various times and places, then lying to all of us about where she'd been."

"Do you know who he was?"

"No. I have no idea. Brianne had always been a one-man-at-a-time kinda gal."

"If you had to take a guess . . . ?"

"Believe me. I'm as inquisitive as you are. I even asked her about it. Several times. She wouldn't tell me, and I don't know. Can't even hazard a guess."

Savannah thought it over for a moment, then said, "So, Brianne was engaged to Paul, about to be married, in fact. But she was having an affair with another man. That could certainly cause a few problems between an engaged couple."

"Yes. Even a namby-pamby like Paul wouldn't want his fiancée meeting another guy and hiding it from him."

She sighed wearily and rubbed her fingers against her temples. Again, it occurred to Savannah that she looked very tired.

"Brianne would sneak out at all hours of the day and night, lying about where she was going," Dee continued. "I heard enough of Paul's screaming and yelling to know that he'd put some sort of tracer on her phone and knew for sure that she'd gone to some bars that are known as pick-up joints."

"Did you hear the names of any of these places?"

"A couple of times he mentioned a bar called The Fisherman's Lair."

"I know the place."

"I can't think of any others right now. I also can't say for sure what Brianne and her secret guy were doing together during those clandestine meetings."

"Apparently, Paul assumed it was hanky-panky."

"Yeah, but Paul couldn't pour water out of a boot if the directions were written on the sole. I'd suggest you don't put a lot of stock in anything he might have said to her. Or you either, for that matter."

"Do you think Brianne was having an affair?" Savannah asked. "Or maybe even multiple affairs?"

"If it had been almost anyone else I know, I'd say, 'Yes.' But Brianne was different. She was one of the few people I ever knew who had true integrity. She did the right thing even when it wasn't convenient for her. That's a rare quality in human beings."

Savannah nodded. "I'm afraid you're right."

Dee seemed to sink lower into the chair, like a parade balloon losing air, as she added, "I don't know what she was doing on those nights when she said she was just going to the library or shopping but was meeting someone at various singles' bars. And now that she's gone, we may never know."

Savannah felt herself sinking a bit, as well. Unfortunately, she was afraid the groom and talented, amateur detective might be right.

Chapter 12

Savannah dreaded coming home to an empty house. Even if she and Dirk might be on the outs, she always preferred him to be home with her, rather than gone.

Puttering around in an empty house reminded her too much of the lonely years . . . those long, solitary days and nights before she and Dirk realized that the precious friendship they'd shared for over a decade had grown into something even deeper.

She had to believe that they were still friends. In spite of the anniversary gift unpleasantness and the quick pecks on the cheek instead of passionate goodnight kisses—and the pleasant activities those kisses frequently initiated—she couldn't bear to think their marriage was actually in trouble, let alone damaged beyond repair.

As she pulled into her driveway, she was pleased to see Granny's latest acquisition parked in the "guest spot." It was an ancient Mercury panel truck, like the one Gran had driven a million years ago, when Savannah and her siblings were just kids. Waycross had found it at an auction, lovingly restored it, and given it to Granny for her birthday.

Just seeing it parked in front of her house made Savannah feel happy and safe and peaceful deep inside. It was exactly the way she had felt all those years ago when the state of Georgia had taken her and her siblings from their negligent, abusive mother and awarded Granny custody of the entire lot of them. From that day forward, they had received nothing but devoted care at their grandmother's loving hands.

Waycross couldn't have given Granny, or their whole family for that matter, a better gift than this vehicle, a reminder of their past.

As Savannah got out of the Mustang and hurried into the house, she was infinitely grateful that she wouldn't be spending the evening alone, eating alone, worrying alone.

Thank goodness for Granny.

In the foyer, she yelled, "Hey, Gran! I'm home."

The cats came running to greet her, winding themselves around her ankles, purring, proclaiming their undying love.

Otherwise known in the Reid household as "Begging for food."

"I'm in the kitchen," Granny hollered in return.

Though her response wasn't necessary. The luscious aroma of something chocolaty baking in the oven was enough to tell Savannah that her grandmother was cooking something quite wonderful.

"I'll be in shortly," Savannah called back as she

removed her Beretta from her purse and stowed it on the top shelf of the coat closet.

Placing her purse on the pie crust table that Granny had given her so long ago, she felt a little of the tension of the day fade away.

Her interviews had gone well. No one had accused her being a liar with bloomers aflame. She had gathered quite a lot of information, though she hadn't figured out yet just what to do with it.

At the moment, none of that mattered terribly. Granny was here, *and* she was cooking for her! Perhaps life was worth all the headaches and nuisance after all.

She bent down to pet the cats and was amused to see them sniff her hand, walk several feet away, and sit there, giving her suspicious, disapproving looks.

"I know," she whispered to them. "I smell like goats. I've got news for you. When you gals eat too many of those spicy tuna treats, you don't smell so great either."

She could have mentioned that the goat pen didn't stink half as much as their litter box, but they were temperamental creatures, these mini-leopards of hers, and she didn't want to push her luck.

Making her way through the living room, she passed the desk and saw the light blinking on her answering machine.

She was the only person she knew who still used one of the old machines, instead of the service provided by her telephone company. But she preferred it because she could still listen to the message in real time, when it was actually being left, and decide whether she wanted to pick it up or not.

Pushing the play button, she hoped it was Dirk with some sort of conciliatory message. That would be all her heart needed to truly feel that all in her world was relatively okay again.

But the male voice wasn't Dirk's.

It was, however, familiar to her—one of her favorite cops, Jake McMurtry. Although he and Dirk didn't always get along so famously, she had enjoyed working with Jake "back in the day."

"Hi, Dirk. Jake here," he said. "I was a little surprised you pulled rank and switched tours on me like that. But the ol' lady was happy to have me home tonight so . . . I guess it worked out. I hear you're taking it again tomorrow night. No hard feelin's, man. Bye."

Her heart sank instantly. Gone was the temporary high of having her beloved grandmother in her kitchen and the smell of chocolate wafting through her house.

Her husband had lied to her. Deliberately, blatantly lied.

Okay, she reminded herself, he might not have outright spoken words that weren't true, but he had led her to believe that the hated captain had forced him to take that late-night stakeout as some sort of punishment for the Vince Muller fiasco.

Now, she knew that Dirk had actually requested that assignment, even bumped a junior officer to get it.

He wants to be away from you, her ugly inner voice shouted. *He's done with you! It's over! He wants out!*

*He's probably with another woman right now. That's
why he didn't want you to come along and keep him company. They're probably in the back seat of his cruiser
doing the same thing you were doing the other night
when—*

"Shut up!"

She didn't realize she had spoken the words
aloud until she glanced toward the kitchen door
and saw her grandmother standing there, a dish
towel in her hand, an astonished and distressed
look on her face.

"Savannah girl. What in tarnation's wrong with
you, sweetheart?" she asked.

Savannah opened her mouth to speak, but nothing came out. Tears filled her eyes as sobs tightened
in her throat, then broke free with an awful, gulp-
ing, sorrowful cry.

A moment later, she wasn't even sure how she
had gotten there, but she found herself sitting on
the sofa with Granny next to her, cuddling her,
cradling her head so that she could weep against
her shoulder.

Savannah felt as though, once again, she was
twelve years old and even though her life might be
falling apart around her, the strongest, most loving
person on earth had her, and she would somehow
make everything all right.

Half an hour later, the worst of Savannah's sobbing had passed, and it occurred to her that she
needed to bring a halt to this new trend of hers—
collapsing into the arms of those closest to her and
blubbering all over their shirts.

It lacked dignity.

But as she looked into her grandmother's eyes, that were the same deep cobalt blue as her own, she didn't see any sign of annoyance or judgment. Only love and concern.

Savannah grabbed some tissues from a box on the end table, wiped her eyes, and blew her nose, then turned to Granny. This was the point in any of their heart-to-hearts when Savannah, having shared her concerns in much greater detail than she probably needed to, with far more raw emotion than was probably necessary, was ready to receive any wisdom her elder cared to share.

Like precious golden honey, the words of wisdom dripped sweetly from Granny Reid's lips. "That's nothin' but a bunch o' hooey."

"Hooey?"

"That's what I said. Bullpucky. Balderdash. Much ado about nothin', or at very least . . . a lotta ado about notta lot."

"But he *lied* to me!" Savannah heard the plaintive tone of her own voice. She realized she sounded like a four-year-old girl at the ice cream counter, complaining that her mom had bought her a single scoop of vanilla instead of a double butter pecan.

She wasn't proud.

"Okay, so your man might've lied to you or stretched the truth a mite, or let you believe something that wasn't quite the whole deal," Gran acknowledged. "But there's also a good chance he's just keepin' somethin' that's private to hisself."

"He's a married man! He doesn't get any privacy!"

Savannah had spoken the words without think-ing.

Since hitting perimenopause, her brain/mouth filter had become frayed to the point of nonexis-tence. But that wasn't always a bad thing. Some-times, she heard her mouth saying things that her heart truly felt. Even if her more logical brain didn't always believe them.

"You know better than that, darlin'," Gran told her with a gently reproving look. "Everybody har-bors a smatterin' of secrets from time to time. That don't mean they're all deep, dark secrets. Just things they don't necessarily share with every Tom, Dick, and Sally in sight."

Granny glanced down at Savannah's shirt cuff with its green stain. "Like not mentioning that a goat recently chewed on them. Most people would probably share that with those around them . . . unless they had a good reason to keep it to them-selves."

Savannah gulped. "How do you know that a—?"

"As you'll recall," Gran interjected, "we lived next to some folks who raised goats. Lord knows, I've had my underdrawers tugged off the clothes-line and chewed more times than I can count. I reckon I should know what goat spit looks like."

Once again, Savannah regretted having taught those she loved her best detective skills. Not that they needed to be taught. Granny's own natural curiosity, bordering on downright nosiness, was quite enough with or without lessons. She didn't need instruction when it came to "sleuthing," as Tammy liked to call it.

"As I was saying," Granny continued, "husbands have the right to keep a few things to themselves, just like we women do. They're entitled to a secret or two, as long as they're not destructive secrets about wrongdoings that'll wind up hurting them and others."

"That's just the point. If he's not doing anything wrong, why does he have to hide what he's doing? A man who has nothing to hide, hides nothing. You told me that yourself."

"Okay, okay. How do you know your man's not on a stakeout, just like he said?"

"He might be. But who's he with, Gran? And what's he doing with them? He made it real clear he didn't want me along with him tonight. I offered to bring food and everything."

Granny gave a little *tsk-tsk*. "I see your point. That's not like Dirk, turning down food. Or your company either. He's mighty fond of you and partial to your cookin'."

"See? That's what I said. He's up to no good."

"No. I don't believe it of him. He's a fine husband, Dirk Coulter is. You'd have to show me a lot more evidence than that for *me* to convict him in a court of law."

"Then you think I'm being unfair to him?"

"I think you're jumpin' to conclusions so high that you'd qualify for the Olympics pole vault."

"Really?" Savannah didn't know whether to feel insulted or relieved.

She decided to embrace the relief.

"I so-o-o hope you're right, Gran. I'd give anything to believe you're right."

Granny reached over and patted her hand. "Then

believe it, sugar. What's the harm in believing the best about those you love?"

"If they betray you when you were busy trusting them, that makes you a fool."

Granny laughed softly. "No, darlin'. It makes *them* a fool for betraying a good person who chose to give them the benefit of the doubt. It's not a bad reflection on you. Making a conscious decision to be patient and kind and to believe the best of folks, that's the act of a strong person, not a fool who's too dumb to know he's bein' taken for a ride on a turnip truck."

"Unless they treat you badly and prove they aren't trustworthy, and you're dumb enough to trust them again."

"Now that's a different story. If they've shown you what they're made of, given you grief, and you go back for more—then that's on you. But I don't think your Dirk falls into that category or even comes close."

"What do you think I should do about this, Gran?"

Granny shrugged. "If I tell you, you won't do it."

"I might."

"You won't. I know you, girlie."

"Tell me anyway."

"Okay. I will, and it'll be like water rollin' off a duck's back." She fixed her granddaughter with a stern eye. "You should let it go, Savannah. If somethin' important is botherin' your husband, sooner or later, he'll tell you about it, or he'll just work it out on his own. Then it'll be over and done with, and the two of you will pick up where ya left off. There. That's the best advice I've got to give you."

Savannah tried to imagine herself "letting it go."
She couldn't.

"I can't."

"I told ya so. I knew ya couldn't. You're good at
a whole heap of things, but lettin' go o' stuff ain't
one of 'em."

"It's really not. So, what's your second-best advice?"

"If you're truly a glutton for punishment and
just gotta open that can o' slimy, crooked worms
and wallow in the mess ya made, then ask him
point-blank what's going on with him."

That appealed to Savannah far more. The direct
approach. "Yeah! I'll grab him by the throat and
shake him till he spills his guts," she said with a
semi-maniacal grin.

"You do what suits ya, sugar. But I'd recommend
a gentler approach. Dirk's a big, strong feller with a
healthy sense of self-preservation. I can't rightly see
him just standin' there, submittin' to a chokin' all
quiet-like. He'd probably call a halt to it with vim
and vigor, and you'd be in a heap o' trouble."

"True." Her brain searched for an alternative
plan. It didn't take long to formulate one. "Okay.
I'll just ask him what in tarnation's gotten into him
lately, and I'm not going to take 'Nothing' for an
answer."

Granny quirked one eyebrow and slowly shook
her head. "Yeah. You do that, sweetcheeks. Good
luck to ya."

Chapter 13

Savannah lay in bed, pretending to enjoy a romance novel on her electronic e-reader. But she hadn't flipped a page for so long that the thing turned itself off, leaving the room dark.

Except for the dim, green light from the digital clock.

It was reminding her that, two hours after his tour had supposedly ended, her husband still wasn't home.

Even after years of doing stakeouts of the same sort that he was supposedly doing that night, Savannah had never acquired the knack for staying awake past her usual bedtime. Her personal circadian clock worked far too well in that regard.

Within minutes of her normal zonk-out time, usually around midnight, her eyelids started to droop and her body seemed to melt into a puddle the consistency of warm apple jelly on a hot sidewalk.

Even if she was sitting in an unmarked car, surveilling a highly dangerous suspect, or spying on someone while lying on a park bench and pretending to be an inebriated street person, or sitting in front of the television with her favorite show playing, she would slide into a deep sleep akin to a coma.

Unfortunately, that night was no different.

In spite of all the adrenaline coursing through her bloodstream, she was dismayed to discover that her exhausted body was less ready for battle than her mind.

Hours ago, she had decided to confront her husband, harangue him, cajole him, twist delicate members of his body into pretzels, starting with his pinky finger or left earlobe and progressing to more sensitive parts if necessary. Whatever it took, she would finagle the truth out of him, once and for all.

She had been fully prepared to do all of these things and more, even before he had stayed out two hours longer than expected. She had her speech all rehearsed.

It wasn't long.

"Are you messing around on me, boy?"

Subtlety wasn't her forte.

After her earlier talk with Dee, the astrologist-groom, she decided to chalk that impulsiveness up to being an Aries. Headstrong, forthright, fearless, totally lacking in even a smidgeon of tact—that was her, all right. She owned it, even celebrated it, even though she knew Granny Reid wouldn't approve.

One of Granny's favorite Bible quotes in such

circumstances was: "When it is possible, as much as lies within you, live in peace with all men."

Savannah appreciated the wisdom of those words, and she tried to abide by them as much as she could manage.

She didn't complain—very often—about the bath towels that were wadded into balls and crammed between the rod and wall, rather than folded neatly in perfect thirds, hung, and then smoothed with the palm of a loving hand before leaving the room.

All day long, as she walked around her formerly neat home, she swallowed words like "Why the hell are your sunglasses in the bread basket?" And "Why on earth did you bother to bring that empty toilet paper roll all the way to the kitchen, only to drop it in the sink?"

No, she tried to live in peace with her man and did. Most of the time.

Nobody was perfect.

She tried to be tactful, but it went against her grain. Tactfulness felt sort of sneaky to her. Even though her Southern heritage and upbringing demanded that sensitivity and diplomacy be employed in almost all circumstances, such "nonsense" didn't come naturally for her.

She wasn't sure if that was a character flaw or a gift. She suspected it was a bit of both.

But in the quiet of the night, speech prepared, dressed for "combat" in a silky nighty that would make him wish he'd been a bit friskier lately, Savannah was ready for him.

Until the clock passed 2:00 A.M., and her eyes closed.

With her arm around Diamante and Cleo curled into a purring black ball on Dirk's pillow, Savannah faded off to sleep.

Yeah, Savannah gal, she thought as she drifted off. *You're a real spitfire hellcat.*

Until midnight.

Then you turn into a punkin.

At 4:14 A.M., she woke with a start, looked at the clock, then turned toward the other side of the bed. There he was, sound asleep.

In fact, he looked dead. He wasn't even doing his usual, bring-down-the-rafters snoring.

That meant one thing to her: he was exhausted.

Telling all those lies and all that fooling around with other women stuff must've plum wore him to a frazzle, her inner witch told her.

Or something substantial happened on the stakeout, and he had to stay late doing paperwork or booking someone, whispered the calm, gentle voice of reason.

As Savannah watched her husband sleep, she could see his features clearly in the moonlight that was now streaming through the lace curtains. He appeared sweet, innocent, untroubled. Far different from the way he had looked in previous days.

Her earlier anger and sense of urgency subsided a bit, and all she really wanted to do was kiss him and snuggle against him. To feel his arm, hard and muscled, slip around her and pull her close to him, into the blissful warmth of his body.

Now that he was actually beside her, still and at rest, she studied him with eyes of love and couldn't believe that these misgivings she had were real.

Their marriage had always been solid. The occasional thunderstorm had cropped up and, from time to time, some impressive squalls had rocked their marital boat.

They were both strong-minded people and were "set in their ways," as Granny would say, both having lived alone for years. It wasn't surprising they would have encountered a few storms along the way. But she had always thought, at least when the nor'easter had passed, that they had weathered the gales well enough.

Was this really the end? Were these "signs" she was noticing true indications that something was badly wrong, as her intuition was telling her? Or were they figments of a menopausal imagination?

More likely, they were echoes of the past when, night after night, a little girl had tossed and turned in a bed filled with siblings and wondered where her daddy was, why she hadn't seen him for so long, and what the townspeople meant when they whispered, "He's a long-distance trucker so's he can stay outta town and chase skirt."

Intuition or imagination? It was hard to know.

Having been a cop for years, Savannah had relied on her innate knowledge to keep her alive. Long ago, she had learned not to disregard what her precious instincts told her.

But this once she hoped, as fervently as she had ever hoped for anything in her life, that it was her intuition that was lying to her.

Not her husband.

* * *

When Savannah woke a few hours later, she turned to the other side of the bed and saw that she was, once again, alone.

At first, she thought he had already left for work, then she smelled the aroma of coffee brewing, and noticed that Cleo wasn't in the bed with her and Diamante.

Cleopatra was always with Mom, unless Dad was available.

Savannah got out of bed, walked to the closet, and chose her new satin Victoria's Secret robe.

It never hurt to look your best when suspecting that your husband was behaving like a two-bit, low-down alley cat. If for no other reason than to remind him of what he was going to miss, terribly, if and when he got nailed for his indiscretions.

On the other hand, if he was behaving in a manner that would qualify him for the Best and Most Faithful Husband of the Year Award, it never hurt to suggest he might have a little reward coming. Something that would prove a sight more satisfying than an engraved, gold-plated trophy for the mantel.

With that in mind and hoping for the best, she left the robe loose, revealing a generous amount of cleavage.

Diamante followed her down the stairs, and when they reached the bottom, she could hear him talking to Cleo in the kitchen. His tone was soft and soothing, as always when he was speaking to one of his "favorite girls."

But before she reached the kitchen, Savannah realized that it wasn't Cleo he was conversing with. It sounded like he was on the phone.

"No, I haven't told her yet," she heard him say. "I will. I'm gonna have to, sooner or later. But it's not a conversation I'm looking forward to. That's for sure."

Savannah stopped so abruptly that the cat ran into the back of her heels. Her heart was pounding so hard that she could hardly hear the rest of what he was saying.

"I have to tell you," he continued, his voice less soft than before, "I don't appreciate you putting me in this position. You know I think the world of you. I always have. But she's my wife and . . ."

He paused to listen for a moment, then said, "Yeah, yeah, okay. I understand. But you need to hear me, too. I didn't sign up for this. You're the one who's putting me in the hot seat, and I don't appreciate it. This is *my* marriage. I'm the one who's going to decide when it's the right time to tell her about you and what's going on."

Savannah didn't even realize that she had gasped, until she heard him say, "She's up. I gotta go."

She heard his phone beep as he turned it off. She could hear her own pulse pounding in her ears.

Before walking into the kitchen, she tried her best to compose herself. It was either that or run in there, grab him, and start yanking out every one of those precious hairs on the top of his head. The ones he was so afraid of losing. The ones she was pretty sure he counted every day.

Savannah drew some calming breaths, and in one of the best performances of her entire life, she squared her shoulders, lifted her chin, and casually strolled into the kitchen.

She caught him shoving his cell phone into his jeans pocket.

Instantly, he donned his "I Wasn't Doin' Nothin' Wrong" look—an expression she was all too familiar with, having seen it on every burglar she had ever caught, holding the loot he'd just stolen in his hands.

It was quickly followed by a "Gee, I'm So Surprised, But Not the Least Bit Upset to See You!" look.

"Good morning!" he said far too cheerfully. "I didn't hear you come down."

"Who were you talking to?" she asked in her most straightforward, headfirst, horns down, Aries tone.

"When?"

On January 32nd, at 12:72 P.M., she thought, *when you were in the shower with that piglet, helping a monkey shampoo its hair. When the hell do you think?*

Instead, she softly, slowly said with her thickest Southern drawl, "Just now."

He fake-thought about it for a moment, then said, "Oh, that. Just work." He glanced at his watch. "Speaking of work, I've gotta report in early this morning."

"You practically live there these days."

He shrugged. "Can't be helped. The stake-out's really paying off."

"Oh?" She was less than impressed.

"Yeah. That dope house I've been sittin' on, it was really hopping last night. I was watching with binoculars from a roof across the street. I took down a bunch of plate numbers. Today we're gonna pick up a dozen or so of that dealer's best customers. Word will get around, and the dude'll be outta business."

When she didn't respond, he continued with a pleading tone. "That's a good thing, Van. He's causing a lot of misery with his operation there. It's gonna feel great to get him and his poisons off the street."

There he was. Her husband.

Just for a moment, Savannah saw the man she loved, the handsome groom she had married as the sun was setting there on the beach, her former partner in law enforcement, the good guy whose favorite thing in the world—next to making love to her, petting Cleo, and telling Vanna Rose a bedtime story—was taking down the bad guys.

In that moment he was telling her the truth.

For all the good that did, after what she had heard before entering the room.

He grabbed his mug off the counter, drank the last bit of coffee from it, then reached for his holster and Smith & Wesson on the table.

"I'm sorry, babe," he said. Again, she could tell he was speaking the truth. He really was sorry.

Unfortunately, it made things worse, not better.

As he passed her, he glanced down at the cleavage she had bared for him.

In a moment of generosity that now seemed so long ago.

He gave her a better-than-average good-bye kiss. A bit longer and sweeter than she'd gotten in a while. She assumed it was in homage to his bird's-eye view of The Girls. Dirk had always been a dyed-in-the-wool boob man.

"Gotta git," he said.

A moment later he was gone, taking her heart and any hopes she had harbored for their future along with him.

Surgeons don't get to cancel people's lifesaving surgeries and take the day off to worry themselves sick when they're on the outs with their mates, Savannah told herself as she drove to a secluded beach not too far from the morgue.

Even if she'd just overheard her husband talking to his mistress, there was no excuse for her moping around the house in the middle of an investigation.

Besides, the quicker she solved this case, the sooner she could get on with her next mission—finding out who the two-bit hussy was and stomping a mudhole in her backside.

Or at the very least, make her fear for her life while administering a fierce tongue lashing that she'd never get over.

That was Savannah's plan at least. Subject to possible adjustments before execution, given future developments.

Granny's skillet might need to be employed.

Time would tell.

Savannah had called Dr. Liu and asked if they could have a clandestine meeting to compare notes and plan her next avenue of investigation. The M.E. had suggested a nearby beach, saying she could slip away, unnoticed, for a half hour or so.

Apparently, "business" was slow.

That was a good thing. A lull in the action at the

county morgue was beneficial for the community at large.

Savannah only had to wait a minute or two, until Jennifer's oversized, black BMW pulled into the lot and parked beside the Mustang.

Eager to enjoy the plush, leather seats of the luxury car, Savannah eagerly jumped out of her vehicle and climbed into the doctor's passenger side.

Jennifer looked a bit forlorn until Savannah handed her a tin that contained some of the triple chocolate cookies that Granny had made the night before.

"You baked!" Jennifer said, reaching for the container. "Bless you!"

"Bless *Gran*," Savannah replied. "They're hers, not mine."

Jennifer raised the lid, looked inside, and took a slow, long breath, smelling the delectable aroma of the tin's contents. "Granny's cookies!" she exclaimed. "Even better."

"Thanks," Savannah said dryly.

"Oh, come on. Don't be jealous. Yours are exquisite. Hers are perfection."

"That's true."

Jennifer held out the tin to her. "Have one?"

"No, thank you. They're all for you. I already had two for breakfast."

"You're going to die."

"With a smile on my face."

"Along with a smear of chocolate, no doubt."

"True enough." Savannah watched as Jennifer made fast work of a couple herself. Glancing up and down the doctor's slender figure, she wondered what it would be like to eat as much as you wanted of whatever you wanted and remain society's rail-thin idea of "slender" and "healthy."

Savannah would never know. She was a "Reid woman," and that was fine by her. "Slender" might be a genetic impossibility. But she figured as long as she could chase down most men, tackle them, and wrestle them to the ground without a spike in her blood pressure or cholesterol levels, she had the "healthy" part covered.

As quickly as she could, to make the best use of the doctor's stolen time, Savannah filled her in on what Tammy had found on the Internet about suicide pacts and what Savannah had discovered during the interviews at Brianne's estate.

Jennifer's mood turned very dark when she heard about the websites where physically healthy people were being encouraged to end their lives.

"If I find out that someone did that to Brianne, God help them," Jennifer said with more anger than Savannah had ever heard her express on any topic. "It's one thing to support someone who's in the final stages of an agonizing disease, in unbearable pain, and has decided to end their lives. But to encourage a depressed person to do such a thing, that's unconscionable."

"Communicating with that sort of website . . . does that sound like something Brianne would do?" Savannah asked her.

"My first inclination would be to say, 'No.' She was an optimistic person, hopeful, resourceful, inclined to work problems out rather than attempt to escape them. But once the Halstead's symptoms began to appear, once she was diagnosed, she became clinically depressed. I have no doubt about it."

"Who wouldn't? To hear that your worst nightmare, the one thing you dreaded, this threat that's been hanging over you most of your life, is finally manifesting itself. That would make even an optimistic person depressed."

"I know. And when people are genuinely, clinically depressed, it changes who they are and how they think. I'd have to say that honestly I don't know what my friend was capable of doing, considering the state she was in."

"Then you may not be able to answer this question either," Savannah said, sorry that she had to ask it. "Do you think Brianne was faithful to Paul?"

Jennifer looked surprised at the question. "I believe so. In all the years I knew her, I don't think she ever had more than one lover at a time and not that many overall. Why do you ask? Did Paul suggest that she had been seeing someone else?"

"No. To hear Paul tell it, they were the perfect couple—other than the Halstead's, that is."

"Then why are you asking about her faithfulness?"

"Because Dee told me she overheard some rather heated arguments between the two of them about that very topic. At least, she heard Paul yelling at Brianne, accusing her of sneaking around and seeing someone else."

"I find that hard to believe," Jennifer said. "Paul might be a bit dull for my taste, but I've never heard him raise his voice under any circumstance."

"Are you saying that Dee was lying to me? That she had some ulterior motive for painting Paul with a black brush?"

"I really don't know. I haven't spent a lot of time with Dee. Mostly I saw her when I went up the hill to play with the goats." She smiled. "Aren't they cute?"

"Adorable. Even when they're chewing the clothes off you."

"Yes, that does happen. One of them swallowed nearly a foot of my sweater belt before I noticed. When I pulled it out of her, it was so gross. All soggy and green. Anyway . . . occasionally, Brianne and I would take a couple of her horses for a ride down the canyon and back. Dee would tack up the horses before we rode and groom them when we finished our ride. She seemed very pleasant and bright."

"Oh, she's very bright. That's for sure. She missed her calling. Should have been a detective of some sort."

Savannah paused, considering the best way to ask her next question. Finally, she decided to just spit it out. "Do you think that Brianne might have been seeing Nels? If she was sneaking out to meet someone, could it have been him?"

With a shrug Jennifer said, "I've already done quite a bit of research myself, and I haven't found anything to connect them to each other. Other than the Halstead's, I couldn't uncover any common element between them, no shared interests, no mutual friends or enemies, locations, events, nothing."

Smiling, she added, "But then, I'm no Tammy Hart."

"Tammy *Reid*. She's one of us now."

"Lucky her. . . ." Jennifer reached into the box again. "An endless supply of delicious baked goods."

Chapter 14

Even though Jennifer Liu didn't seem to think there was a connection between Brianne Marston and Nels Farrow, Savannah had to check it out herself. In any investigation, she left no rock unturned, and in this particular case, she only had two rocks: Nels Farrow and the bar called The Fisherman's Lair. Since there was no rush to visit The Lair, as it would be open until 2:00 A.M., she decided to start with Nels Farrow's widow, Candy.

Before leaving the beach parking lot, Savannah gave Tammy a call to see if she could find the Farrows' address.

Tammy sounded worried when she answered with a rather abrupt, "Hi, Savannah. What's up?"

"I was going to ask you if you could find an address for me, but I'm just being lazy. If you're busy, I can do it myself."

"No. I'm not . . . well . . . I'm sort of busy."

"My little namesake keeping you on your toes?"

"No, your brother is."

"What's wrong with Waycross?"

"He's got the flu. A pretty bad case of it, too, poor guy."

Savannah cringed at even the thought of her little brother being sick. Of her eight siblings, Waycross and Alma were, hands down, her favorites. Sweet, sensible, generous, and loving, he had always been dear to her heart.

She asked, "Tummy or muscle cramps or headaches or—?"

"All of the above."

"O-o-o, that's rough. Can I help? I could run to the drugstore for you or bring some chicken soup or . . ."

"No. I think we're okay."

Savannah thought of little Vanna. "How about you and the baby?" she asked. "We wouldn't want either of you to catch it, especially the little one."

"I know. I was just going to suggest that to Waycross."

"Do you and the baby want to stay at my house until he gets a bit better? He might appreciate the peace and quiet."

"No, it's worse than that. I'm afraid to leave him alone. He's really sick. Throwing up constantly, dizzy, weak. He's a disaster. Couldn't even keep down the herbal tea or miso soup I gave him. He threw up when I even mentioned a seaweed smoothie."

"Oh, wow. I hate to hear that. I know how much he loves those."

"I know, right?"

"What if I come get Vanna and take care of her for you while you tend to my brother?"

"But you have"—Tammy dropped her voice to a

whisper—"that thing you're working on. You don't
have time to babysit."

Savannah was about to tell her that family came
first and the investigation would have to wait, but
then she thought of a better plan. "Pack that little
puddin' cup a diaper bag with some bottles of that
special momma milk of yours, and I'll swing by and
get her. I'll ask Gran to come to my house, and
she'll help me watch her."

"But if Gran's around you very long, she'll figure out that you're up to something."

"That ship done sailed," Savannah said with a
sigh. "One glance and she knew I'd been chewed on
by a billy goat."

Savannah only needed a few minutes to get to
the charming little storybook house on Pelican
Lane where Tammy lived with Waycross. Two doors
from the beach with a steeply pitched roof, horseshoe-shaped door, rustic stonework, and leaded
glass windows, the fanciful cottage had been
Tammy's home for quite some time before Waycross had relocated from Georgia to San Carmelita.

The house had been a gift from Savannah after
a particularly lucrative case had closed. Savannah
had happily bestowed it upon her faithful friend
and assistant as a reward for all the uncompen-
sated time and love that Tammy had given the
agency for so long.

Sometime later, to Savannah's delight, Waycross
had visited California and promptly fallen in love
with the Golden State and his golden girl, though
not in that order. Fortunately, Tammy and he had

figured out that they were in love far more quickly than she and Dirk had.

Savannah couldn't have been happier when the sister her heart had chosen became her honest-to-goodness sister-in-law.

It was always a pleasure to drive down here to this picturesque cottage and recall the good times they had shared over the years. But today, Savannah had more serious things on her mind. The case, her marriage, and if those weren't enough, her younger brother's health.

No sooner had she pulled into their driveway, than the door opened and Tammy appeared on the porch with Vanna Rose in one arm and the diaper bag in the other.

Savannah got out of the car and hurried to her.

"Give that little fairy princess to her auntie Savannah," she said, taking the excited, wriggling child into her arms.

Savannah looked into the baby's bright eyes, sparkling with joy at seeing her, and her heart melted.

Children, dogs and kitties . . . the purest sources of true, unconditional love on earth. It was the sort of affection that healed the heart in an instant and brought peace to the most troubled soul.

She kissed the baby's chubby pink cheeks, then turned to Tammy. "How's that little brother of mine doing?"

"He refuses to go to the doctor," Tammy replied, a worried scowl on her pretty face. "I told him if he gets any worse, I'm going to make him go, if I have to drag him there myself."

"Good for you. If he kicks and screams too

much, give me a call. Between the two of us, we'll get him there. You can't fool around with the flu. It can be serious."

"I know. But you know how guys are about going to the doctor."

"If duct tape and staples won't hold the severed limb on, they'll think about it."

"Exactly."

Savannah opened the Mustang's passenger door, flipped the seat forward, then tucked Vanna Rose into her own carrier that had been installed in the rear seat even before the baby was born.

The Reid clan had been ecstatic to welcome a little one into their midst after a long, dry, boring spell of "adults only" family gatherings.

A baby reminded everyone that, amid all the heartaches in the dark, bitter world, there was also sweetness, innocence, and light.

Vanna cooed and shrieked a good-bye to her mother, as Savannah climbed inside and started the car.

"Call me if you need me," Savannah shouted to Tammy as she pulled out of the drive.

"You, too," Tammy yelled back.

As Savannah drove away, she glanced at her rearview mirror and saw Tammy walking back to the arched front door of her Three Bears cottage. Her head was bowed, her steps faltering and slow, not at all like her usual, bouncy, energetic gait.

An unsettling thought occurred to Savannah. *Maybe my little brother's flu is even worse than she's letting on.*

* * *

No sooner had Savannah gotten Vanna Rose settled back at her house, than Granny arrived to attend to the wee fairy princess. So, Savannah wasted no time getting the Farrows' address from Dr. Liu and heading that direction to interview Nels's widow, Candy.

Savannah wasn't looking forward to it. Dealing with grieving families had always been the worst part of being a cop for her. As a private investigator, too.

At least this time, she wasn't having to make the much-dreaded notification.

She headed up the hills that bordered the east side of town, into an older, quaint area above the historic, adobe mission. Here, homes were smaller, a bit more modest than the mansions on the beach or perched at the top of the highest hills, enjoying the best ocean view—or wildfire view, depending on the season.

It wasn't hard to find the small, Spanish-style house, not unlike her own, with its white plastered walls and red clay tile roof. The Farrow home even had an impressive, red bougainvillea climbing across the front porch. Though the colorful vining plant wasn't nearly as robust as Ilsa and Bogie, the pair that graced her own entryway.

As she got out of her Mustang and walked up to the house, she couldn't help noticing the well-tended landscaping in the front yard. Ice plants abounded, as was common in a drought-prone area, as they could survive with very little water. But the floral beauty didn't stop there. Everywhere Savannah looked, she saw purple irises and crane-shaped birds-of-paradise flowering in profusion, along with bottlebrush plants that looked like giant pink caterpillars.

Behind the flower beds, framing the property and providing privacy, were thick, lush Oleander bushes that were at least six feet tall.

Omnipresent in Southern California, Oleander was known as a plant that was used to make medicines and, unfortunately, occasionally, a lethal poison.

That was a fact Savannah was all too familiar with, having solved a case where it had been used as a deadly weapon.

She knocked at the door several times. Eventually, it was answered by a pretty, young woman, whom Savannah guessed to be in her early thirties.

At least, she would have been pretty, if her eyes had not been red and swollen nearly closed from crying.

The petite blonde was dressed in a shirt that had long sleeves, which was unusual, considering the heat of the day. In Southern California, long-sleeved shirts were usually reserved for the bitterest cold, winter day, when the temperatures plummeted to sixty-nine.

Savannah noticed that in her left hand, she carried a pair of long-handled rose-pruning shears.

Savannah didn't need Tammy the Super Sleuth to explain the reason for the long sleeves.

"Hello. May I help you?" The woman looked a bit guarded and suspicious, and Savannah couldn't blame her. No doubt, the lady of the house was mistaking her for some sort of vulture, who had read the obits, and was now swooping down onto her front doorstep with the intention of selling her something related to her husband's passing.

"My name is Savannah Reid. Would you happen to be Candy Farrow?"

"I am."

Trotting out the same old story that she had used on Paul Oxley and Dee the groomer, Savannah said, "Mrs. Farrow, I'm sorry to bother you at a time like this. But I'm an investigator, doing some research that will hopefully benefit people who suffer with Halstead's. I know you're busy, and this is probably the worst time of your life to entertain an uninvited guest. But if you could answer just a few questions for me, I promise to make it as quick and painless as I possibly can."

"I was pruning my husband's roses" was the lackluster reply.

Savannah smiled. "Yes, I see that. I raise roses myself, and I'm quite familiar with the equipment—not to mention the battle wounds. Pruning roses ain't for sissies."

That brought a slight smile to Candy's face. "That's for sure." Her guard seemed to drop a bit, and she opened the door. "Come on in. I don't mind answering a few questions if it will help people with that horrible disease. As long as you don't mind me pruning while we talk."

"I won't object one bit. I'm convinced that the best conversations are the ones conducted in a flower garden," Savannah assured her, as she followed Candy through the living room, the kitchen, and out the back door.

"My husband would agree with you. I mean, he *would have agreed* with you."

"I understand. It's hard . . . remembering, I mean."

Savannah looked around and realized that she wasn't the only one in San Carmelita with a green thumb. The Farrows' backyard was quite different from hers. It was far more masculine with its raised flower beds bordered with carefully laid stones, assorted cacti arrangements, coyote bushes, Manzanita, and sunflowers. But it was just as impressive in its own way.

Candy led her toward the rear of the yard, to an area enclosed with a white, picket fence. Its entrance was a sturdy, arched trellis that supported a glorious burden of climbing roses the soft color of lilacs.

Savannah remembered what Dr. Liu had said about Candy finding Nels in the rose garden. She was a bit surprised that the woman could bring herself to be in this place, beautiful though it was, let alone work here in the hot summer sun.

Many people found it difficult to revisit a scene where they had experienced a trauma. But then, human beings mourned in many different ways, and she had learned long ago not to judge their choices.

Savannah was also surprised to see that every blossom in the rose garden was a delicate shade of lavender. She had never seen anyone plant only one color of roses. There were so many beautiful varieties, that when she had planted her own, she had found it difficult to choose and had limited herself to one of each type and color.

As Candy led her beneath the trellis and into the garden, the new widow said, "Everyone is surprised to see an all-purple rose garden. But Nels planted this for me the first year we were married, and I wouldn't change it for anything. Especially now that he's gone."

"Your husband must have been a very romantic man," Savannah said.

Candy laughed softly, even as tears moistened her eyes. "He was. Though not in the traditional ways. He frequently forgot anniversaries, was worthless at gift giving, and I could probably count on one hand the times he uttered the words, 'I love you,' I'd have to say he wasn't much of a snuggler either."

Savannah gulped, thinking of her own nontraditionally romantic man. "Women place such great store on the words and the presents and cuddling," she observed. "Men . . . not so much. Not most of them anyway."

Nodding, Candy replied, "True. Instead, when mine found out that lavender roses were the symbol of love at first sight, he planted this garden for me and then lovingly tended it, year after year. I always knew what that meant, what he was saying to me. Every time I walk into this beautiful place, I remember the moment we met."

"You two were instantly smitten?"

"Absolutely. On the spot." Candy glanced down at Savannah's wedding band and engagement ring with its enormous, princess-cut diamond. It was the one gift that Dirk had definitely gotten right. "How about you and your husband? Was it love at first sight for you two?"

"Um, no. For a long time, we were just buddies. Good buddies, then best friends. We knew each other for years before we realized there was something more there. He sorta grew on me gradually."

"But it's working?"

Savannah felt a knot in her throat when she replied. "I think so. I sure hope so."

A look of urgency came into Candy's eyes, along with some fresh tears. "Don't take your husband for granted. Make the most of every day you have with him. You never know when—"

She choked on her words and had to pause to tamp down her emotions.

"Thank you," Savannah said, filling the awkward silence for her, while fighting some unpleasant feelings of her own. "I appreciate that. It's good advice that we can all use."

Chapter 15

As Savannah was driving home to check in on Granny and Vanna Rose, she used the car phone to call Jennifer Liu. Again, the doctor answered after only one ring.

She must be sitting on that phone, Savannah thought. *Poor girl. I sure wouldn't want to be in her shoes. Not even her best Jimmy Choo, crystal rhinestone embossed stilettos.*

Savannah wished she had some good news to share with her. Unfortunately, she had no news at all, which in this situation was the same as bad news.

"Savannah! How's it going?"

"I just left Candy Farrow."

"Did you find out anything helpful?"

Savannah hesitated, trying to think of how to put the best spin on what little she'd uncovered. "She and Nels were very close. If he was having an affair with Brianne or up to no good in any substantial way, I don't believe she suspected it at all."

"Did she seem like a savvy woman who would have known if he was?"

"Yes. She's intelligent. Wise, too. She gave me some good advice that I'm going to do my best to follow."

"But she didn't suggest any connection between the two of them?"

"Not at all. I told her about Brianne passing from the same illness and asked if she'd ever heard of her. She said she hadn't."

"How about Nels and his recent behavior?"

"She said that he was depressed, as one might expect, considering he'd received a death sentence."

"Any suggestion of suicide plans?"

"Quite the contrary. She said he was determined to cherish and make the most of every day he had left. The night before he died, they sat at the kitchen table and wrote a bucket list of things they wanted to do together, while he was still able."

"That doesn't sound like someone who was intending to end it all the very next day."

"I know."

For a moment, the two women were silent, grappling with this new piece of evidence that supported their worst fears.

"They really were murdered," Jennifer finally said.

Savannah could tell by her tone that the brutal fact had just become even more real to her grieving friend.

After years of observing other people's worst trials and experiencing some of her own, Savannah had discovered that some of life's harshest truths were too painful to swallow in one moment and had to be sipped gradually, taking in only as much as the heart could bear at the time.

Apparently, this was one of those circumstances for Jennifer.

"I hate to say it, Jen," she said. "But I do believe that's what we're looking at."

"But we're no closer to finding out who did it."

"I still have a couple of leads. I'm going to go home for a pit stop. Gran's babysitting my baby niece there. I'm going to pop in and see how it's going."

Savannah didn't mention the other reason she wanted to stop at the house.

Sometimes, if Dirk was pulling a double shift, he would come home around that time to shower and grab a bite to eat before going out to tackle the second part of his workday.

Savannah had tried to convince herself that she wanted to be there to feed him, to touch base, and show him some wifely kindness. But she knew herself better than that.

Her intentions were far less admirable. She had puredee no-good on the mind.

All day, the good wife inside her, the one who believed it was important to trust one's spouse and give them the benefit of the doubt in almost all circumstances, had been wrestling with her basic nature, the core part of her that made her a good detective.

Her nosy self.

She knew, all too well, who would win the battle in the end. There was no question about the outcome. She wasn't going to have a moment of inner peace until she found out whom he had been speaking to on the phone that morning in the kitchen.

No matter how many times she scolded herself for even thinking of sneaking a peek at her husband's phone while he was in the shower, she knew she was going to do it.

She had already convinced herself that, having eavesdropped on the conversation she'd overheard that morning, ninety-nine out of one hundred wives would do the same. And the one who wouldn't just didn't know how to look up the call history on a smart phone.

But she decided not to burden Dr. Liu with her marital problems. The woman had enough on her mind and thought precious little of Dirk as it was. No point in deepening her dislike for him.

Savannah took momentary comfort in the fact that she was a loyal wife, if not a great respecter of her husband's privacy.

"After I see how Gran's doing with the baby," she told Jennifer, "I'll head over to The Fisherman's Lair to see if I can find out the name of the guy Brianne was meeting there."

"That's a rough place. Watch yourself."

"I will."

"Okay, you said you have a couple of leads. That's one. What's the other?"

Savannah thought hard but came up blank. "Okay. You got me. There isn't another one. That's all I have."

"Then you'd better wear your undercover hooker garb when you go fishing at The Lair."

Savannah chuckled. "I'm not quite as alluring in my leather miniskirt and fishnet stockings as I was twenty years ago. Cellulite is definitely having its way with me, or at least my thighs, these days."

"Don't worry about a little lump and bump here and there. I assure you, with abundant cleavage like yours, it won't be your thighs that The Lair's clientele will be drooling over."

When Savannah arrived back home, she entered her house and found a most peaceful, soul-satisfying sight. Gran was sitting in Savannah's chair, her feet on the footstool, bookended by Diamante and Cleopatra.

The reason they were next to Gran's feet and not on her lap, as usual, was obvious. Vanna Rose was sound asleep, lying on her tummy in Granny's arms, her head on her great-grandmother's shoulder, her tiny hand resting on Gran's cheek.

Savannah couldn't help recalling the bliss she had experienced as a child, snuggling against her well-rounded grandmother. Lying on Granny was like melting into a large, warm, soft pillow. Nothing bad could ever happen to you there in the circle of her loving arms. Surely, there was no sweeter, safer place on earth.

Granny gave her granddaughter a smile when Savannah walked over to the sofa and sat down.

"Sorry for takin' up your chair," Gran said, speaking low. "I'd get up and give it to ya, but—"

"No, no. Don't be silly. I wouldn't ask you to move a hair on that child's head or your own either, for that matter. The two of you are the most peaceful sight I've seen in ages."

"I must admit, I am enjoying every second of this. What a blessing it is, having a little one in the family again. It's been too long."

"It has been," Savannah said somewhat sadly.

She couldn't help thinking of her and Dirk's unsuccessful attempts at becoming parents. It was the one cloud hanging over an otherwise mostly-sunny marriage. At least, until lately.

Savannah's early-onset menopause and its resulting infertility was one of the few regrets that she had, concerning her husband. For all the years she'd known him, the otherwise rough, tough street cop had demonstrated a deep affection for all things that were truly sweet and innocent: dogs, cats, and especially children. She had no doubt that he would have made a wonderful father, and she would have loved to have given him a son or daughter of his own.

Apparently, some things just weren't meant to be.

Maybe if you'd given him a kid or two, you'd mean more to him now, barked her internal tormentor. *He's probably going to dump you. It's not like he's got a cute little kid to stick around for and—*

If I ever manage to get my hands around your throat, you nasty, evil woman, she told the voice, *you are done for. Kaputz. Toes pointing at the sky and on your way to hell in a handbasket!*

"Who's going to hell in a handbasket?" Granny asked.

"Oh, I didn't realize I was talking out loud."

Gran chuckled. "That happens more and more as you get older, so get used to it."

"Then I'm going to be in trouble, considering what I'm thinking half the time."

"It's probably no worse than the rest of us. If we could read each other's thoughts for ten minutes, most of us would never speak to each other again."

"Present company excepted," Savannah said, giving her an affectionate smile.

"Of course," Granny replied. "You just might be the one person I've never had one cranky thought about in my entire life."

"Not even when I threw my muddy shoe at Marietta, and it landed in the middle of that beautiful, big, banana-nut cake you'd just baked for the pastor?"

"Well . . . okay . . . I've never had *two* cranky thoughts about—"

"Or that time when I snuck your only pair of earrings, the ones you only wore to church and weddings and funerals, out of your drawer and then dropped one of them down the hole in the outhouse seat?"

"I reckon that was the height of your career as a juvenile delinquent, so—"

"Then there was the other time when—"

"Savannah, girl, you need to learn how to stop when you're ahead."

Savannah laughed. "I've heard that before."

"I'm sure you have. But then, we've all got our life lessons that we're workin' on."

"When do you suppose we get them all learned?"

"About the time that we look around and realize that we're starin' *up* at the grass, rather than *down* on it."

"Hmm, something to look forward to."

Savannah heard a familiar sound in the driveway—the rumbling of Dirk's cruiser as it pulled next to her Mustang and stopped.

Cleo flew off the footstool and ran to the front door. No doubt about it; Daddy was home.

Rather than her usual pleasure at hearing that sound, Savannah experienced an unpleasant mix of sadness, anger, and fear. In all the years she had known him, she had never felt those emotions in his presence. At least, not on account of him or his actions.

She hated the change.

When he walked through the door and into the foyer, she wanted to run to him, like Cleopatra, throw herself into his arms, and then—remembering the phone call she had overheard that morning—beat the ever-lovin' daylights out of him.

But she fought the urges and just sat there, waiting for him to finish greeting Cleo and walk into the room.

When he finally did, after what seemed like about twelve hours, he gave her a brief nod before directing his attention to the baby on Granny's lap, who was stirring from her sleep.

"Uh-oh," he said. "Uncle Dirk didn't mean to wake you up, little fairy princess."

The baby quickly stirred, her blue eyes wide open with excitement at seeing him. She turned in Gran's arms to face him and held out her hands to him.

A second later, he had scooped her up and was holding her over his head, calling her "Tinkerbell" and asking her if she wanted to go to never-never land.

Savannah couldn't help but smile as she watched her husband "fly" the child around the room on a "fairy adventure." It was a common game they played, where the sofa became a pirate ship, the television a giant crocodile, and the coffee table was transformed into a lagoon inhabited with mermaids.

Although little Vanna Rose couldn't yet understand his vivid descriptions of the scenes she soared over, she loved the excitement in his voice and squealed with glee as they barely escaped the snapping jaws of the mighty "croc."

When their trip finally ended, Dirk landed himself and the child in his recliner, where they began a serious game of patty-cake, that included her slapping him on the cheeks and ears—much to her delight.

"So, what's going on?" he finally asked the adults in the room. "How come we get to babysit the munchkin? Are her folks out on one of their date nights again?"

"I wish," Savannah said. "But no such luck. Waycross is sick."

Dirk halted their game and gave Savannah a

deeply concerned look. "What do you mean, 'sick'? What's wrong with him?"

"Apparently, he's got the flu," Granny offered, "and a pretty bad case to boot."

"That's why the baby's here," Savannah told him. "We were afraid she might catch it if she stayed there."

"What's he doin'? You know, like what're his symptoms?" Dirk asked.

"He's throwing up. A lot. And he's got the Green Apple Quick Step out the other end, too." Savannah rolled her eyes. "Shakes, chills, muscle aches, and all that good stuff. Tammy says he's really miserable. She's been plying him with herbal concoctions, but he's just getting worse."

Dirk jumped up from his chair and handed the baby back to Granny. He took his phone from his jeans pocket and punched in a few numbers.

"Yeah, Tammy," he said when she answered. "I hear your guy's sorta under the weather. Can I talk to him?"

As Tammy replied, he gave a quick glance toward Savannah and Granny, turned his back to them, and walked into the kitchen.

From the other room, they heard him say, "No, don't get him out of the bathroom if he's busy. I just wanted to check on him and tell you . . . if he gets any worse, like *at all*, you should get him to a doctor right away."

He paused, listening, then said, "I don't care if he doesn't want to go. If you see him doing . . . well, anything that you don't like the looks of, and he won't go to the hospital, you give me a call. I'll come over there and take him in myself."

A moment later, Savannah couldn't miss the urgency in his voice when he added, "I don't mean to scare you, honey, but there's a nasty bug going around town at the moment. You can't mess with it. He could take a turn for the worse real fast. Try to talk him into going to a doctor. I'll call back in a while and see what's going on. Okay? All right. Take care, darlin'."

Savannah sat, shocked by all she had just heard. Like most men, Dirk had a tendency to whine a bit more than necessary when he caught a common cold. But, in general, he didn't tend to overreact when it was someone else who was sick.

Of course, she felt sorry for her little brother and was moderately concerned about his health. After all, influenza could be serious, even deadly, and shouldn't be taken lightly. Heaven knows, that particular disease had taken millions of lives over the course of human history.

But while she appreciated Dirk's touching concern for his brother-in-law, she couldn't help feeling that he was being a tad overly dramatic in this case.

Other than his broken leg, which was finally on the mend, Waycross was an extremely healthy guy. She had no doubt he would shake this off in a few days, considering the benefit of Tammy's loving care and in spite of her green-glop concoctions.

When he walked back into the living room, Savannah saw that the look of concern on his face was even more pronounced than before he had made the call.

"Well? What'd Miss Tammy have to report?" Granny asked. "How's my grandson doin'?"

"Some worse," Dirk told her. "She says he's not acting like hisself . . . whatever that means."

"But he won't go to the doctor?" Savannah asked.

"Nope. But that's no surprise."

"Why?"

Dirk looked uneasy, like a felon who was deciding whether or not to confess. "Because he's him . . . a guy. You know how we are."

"Waycross ain't like that," Granny said. "I raised him not to be ashamed to admit it when he needs help. Maybe I should hightail it over there and talk some sense into him myself."

"No, don't do that," Dirk said most emphatically.

A bit too emphatically, Savannah thought.

"I'm gonna grab a shower," he said, "and then I'll stop by their place on the way to my stakeout."

"Thank you, son," Granny told him with her most gentle, loving voice—the one she usually reserved for her grandchildren and their babies. "I'd sure appreciate you doin' that. T'would set my heart to rest, knowing that you're takin' charge o' things over there."

"Me, too," Savannah added gratefully.

Without replying, he walked over to Vanna, softly ruffled her red curls with his fingertips, gave her a sweet, if somewhat worried, smile, then headed out of the living room and up the staircase.

Savannah watched him, thinking, plotting.

She knew his routine. He would go into their bedroom, get a clean shirt, underwear, and socks from the dresser drawers. Then he would peel off his jeans, throw them across the foot of the bed, and walk into the bathroom next door for his shower.

His phone would be in his jeans pocket.

She could feel her heart racing. In her line of work, she was all too familiar with the art of covert operations. She was quite good at that sort of thing. But she wasn't used to sneaking around on her husband, and that was probably a good thing, since he was a detective. A darned good one.

Reluctantly, she would admit that, on one of his better days, he was a fairly even match for her. If she was going through chocolate withdrawal or was in the throes of some sort of menopausal meltdown, he might even be a wee bit better.

So, if she intended to do this deed, she'd have to be careful about it.

Also, she wanted to hide the fact from Granny, whom she was pretty sure wouldn't approve of such an underhanded deed.

She tried to keep a neutral, innocent, I'm-Not-Up-To-A-Darned-Thing look on her face as she sat there on the sofa, waiting to hear the shower begin upstairs.

Of course, having raised two sons and nine grandchildren, Granny was all too familiar with that particular expression and fixed her with a suspicious look of her own.

Finally, Savannah heard the burbling sound of water flowing through the house's old pipes.

Okay, she told herself, *it's now or never.*

"Excuse me for a minute," she said to her grandmother as she headed for the staircase. "I've got something I need to take care of. I'll be back in two shakes of a lamb's tail."

But as Savannah headed up the stairs she knew it would take longer than two shakes. First Degree Skullduggery, especially of the domestic variety, took ten. At the very least.

Chapter 16

Even though Savannah knew that Dirk would never hear her footsteps above the sound of the shower running, she found herself tiptoeing past the bathroom door on her way to the bedroom.

One could never be too careful about these things.

If worse came to worst, and she found something heartbreakingly conclusive on his phone, she didn't want to compromise her own role as the offended party by getting caught doing something less than angelic.

Like that would matter one hoot, she told herself as she snuck through the bedroom door and quietly closed it behind her.

If I find something on that phone that would stand up in court and convict a guy of adultery in the first degree—a capital crime with special circumstances—he's gonna wish he had a state-administered execution compared to what I'm going to give him.

"After I pick up the broken pieces of my heart off the floor," she whispered.

Her pulse thundered in her ears as she walked over to the bed where, as predicted, his jeans had been tossed across the foot of it.

For a moment she looked at the worn denim, the threadbare knees, and ragged hems. She thought of all the work he had done in those jeans, bringing them to that tattered state.

Protecting. Serving.

His city.

Her.

Over the years, through all of their ups and downs, there had never been a moment when she had considered her best friend and then husband-to-be anything less than a truly honorable man.

Detective Sergeant Dirk Coulter was one of the good guys.

Knowing that fact had been important to her. She had relied upon it. Taken pride in it.

For years, she had felt safe—physically, mentally, and emotionally—because Dirk Coulter was a good man.

Good men don't lie to their wives, said one of the voices inside her head. She wasn't sure which one it was this time . . . the nasty, accusing gal, or her quiet voice of reason.

A good man doesn't have a mistress who puts him in a position he doesn't appreciate, the voice continued. *A good man doesn't stand in the kitchen, talking to his "other woman" on the phone, ensuring her that he'll tell his wife about her sometime soon.*

And a smart, strong woman with investigative skills

doesn't wait around, wringing her hands and wondering what's going on, when she's got good reason to believe her man's stepping out on her, she told herself.

If he's innocent, then let's find out now and put this whole thing to rest. If he's guilty, it's better that you know about it now than that you find out farther down the road, after you've developed an ulcer or he's passed away from a brain hemorrhage, brought on by exposure to a fourteen-inch, cast-iron skillet.

It's now or never, Savannah girl. Do it!

She couldn't help noticing that her hand was shaking when she slid it carefully into the jeans pocket and pulled out his cell phone.

In fact, it was shaking so badly that she held the phone over the bed as she turned it on, just in case she dropped it.

All the while, she kept her ear tuned to the sound of the shower running.

She had already decided that if, for some reason, he exited the bathroom early and came into the bedroom before she was able to replace the phone, she would claim she had come upstairs for a sweater.

Lying to your husband, she thought, *that's a new low. I thought that was something we just didn't do.*

Just like I thought we would always be faithful to each other, the way we promised we would that day on the beach in front of God and everybody we loved.

A second after she pushed the "On" button, the phone lit up, and she burst into tears when she saw the picture he had chosen for his home screen. It was a photo she had never seen before. One he had obviously taken secretly.

The picture was of her in her pink Minnie Mouse pajamas, asleep amid the tousled sheets of their bed, her arm draped over Diamante, and Cleo lying on Dirk's pillow next to her.

Then and there, Savannah decided to turn the phone off and replace it in his jeans. What man who was fooling around on his wife would have a picture like that on his phone? A photo for the world, and more importantly, his "other woman," to see anytime his phone rang?

No man.

Certainly not her Dirk.

Whatever that phone call she had overheard might have meant, there had to be an innocent explanation.

She would ask him for it, somehow, some way. But when she did, it wouldn't be an accusation, because now, in her heart, she knew he was still hers—body, heart, and soul.

She was reaching for the jeans, when suddenly, the phone rang. It startled her so badly that she dropped it.

Fortunately, it landed on the quilt Granny had given them for their wedding.

She snatched it up off the bed and started to turn it off. Then she recognized the ring tone. It was one of Dolly Parton's old tunes named "Dumb Blonde," a song whose lyrics contradicted the offensive title. Dirk had chosen it long ago for Tammy.

Torn, Savannah hesitated, reluctant to turn the phone off, as planned. The call might be important. An emergency even. She couldn't ignore it, even if it meant her getting caught.

"Hi, Tams," she said, keeping her voice low.

"Savannah? Oh, I thought it would be Dirk."

"He's in the shower, sugar. What's up?"

To her dismay, she could hear Tammy start crying on the other end. "It's Waycross."

Savannah's heart sank. She fought the urge to panic. Whatever was wrong, it would require a calm mind and spirit. "Okay, honey. Tell me what's wrong."

"I don't even know. It's as if he's gone crazy or something. He's not even . . . him!"

"I hear you. Now, take a deep breath and tell me exactly what's happening."

"A few minutes ago, he found out that I'd sent the baby over to your house, so you and Granny could take care of her, and he just flew into a rage about it."

A rage? Savannah thought. *Waycross?*

She could count on one hand the times she had ever seen her brother mildly annoyed. He was the calmest, most peace-loving person she had ever had the pleasure of knowing.

"Did you explain to him that we just wanted to keep the baby from catching his flu?" Savannah asked.

"I tried to. But he seemed to think that we thought he was an unfit father, not capable of taking care of his own child. He says you and Dirk are trying to take her from him, like a custody thing, permanently."

"What on earth would make him think such a thing?"

"I'm afraid he's got a fever, and it's addled his brain or something. I'm telling you, he's just not himself. Something's badly wrong with him. I'm starting to think he had a stroke or—"

"Put him on the phone," Savannah told her. "Let me talk to him. I'm his big sister. He'll listen to me."

"That's just the problem. He's not here."

"Not there? Where is he?"

"He took off. Drove out of here like a bat out of hell a few minutes ago. I tried to stop him from getting into the car, but he shoved me to the ground!"

"Are you hurt?"

"No, but he's never, ever done anything even close to that!"

"Did he say where he was headed?"

"That's the craziest part of all. He said he's going to your house to get his baby and bring her back home where she belongs." Tammy's voice was getting higher, more frantic by the moment. "Savannah," she said, "I'm so afraid. I can't believe I'm saying this, but I honestly don't know what Waycross is capable of right now."

"Try to calm down, sweetie. I can tell you one thing that's *not* going to happen. He's not going to get anywhere near this baby in the state he's in. We're not going to allow that. You know we won't let any harm come to either one of them."

Tammy's weeping subsided a bit as she said, "I know you won't. But I don't want you or Dirk to get hurt either."

"We won't. I promise you. Nothing bad is going to happen to anybody you love. I won't let it."

"Thank you, Savannah. I love you."

"I love you, too, sweetcheeks." Savannah heard Dirk turn the shower off in the room next door. "I know you can't help it but try really hard not to worry."

"Okay" was the weak, unconvincing reply.

"I'm going to tell Granny to bring the baby upstairs and keep her here in our bedroom. Dirk and I will go out on the front porch and wait for Waycross. We'll deal with him."

"Be gentle with him, please. You know something's got to be wrong with him. Our Waycross . . . he's not like this. He's the sweetest—"

Her voice broke, and she couldn't continue.

"You know we wouldn't hurt him for the world. We'll take good care of him and get him to a doctor, I promise. All will be well, honey. I give you my word. I'll call you as soon as things settle down, and we know what's going on."

"Maybe I should come over there myself."

"No, you stay there in case he comes to his senses and goes back home."

"Okay. Keep me posted. Please."

"I will. I promise."

As soon as Tammy ended the call, Savannah shoved the phone back into Dirk's jeans and ran out of the bedroom.

She pounded on the bathroom door. "Dirk, you've gotta come out, darlin'."

He didn't open it fast enough, so she barged in, to find him wrapping a towel around his waist.

He took one look at her face and said, "What's wrong?"

"Tammy just called, all upset, crying. Waycross has plum lost leave of his senses. He roared out of the house, knocked Tammy to the ground, said he was driving over here to get his baby. He claims she belongs at home with him, and that we're trying to take custody of her."

"Damn."

"Where would he even get a stupid idea like that?"

Instead of answering, he pushed past her and hurried into the bedroom. She followed him and, as he pulled on some underwear and a T-shirt, she said, "I told Tammy we'll take care of the situation once he gets here. I promised her that we'd make sure he comes to no harm. I said we'd bring Gran upstairs with the baby, then wait for him on the front porch."

"Good," he said, sliding into his jeans. "Go get them. Now."

"Okay."

She turned to rush out the door, but as she did, she heard the phone in his pocket ring once again. As he answered it, she waited anxiously to see if it was an update from Tammy.

"Yeah, Coulter here," he said.

Almost instantly, a deadly serious expression crossed his face . . . one that chilled her heart. Then he sent her an alarmed look that she could feel through her entire being.

"Okay," he said. "Where?"

The other person spoke. She could hear the voice enough to know it was a male, but not Waycross.

She felt slightly relieved.

"Right," Dirk replied. "Thanks."

He hung up, and for what seemed like forever, she hesitated, wanting to know what had been said and why her husband's tanned face had turned several shades lighter but feeling the urgency to get on with her task at hand.

"Whatever that was, I've got to get Granny and the baby upstairs," she said, more to herself than to Dirk.

"No, you don't," Dirk said, his voice flat, as though he was stunned into an emotional numbness.

"But Waycross . . ."

"He's not coming."

Time slowed for Savannah. What felt like an eternity passed as she listened to Granny talking to Vanna downstairs and the baby jabbering sweetly in return.

"He went back home?" Savannah asked, knowing that her words weren't logical. It hadn't been Tammy who called. The male hadn't been Waycross. There had been no soft, Southern drawl. Why would someone, whose voice she didn't recognize, call to tell them that Waycross had returned to Tammy and was perfectly safe and sound?

"That was the dispatcher. He told me my brother-in-law's been in an accident."

Savannah felt a flood of adrenaline hit her bloodstream, turning her insides to quivering jelly. "Where?"

"'Bout a half mile from their house."

"How . . . how bad?"

"I don't know."

Dirk reached for her, pulled her into his arms, and held her tightly against his chest. Too tightly. She could feel his heart pounding and his breath coming as fast and hard as hers was.

But the embrace was only for a moment.

He released her, grabbed her hand, and headed for the door. "Come on, babe," he said. "Let's go see for ourselves."

Chapter 17

"Let him be okay. Please, please, please. Let Waycross be okay." Savannah whispered the heartfelt prayer as she yanked the cruiser's door open and slid onto the passenger's seat.

Dirk had gotten in seconds before her, and even before she could get her door closed, he punched the gas and sent the powerful vehicle hurtling out of the driveway and down the street.

"He's okay," he told her. "He'll be all right."

She thought of all the times she had uttered those empty, worthless words to people fearing the worst, and a sense of desperate anger rose, hot and spirit-scalding inside her.

"You're just saying that to make me feel better. You don't know it's true," she shot back. "For all you know, he could be—"

"He's not dead. He's fine!" was Dirk's equally emotional reply.

"Until we find out he's not," she said, fighting back tears.

"Yes." Dirk's tone softened as he reached over and patted her thigh. "Unless and until we know he's not . . . he's okay. Okay?"

Once they were a few blocks away from the house, Dirk flipped on the patrol car's siren and lights and increased his speed.

Savannah knew he had waited because he didn't want Granny to hear the siren and become any more alarmed than she already was.

"I think you did the right thing, babe, not telling your grandma," he said. "There's no point in her being worried sick until we know, well . . . what we're dealing with."

"She knew something was wrong. She's a smart cookie, and the two of us came tearing down the stairs and out the door with nothing but a 'We gotta go. See ya later.' Of course, she's worried."

"But not nearly as worried as she'd be if she knew what's actually happened."

"True. No point in her being all upset until she has to be."

"She may not have to be."

"From your mouth to God's ears."

He took a hard turn onto Seaview and headed toward the beach, squealing the tires and running a red light.

Savannah held on to the armrest with her right hand and the console with her left.

This was hardly her first wild ride with Dirk at the wheel of a squad car. He was a skilled driver, and she wasn't worried about him wrecking it. But not all members of the public respected the sound of a siren and pulled over as they were supposed to. She knew more than one cop who had been injured, or worse, when T-boned at intersections by impatient drivers who were determined to take their supposed right of way, no matter what the cost.

"Should I call Tammy?" she said, thinking aloud. "I told her I'd let her know when things had settled down."

"We will. When things have settled down. Once we know what's going on, we'll call her."

"Or go over there in person if the news is . . ." A hard knot formed in Savannah's throat, and she couldn't finish the statement.

He finished it for her. "Yes, we'll probably wind up going there in person."

When she gave him a horrified look, he quickly added, "When we need to give Waycross a lift back home."

Again, he squeezed her thigh. "Relax, darlin'. We ain't gonna be doin' no notifications today. It's a wreck. Just a plain ol' 11-79. We used to answer those calls a dozen times a day."

Her anxiety level soared. "An 11-79? Not an 11-78? You didn't tell me an ambulance was sent!"

"Probably just a precaution," he added quickly. "Or maybe for somebody in the other vehicle. Please, sugar, don't borrow trouble. We'll be there in less than a minute. Just hang on and try not to torture yourself with worst-case scenarios. Okay?"

The hot tears that had been forming in her eyes spilled down her cheeks as she grabbed his hand, which was still resting reassuringly on her thigh, and squeezed it between both of hers.

"What would I do without you?" she said.

He gave her a quick look, filled with love, as he reluctantly pulled his hand back and used it to squeal around another corner, taking them onto Anchors Way.

"It doesn't matter," he said. "You won't ever have to find out what you'd do if I wasn't around. I'll always be here. You're stuck with me, kid. This marriage thing—for us, it's a life sentence."

"One I want to serve. Every day."

She thought of his cell phone, the picture of her and the kitties sleeping, and she felt ashamed of herself for doubting him.

Unfortunately, she hadn't had time to savor the feeling of relief. Tammy's call had come too quickly on the heels of her comforting reassurance, turning her world upside down all over again.

Now, instead of experiencing a sense of blissful respite at having solved a potentially disastrous problem, she was imagining paramedics doing CPR on her little brother as they loaded him into the back of an ambulance.

Then, she didn't have to imagine it anymore.

They turned the corner onto Pelican Lane, and she saw it. Thankfully, minus the CPR.

Ambulance attendants were, indeed, strapping her brother to a gurney. She was grateful to see that he was conscious, though flailing about as they secured him.

No doubt, that was the reason for the restraints.

Nearby, his beautifully restored old Charger was a mess, its front half on the sidewalk, its left fender crushed. Beneath its crooked tire lay the sad, blue remains of what had once been the corner mailbox.

Envelopes of various sizes and colors floated down the street, riding the early-evening sea breeze.

"Looks like the only fatality was the United States Postal Service," Dirk said.

"Thank goodness," she whispered.

"Yes," he agreed.

He had barely brought the cruiser to a stop when Savannah threw open her door and jumped out.

She ran to the gurney and, much to the male and female attendees' surprise, pushed them aside to get to her brother.

"Waycross, darlin', are you all right?"

He looked up at her with wild, unfocused eyes.

Grabbing his hand, she squeezed it and said, "It's me, honey. It's Savannah. Don't you worry. Everything's okay now. The worst is over. You're gonna be all right."

She turned to the paramedic whom she had just shoved, an enormous black man with a round face and kind eyes. His name tag identified him as Glenn Hodges. She whispered to him, "He *is* going to be all right, huh?"

He didn't answer her at first. Then Dirk, standing behind her, flashed his badge and said, "She's his sister. His *older* sister."

Glenn smiled knowingly and patted Savannah on the back with his big hand so hard that he nearly knocked her down. "Aww. You're the Big Sis. I should've known. I've got a few of those myself."

He grabbed the end of the gurney and began to pull it toward the back of the ambulance.

Before the petite female EMT, standing nearby, could offer assistance, Dirk grabbed the other end and started to push.

As they slid the stretcher into the vehicle, Glenn told Savannah, "Your little brother's bum leg needs to be checked, just in case it got re-injured. Plus, his heart rate's elevated."

"Probably from the adrenaline, right?" she asked hopefully. "After all, he was just in an accident so you'd expect his pulse to be—"

"Higher than that. Plus, arrhythmia." He paused for a moment, and when she didn't reply, he added, "That's an irregular heartbeat."

"I know what arrhythmia is," Savannah said. "Thank you."

"Does he have any heart disease?"

"He's as healthy as Farmer Doolittle's best plow mule."

"What? Whose what?"

Dirk translated. "No diseases. Heart or otherwise."

"Oh, okay. Good. But he still has to be checked out."

With the gurney inside and secured, Savannah got ready to climb inside with her brother.

"Wait a minute," she heard Dirk say.

Assuming that he was talking to her, she turned around, ready to give him an argument about why she should accompany Waycross to the hospital. But instead, she saw him reach out and grab the paramedic's burly arm. She realized Dirk was speaking to him.

"Before you go," he continued, "there's something you need to know. They'll need to be informed at the ER, too."

"Okay. What's that?" Glenn asked.

Dirk gave Savannah one of his now all-too-familiar, guilty looks. Then he said, "He has another medical issue going on. He—"

"Oh, yeah!" Savannah interrupted. "He has the flu. Really bad. The one that's been going around. That might be what's causing his arrhythmia. My husband's right. The ER needs to be aware of that."

Dirk reached over and put his arm around Savannah's shoulder. He hugged her tightly against his side.

"He doesn't have the flu," he said softly. "He's going through opioid withdrawal. A pretty severe case of it. Cold turkey, I suspect. Be sure to tell them that at the hospital."

The paramedic didn't look particularly surprised. But if Dirk hadn't been supporting her, Savannah was pretty sure she would have hit the ground, like a weeping willow struck by an F-5 tornado.

"Opioid withdrawal?" she shouted. "What the hell are you talking about?" She shook off Dirk's arm and pushed him away from her. "What are you saying? My brother's no drug addict! He's as clean as they come. Hardly even drinks. Why would you accuse him of—?"

Even though she resisted, he pulled her back

into his embrace and said, "I'm not *accusing* anybody of anything, Van. It's just a fact, and they need to know it. You get in the ambulance and ride with him. I'll follow along. We'll talk about it once we get him checked out and settled in."

She looked up into his eyes and his love, concern, and affection touched her heart and calmed her anger. A sense of deep despair took its place.

"Everything will be okay," he said. "Go on now. Get inside." He turned to the paramedic. "She's riding along."

When Glenn looked less than enthused, Dirk added, "She'll behave herself. She promises."

"Okay," he said, somewhat reluctantly. "Let's go."

Savannah didn't wait for him to change his mind. She jumped into the back of the ambulance and sat where she was directed, on a bench seat next to her brother.

She took Waycross's hand and laced her fingers through his. "You're okay, darlin'," she said, summoning her most soothing, older sister voice. "No matter what's going on with you, your family loves you to pieces, and we're going to stand by you every step of the way. You're not alone, and you'll be all right in the end. You'll see."

The little female EMT got into the driver's seat, and Glenn climbed into the back after Savannah, filling the interior.

She released her brother's hand and leaned away from him, making room for the paramedic as he started an IV on Waycross. That finished, with a series of wires and straps, he connected Waycross to various instruments on the wall that began to register his vital signs with beeps, blinks, numbers, and colorful screen graphs.

Once those duties were fulfilled, Glenn turned away from them and busied himself with a portable computer, inputting data.

Savannah sensed that he was providing her and his patient with a bit of familial privacy to discuss some delicate topics.

As she was wondering how to broach the difficult subject, Waycross squeezed her hand tightly and looked up at her, his large, sensitive eyes filled with tears.

"I'm sorry, Sis," he said. "I'm so, so sorry."

"Shh, you don't need to talk if you don't feel up to it, and you don't have to be sorry. You haven't done anything wrong."

"Yes, I have," he argued weakly. "I *did* do wrong. Way wrong. Dirk knows it."

Savannah weighed his need to rest and remain calm against her desire to know the answers to the questions that were now sweeping over her in suffocating waves.

As usual, her insatiable curiosity won the battle. "What did you do, darlin'?" she asked, not particularly proud of herself. "Tell me what is it that Dirk knows . . . if it's not too much for you."

"After I hurt my leg, those pills that the doctor gave me, they worked pretty good. At first. But then, it got to where they didn't help so much. Then not at all. I tried not to take more of 'em than the doctor said. But my leg was hurtin' somethin' fierce. Like it was gettin' hit with bolts o' lightnin'. Remember?"

She nodded. "Yes, I know. It was plum awful, what you were going through. I felt so sorry for you. We all did."

"I couldn't stand it. I couldn't sleep or eat, and I couldn't bear it throbbin' all the time. So, instead of taking what my doctor told me, I doubled up on them pills. It was the only way I could get any relief."

"I understand."

"Then that wore off, and I needed three at a time and closer together. Of course, I ran out early, and my doctor wouldn't let me have any more."

"Those opioids are controlled substances, sweetie. He could only prescribe a certain amount."

"I know. That's what he told me. He said they were only meant to be used for a short time, to get me past the worst of the injury. But I was still in the worst of it!"

"I understand." She laid her palm against his cheek, as she had when he was a small child and had skinned his knee.

Unfortunately, his grown-up problems were so much greater, and she knew that nothing she said was going to minimize them. He had a difficult path ahead, and all the loving support his family and friends could muster wouldn't smooth the rough road he would have to walk.

"What was even worse than the pain was, when I ran outta them pills, I'd get sick somethin' fierce," he continued. "It's like havin' the worst case of the flu you ever had in your life. Times ten."

"It *is* like that," Glenn interjected, looking up

from his computer screen. "You've got a lot of company, brother. I hate to say it, but I see this sort of thing all the time."

"Did you tell your doctor that you needed some help withdrawing from them?" Savannah asked Waycross.

"No."

"Why not, sugar?"

"I was ashamed."

His eyes were haunted when he added, "I didn't want to admit I had a drug problem. I didn't want anybody to know that I was like . . . you know . . . like her."

Savannah didn't have to ask who he was talking about. She knew instantly.

"Waycross, you are *not* like Shirley," she told him. "You never were, and you never will be."

"But they say drug addiction and stuff like that runs in families," he argued. "She's our mother and—"

"You just stop it right now, Waycross Reid. I don't want to hear another word of that foolishness. If ever there was a young man who rose above his raising, that'd be *you* in a nutshell."

She leaned over so that she could look directly into his eyes, all the better to make her point. "You are a loving, devoted husband to Tammy and the best father on earth to little Vanna Rose. Never in a million years would you raise your hand to your child the way Shirley used to whack us around when she was in a bad mood or just had a mind to. You'd never neglect your family the way she did us, letting us go hungry and dirty, sitting alone in our bedroom for days, while she partied. So, I don't want to hear you comparing yourself to her ever again. You hear me, boy?"

"But I went to a drug dealer, Savannah, just like she used to do. I was in so much misery that I couldn't stand it. I wasn't man enough to just buck up and take it. I went and bought what I wanted from hard-core criminals. And the worst thing is: Dirk saw me. My own brother-in-law saw me walkin' in, then back outta that drug house. The one he was stakin' out."

Savannah caught her breath as several of her mental puzzle pieces snapped into place, forming a clear picture that explained so many things she had been worrying about.

Wracked with shame, Waycross continued. "He followed me when I left that place. Once I'd got a few blocks away, he pulled me over, and searched me, like he would've any other common criminal."

"Did he cuff you?"

"No."

"Then he didn't treat you like his usual 'common criminal.' He cut you some slack."

"Maybe, but he found the pills in my pocket."

"Yes, I imagine he did. Dirk's good at frisking folks," she added.

"He told me he should arrest me, but I begged him not to."

Visions of the scenario, as he was describing it, filled Savannah's mind and broke her heart. No wonder Dirk had been acting strangely. No wonder he couldn't meet her eyes.

He had been hiding something from her all

right, harboring a guilty secret. But it hadn't been his own.

"I don't blame him, mind you," Waycross added. "I put him in an awful spot. With his job and with you. He knew he oughta arrest me, but with me being your brother and all . . . what could he do?"

"What *did* he do?" she asked, fearing the answer.

"He told me in no uncertain terms that I had to stop. He snatched the pills right off me and said I wasn't ever gonna take another one. Or else there'd be hell to pay."

"That sounds like Dirk."

"I promised him I'd swallered my last one, and he didn't have to worry about me showin' up at that there drug house ever again. I don't think he much believed me, because he assured me that he aimed to sit on that house ever' single night and keep an eagle eye on it, just to make sure I didn't set foot inside."

"That's why he pulled rank on McMurtry to get that particular assignment every night," Savannah said, more to herself than to her brother.

"I reckon so. He also stressed the point that I should get some kind of rehab help. When I told him that I couldn't afford it on what I make, he offered to pay for it."

"That doesn't sound so much like Dirk, but . . . well . . . he loves you, kiddo."

"I know. He showed it all the way."

She recalled Dirk's reaction earlier when she and Granny had reported that Waycross was sick. "That's why he was so worried when we told him you had the flu."

"He probably figured out I was sick from tryin' to kick those pills cold turkey."

Glenn spoke up. "That's a dangerous thing to do, Mr. Reid. That's why your heart's going crazy. You should have weaned off them gradually under a doctor's care. With supplemental medications if necessary."

"I know," Waycross replied. "But I thought I could do it by myself. I figured the least amount of people who knew about it the better. I didn't want Tammy to find out."

He began to cry as he gripped Savannah's hand. "Oh, Lord," he said between sobs. "My Tammy. My sweet, precious girl. I pushed her outta my way when I stormed out of the house. She fell right on her backside, and, horse's backside that I am, I didn't even stop to help her back up. She'll kill me for sure. Worse yet, she'll never forgive me."

"You're underselling our Tamitha by a long shot, boy. I'd bet dollars to doughnuts that she's forgiven you already. And if she does kill you, it'll be from smothering you with kisses, and that ain't such a bad way to go."

Waycross thought that over and seemed to feel a little better. He even smiled a tiny bit.

But his good cheer was short-lived. A moment later, his face clouded over again. "Dirk's really mad at me. He said that, because of me and my nonsense, he had to tell his wife a dozen lies. He don't cotton to that. Not to mention him having to pull a lot of double shifts and miss a bunch of your good suppers."

"Yeah. Dirk's a bit of a Rottweiler when it comes to food. Getting between him and his dog dish is a dangerous proposition. It's a wonder you're alive."

"I know. But I don't blame him. I'm mighty grateful to him, in fact. No brother could've done better, standing by me like that and settin' me straight. If it weren't for your husband, I'd be back at that drug house, doing business with a passel o' seriously bad dudes that a country kid like me's got no business doing business with."

"Uh, yeah. That's for sure, and don't you forget it."

As they pulled into the ambulance bay of the hospital, Savannah had only one more question to ask her brother.

"Waycross, tell me something. . . . Did you and Dirk have a phone conversation, when he told you that he didn't appreciate you putting him in this position? When he said that I was his wife, and he would tell me about you and what was going on when he thought the time was right?"

"We sure did. It was a doozy! Boy howdy! That's when I knew how mad he was at me. I'm gonna have to work mighty hard to get back on my brother-in-law's good side again."

Savannah laughed. "I wouldn't worry about it too much, if I was in your shoes. Dirk's always been a big fan of yours, and you've got bigger fish to fry at the moment. But don't worry. We're gonna make sure you get all the help you need to get over this next hurdle."

Waycross sighed and rolled his eyes. "Jumpin' hurdles never was my strong suit back in high school. I was famous for gettin' only halfway over and smashin' my dangly bits to smithereens."

Savannah laughed. "Smashed, black and blue, dangly bits aside, you'll make it. This is one race you're going to win, Waycross Reid. We gotcha, and we ain't letting go."

A few seconds later, the rear doors of the ambulance opened. There was a flurry of activity as Savannah scrambled out, then stood back and watched as the ambulance attendants, along with the ER personnel, pulled Waycross and his gurney from inside and rushed him to the hospital's emergency entrance.

So intent was she on what they were doing that she didn't notice Dirk, until he walked up behind her and put his hands on her shoulders.

Instantly, she whirled around and grabbed him around the waist. Burying her face against her husband's broad, warm chest, Savannah allowed herself to cry. She let the pain and fear of the last few days, and especially the past hour, wash through and out of her.

Finally, when she was finished, she pulled back a bit and looked up at him. She was both surprised and touched to see tears in his eyes, too.

"Waycross told me what you did," she said.

"I'm sorry, Van. I really am," he began. "I wanted to tell you, but your brother was dead set on working it out on his own. He begged me not to tell you and—"

"You've got nothing to apologize for," she assured him. "You were in a rotten spot, but you did what you thought was best all the way down the line. I couldn't ask for more."

He looked enormously relieved. "Really? You're not mad at me?" He gulped, then added, "You still love me?"

"Oh, darlin', I swear, I've never loved you more than I do right this very minute."

To prove it, she kissed him. Long and hard. Right there in the ambulance bay, in front of God and everybody who had nothing better to do than watch a middle-aged couple make out in public.

Chapter 18

In general, Savannah wasn't fond of hospitals. She was even less happy to be inside that one, because she had nearly died inside those dull, beige walls.

They also saved your life here, she reminded herself, recalling how close she had been to death when she'd arrived there, riddled with bullets.

She decided she really should cut the place some slack, in spite of the bad memories, bland paint choices, and depressing gray furniture. Lives were saved here daily, babies born, deadly diseases treated, and some very special people performed those miracles without fanfare and, in many cases, with precious little pay.

Ordinarily, under such circumstances, she would have called a loved one to come, sit with her, and distract her with nervous chitchat, while she waited for the results of her brother's initial examination.

But Dirk was on his way to Tammy's house, to

tell her what was going on and to give her a ride to the hospital.

Savannah would have called Ryan and John. Two of her closest friends for years, they were excellent company at a time like this. Kind, supportive, while not intrusive. But she knew that Waycross wanted as few people as possible to know about his situation, and she would find it awkward to have them come and yet tell them only half a story.

Then there was Granny, but she was watching the baby and—

Gran!

Savannah wanted to smack herself! How could she have forgotten poor Granny?

She glanced down at her phone, which she had muted, complying with the sign on the wall of the waiting room.

One look told her that she had missed four calls from her grandmother in the past fifteen minutes.

No doubt, Granny was fit to be tied, and Savannah couldn't blame her. Every Reid woman knew, all too well, how much the other ones hated to be kept in the dark about important family matters.

Yes, Savannah knew she was in trouble now, for sure.

She glanced around the ER's waiting room at its other occupants. They all wore the haggard, troubled looks of people whose daily lives had been turned upside down by one of the many events that life tossed onto the paths of unsuspecting human beings.

The sad folk assembled there had troubles that ranged from a finger that needed stitching—cut while its owner was slicing an avocado—to far, far worse.

She took a moment out of her pity parade to be grateful she wasn't the group in the corner whose father had collapsed with what appeared to be a heart attack or the young man getting a soda from the machine, whose pregnant wife had begun labor far too early.

Waycross would be all right.

His leg, definitely.

The addiction . . . Like many chronic diseases, there would be no cure. But with a lot of hard work, and the support of his loved ones, maybe he could keep it under control.

Time would tell.

Meanwhile, she had to make some phone calls.

She walked over to the ER admitting desk and asked the nurse there, "Can you tell me how long it might be until I can see my brother? We brought him in a while ago."

"The one who was in the auto accident."

"Yes. The redhead. Waycross Reid."

The nurse typed his name into her computer and said, "They've taken him to radiology, probably to X-ray his leg. It'll be half an hour, at least."

"Okay. Is there someplace I can make a couple of phone calls without bothering anyone?"

"Our new serenity garden," she replied. "Down the hall, through the exit doors on the left."

Serenity garden. She liked the sound of that. If there was anything she could use right now, it was a big plateful of serenity. Maybe she could take a doggy bag full of it back home with her.

She checked her watch, marked the time she should return, and set off in search of peace.

Savannah found the tranquility she was looking for the moment she exited the building and entered the beautiful garden. While not particularly large—about the size of her living room and kitchen—the space was beautifully designed and landscaped.

Tropical plants flourished, providing shade and grace, along with beddings of native plants and succulents in attractive arrangements. A koi pond in the center of the garden was filled with pink lotus blossoms and tiny brass bells that floated among the flowers, circulating in the swirling water and chiming softly when they met.

Comfortable chairs invited visitors to sit and drink the beauty of the place into their troubled minds and spirits.

Savannah was relieved to see that she was the only one there at the moment. She didn't want to disturb anyone's much-needed meditation with the calls she had to make.

Settling into one of the chairs, she took out her phone, and the first thing she did was text both Dirk and Tammy with a quick message: **"Waycross good. I'm in Serenity Garden."**

In seconds, Dirk answered with his standard **"K."**

Her husband had always been a man of few words, and Savannah figured that was probably a good thing, considering how many she had of her own.

A moment later, Tammy sent **"Thx. CUS."**

Savannah assumed that Tammy was not inviting her to curse but was thanking her and letting her know that they would "see you soon." But she wasn't sure. She was pretty proud of herself for even learning how to text at all, considering that it required a certain amount of typing . . . and she had flunked typing class.

Someday, she had frequently promised herself, she would learn the official language of texting, and then her messages would no longer be a source of amusement for her younger, more tech-savvy friends.

Not anytime soon though, she had decided. Maybe after she learned French, Latin, flamenco dancing, and advanced origami.

She punched in her own home phone number and steeled herself for the confrontation to come.

Gran wouldn't yell at her. No, she would be kind and speak in a soft voice as she made you feel lower than a burrowing worm in a well, all because you'd made the best person on earth feel bad or worry about something.

Granny Reid was a gentle person, a peace-loving woman, unless you lied to her, used the Lord's name in vain, spit while in her presence—especially if you weren't outside at the time—or even worse, left her out of the loop concerning family business.

Savannah wasn't expecting an easygoing, just shooting the breeze "Why, hi there, sugar pie. It's so good to hear from you!"

But neither was she prepared for what she got.

"What in tarnation is going on? Tell me right now, before you're a minute older, Miss Savannah!"

Okay, Savannah decided. Maybe gentle Gran *did* yell once in a while, if she was riled enough.

"Well . . . I . . ."

"Well, you what? You and your man lit out of here faster than a sneeze through a screen door. I've been trying to call you for nigh on an hour. Didn't you get my messages?"

Savannah drew a deep breath. If there was anything she hated it was having her grandma upset and knowing she was the cause of it.

"Everything's okay, Granny," she said softly. "Everybody's fine. But Waycross had a bit of an accident with his car and—"

"Oh, Lord've mercy! Is he hurt bad?"

"No, I don't think so. He looks fine, but just to make sure, they brought him to the hospital to check out his bad leg and such. They are doing an X-ray or CT scan or whatever on it right now. But swear to you, he didn't have a mark on him."

"Was anybody else banged up?"

"Not at all. It was a single-car accident. He mashed one fender of his Charger and took out a mailbox. But that was the worst of it."

Savannah heard her grandmother sigh with relief on the other end. "Reckon we can all be thankful for that," she said. "But what in Sam Hill was he doing behind the wheel? It was hard enough for him to drive with his busted leg, but with the flu, too? What was that boy thinking? He should've been back home in bed."

Savannah weighed her response carefully, trying to choose words that were true but delaying the moment when she would have to tell her grandmother everything. That would be much better done face-to-face than over the phone.

"I'm sure he has his regrets," Savannah said. "But the important thing is that he's okay, and nobody else got hurt." She hurried to change the subject. "How are you and the baby doing?"

"Vanna Rose is just fine and dandy. Taking a nap here on my lap. Needless to say, I missed my own nap. Didn't get a wink o' sleep, worryin' myself downright silly over y'all."

"I'm truly sorry, Granny," Savannah told her. "I didn't want to call you until I knew for sure that he was okay. You'd have done the same, if it'd been the other way 'round."

She could practically hear Granny thinking it over. Finally, she said, "That's true. I would've held it back from you until I knew. You did good, Savannah girl. Thank you for taking care of your little brother for me."

Savannah smiled, feeling twelve years old all over again. Gran was proud of her and, at the moment, that was all that mattered.

This evening, when she finally made it home, she would have to break her grandmother's heart with the news of their family's latest challenge. But for now, all was well. At least, as well as could be expected under the circumstances.

"I'll talk to you later, Gran," she said. "I'll call you if there's anything new to report."

"Thank you, darlin'. I love you."

"I love you, too. Bye."

No sooner had Savannah hung up, than she made her next call.

When Jennifer Liu answered, Savannah said, "Hi. Can you talk now?"

"Just a minute. Hold on. . . ."

Savannah heard the clicking of high heels on tiled floor, then a door open and close.

"Okay," the doctor said. "I'm in my office now. What's up?"

"Unfortunately, nothing to do with your case at the moment. We had a nasty scare. As a matter of fact, I'm at the hospital and—"

"The hospital? Are you all right?"

"I am, thanks. But my brother, Waycross, was in an auto accident. It appears he's okay, at least for the moment, but I'm afraid the whole thing kind of derailed me from working on your case. I'm really sorry. I know how important this is to you."

"Don't be ridiculous, Savannah. Family comes first. Especially in a situation like this. Is there anything I can do for your brother or for you?"

"Thank you. But I'm sure they're taking good care of him. In fact, Dirk went to get Tammy and bring her here. As soon as they arrive, and I know that she's okay, too, I'll get back to work for you. I still need to go over to The Fisherman's Lair and see what I can find out there."

"Are you sure? Really, I don't expect you to—"

"Hush now. I don't want to hear another word

about it. Your situation is extremely important, and we consider you family, too."

Savannah could have sworn that she heard the usually stoic medical examiner sniff before replying, "Thank you. It's an honor being part of your family, Savannah."

"Can I check back with you later this evening, after I've been over to The Lair?"

"Sure. I've got an autopsy that'll probably keep me late, but if you text me when you're ready, I'll duck out and meet you at the beach. I need to talk to you about something anyway."

Savannah wanted to ask, "What about?" But at that moment, she saw the hospital exit door open and Tammy and Dirk enter the garden.

"Um, I've got company," she told Jennifer. "Talk to you later."

She stashed her phone in her purse, jumped up from her chair, and ran to Tammy.

Enfolding her in a hearty hug, Savannah said, "How are you, sweetie?"

"I'm okay," Tammy said with more poise and strength than Savannah would have expected.

Yes, Tammy was growing up, Savannah realized. Motherhood was good for her. Now that she was a married woman, her concerns stretched beyond which organic vegetable she would have for lunch and how much farther she would extend her daily run.

Although, with Miss Health-First Tamitha, those things would always be high on her list of priorities.

"How is he?" Dirk asked, looking more worried than Tammy.

"Last I heard, he's okay. Getting his leg X-rayed." She glanced at her watch. "We might find out something in ten more minutes or so. Maybe we should go back into the waiting room."

"I can't wait to see him," Tammy said as they walked out of the garden. "To see if he's my old Waycross again. I guess it was the fever that made him act that way earlier. That had to be it."

Savannah gave Dirk a quick glance. He lifted one eyebrow a notch and shrugged.

He hasn't told her about the meds, Savannah thought. *That's all right. Let Waycross tell his wife himself, in his own time and in his own way.*

Only seconds after they had taken seats in the waiting room, a nurse in blue scrubs came out to meet them. She walked over to Tammy and said, "Are you Mrs. Reid?"

Tammy jumped up from her chair. So did Savannah and Dirk.

"Yes. I'm Tammy Reid. How is my husband?"

"The X-ray of his leg showed no new injuries."

Tammy beamed. "Then he's okay! Can I take him home now?"

"No. We'll be holding him for a while yet. He has some other issues that need to be addressed."

Savannah studied the nurse's face, trying to get a read off her expression. But Savannah classified it as "Professionally Inscrutable."

Savannah decided that, if the nursing gig didn't work out, the woman could make a fortune in Las Vegas, playing poker.

"What kind of issues?" Tammy wanted to know.

"Mr. Reid would like to discuss that with you himself. Come with me, please."

Looking flustered, Tammy said, "Can my sister-in-law and brother-in-law come with me?"

"No" was the curt response. "Your husband asked for you to come alone."

"Oh. Okay." Tammy turned to Savannah and Dirk. "Thanks, you guys. I appreciate you bringing me over here. Why don't you go on home?"

She stood on tiptoe and kissed Dirk on the cheek. "I know you have to get to work. Thank you for bringing me over here and taking good care of me."

He returned the kiss. "No problem, kid. But how are you gonna get home?"

"Don't worry about us, Dirk-o. We're grown-ups. We can take care of ourselves."

She turned to Savannah and gave her a quick hug and peck. "And I know you've got things to do, too. I sent you some emails about that stuff you needed me to research. Be sure to read it as soon as you get home."

Savannah couldn't help being curious about what Tammy might have found. Also, she was surprised that her young friend had managed to get some work done on her behalf, while nursing her husband and dealing with the miseries of the past few hours.

"Mrs. Reid," the nurse said in a distinctly grumpy tone. "Do you want to see your husband or not?"

"What a ridiculous question," Tammy snapped back. "Of course, I do. Take me to him." Without another word Tammy scurried after the retreating blue scrubs, blowing kisses over her shoulder back to Savannah and Dirk.

As they stood there, watching her disappear down the hallway, Dirk shook his head and said, "You know, if this keeps up, I might have to change my ring tone for her. Our fluff-head bimbo's not such a dumb blonde after all."

Chapter 19

By the time Savannah and Dirk pulled into the driveway of their house, he was already late for his shift. He dropped her off with a hug and a kiss and immediately left for the station house.

Considering their recent state of détente, she would have much preferred to have him home for the evening. It would have been nice to connect and make up for lost time . . . except for the fact that she, herself, had work to do.

Covert work.

She couldn't help being uncomfortable with the fact that she was doing exactly what she had been angry with her husband for doing only hours ago—keeping secrets from her spouse.

Was it ever okay?

When she kissed him good-bye, wished him a good, safe evening, and didn't mention that she was going to the town's roughest bar to do some under-cover work, it felt like she was lying.

She couldn't help wondering if he was picking up on her guilt, the way she had sensed his.

She wouldn't be at all surprised. He knew her far too well for her to get away with much, just as she knew him.

As she trudged into the house, laden with her heavy load of shame, she couldn't help thinking it would be easier to just be regular folks . . . unburdened by the inconvenience of having not one but two detectives in the household. Not to mention Granny, Tammy, Waycross, Ryan, and John running in and out.

Shoot f'ar. Nobody can get away with anything in this dadgum place, she thought as she opened the front door.

The kitties came running to her, as always. She bent down to pet them and ask about their day. Then, putting her purse on the pie crust table, she started to call out to Gran. But the house was uncharacteristically quiet, and it occurred to her that the baby might still be asleep.

Quietly, she walked into the living room, expecting to see Granny sitting in her chair. But it was empty.

So was the kitchen.

Savannah tiptoed upstairs, and that was where she found them—two of her favorite people in the world—stretched out, both sound asleep, on her guest room futon.

She watched them for a moment, allowing the sweetness of the sight to soften the harshness of the day. Even when Life was unkind, she bestowed the occasional blessing along the way. Sometimes, you just had to look for it.

After soaking in her fill, Savannah went to her bedroom and exchanged her simple T-shirt for a blouse that could be unbuttoned a notch or two, once she was out the door and no longer in danger of encountering Granny.

While she wasn't in the mood to go all the way with full-on hooker garb in hopes of dazzling The Lair's ruffians, she knew the effect an inch or two of cleavage could have on the male brain. Especially if that gray matter was addled by alcohol.

Having donned the blouse, some slightly tighter jeans, and a pair of strappy high-heeled sandals that showed off her tart red toenail polish to its best advantage, she snuck back down the stairs to the living room and switched on the computer.

Fortunately, she was better at retrieving her emails than she was at texting, and it didn't take her long to find the one that Tammy had sent.

As quickly as she could, she scanned its contents.

Tammy had done her work well. The attachments contained a plethora of personal information on Brianne Marston's brother, Henry, and his wife, Darlene.

On the surface, they appeared to be extremely wealthy people, after receiving an enormous inheritance from Brianne and Henry's father some time back. But Tammy had uncovered numerous facts and figures that demonstrated Henry and Darlene's lack of restraint when it came to spending that fortune.

Savannah was no accountant, but it didn't take a

financial expert to see that they had mowed through the monies left to them and were now deeply in debt.

As she was reading, it occurred to Savannah that Brianne's heir would probably be her brother, her next of kin.

If Brianne had died after the wedding, rather than a short time before, as her new husband, Paul might have inherited the estate instead.

Savannah tried to recall the specifics of her conversation with Dee, Brianne's groomer. What was it she had said about Paul allowing only Brianne's brother and sister-in-law to see her in her final days?

Had Henry and Darlene merely visited with Brianne? Or had they helped Paul in nursing her?

Suddenly, Savannah had two suspects with both motive and opportunity to poison Brianne. What that might have to do with Nels Farrow, she had no idea.

But it was something.

At least, it was *possibly* something and, thanks to Tammy's diligence, that was more than she'd had five minutes before.

As she headed for the foyer, took her leather coat from the closet, and slipped her Beretta into her purse, it occurred to her that her day might be turning around a bit.

"It wouldn't take much," she muttered to herself. "Some days, you gotta figure there's no place to go but up."

* * *

The Fisherman's Lair reveled in its reputation as the seediest bar in town, much the same way a schoolyard bully enjoyed being considered the kid most likely to give you a bloody nose if you looked at him crossways or, God forbid, tried to steal his favorite marble.

The owners and workers at The Lair thought that being a "bad ass joint" made them special somehow. In Savannah's estimation, the place's only true distinction was that of having the oiliest French fries in town.

But then, the fries complemented the oily characters who ate them and the layer of grease scum on the bar counter that received a quick wipe-down once every month or two, whether it needed it or not.

Yes, The Lair was consistent, if not overly sanitary.

When she sashayed into the place, around ten o'clock that night, she eyed the hundreds of fishing lures that had been nailed to the knotty pine walls over the years. Not for the first time, she wondered if the owners had known—back in the day when they'd named the place and painted its tacky sign—the difference in the words *lair* and *lure.*

Probably not, she decided, and that gave her a chuckle each time she entered.

In her estimation any place that gave you a laugh, or even a self-righteous snicker every time you walked inside, wasn't a complete write-off.

She looked around the place, sizing up the crowd, and figured she'd done the right thing by only undoing one button of her blouse.

One caught their interest. Two might've sent them into a testosterone-fueled frenzy—boob grabs, rear pats, the works.

She wasn't in the mood for that sort of thing. The last thing she needed was to make the front page of the local newspaper with a headline like:

FORMER SCPD DET. KILLS 7 OVER PINCHED BUTT

No, she definitely didn't need that kind of publicity. Not to mention how hard it would be to explain to Dirk.

He would, no doubt, howl for a month, complaining that she hadn't taken him along for the fun.

She sauntered over to the bar and perched herself on a stool to the left of a cowboy wannabe, who seemed the chattiest of The Lair's patrons. With flushed cheeks and glazed eyes, he was regaling the bartender and the fellow to his right with a joke in which he was managing to denigrate women in general, minorities at large, and the entire feline species in particular.

Briefly, Savannah wondered if she could slip her Beretta from her purse, shoot him in his left buttock, then scurry out the back door without being seen.

On an average day, she might've considered it more seriously. But after the trials of the past few hours, she was tired, and she hadn't been to the shooting range for a while. She was afraid she might miss.

No point in taking chances.

At that moment, he turned in her direction and something akin to the fabled "Lightning Bolt of

Love" must've struck him. He did such a violent double take that the action seemed to make him dizzy. He nearly tumbled backward off his stool.

"Well, hi there, pretty lady," he said, sucking in his beer gut and squaring his shoulders. "Aren't you a pretty thing, sitting there, looking all prettied up."

She gave him a bright smile. "Aw, shucks. You sure know how to turn a girl's head. I might just send you a little present, come Christmas."

Leering at her cleavage, he said, "That'd be great. I'd love to see more of you."

"No, no, no. I was thinking maybe a thesaurus."

He looked baffled. "Huh? Oh, okay. That'd be nice, too. You're the prettiest thing that's ever walked through those doors. And I should know. I've been sitting on this here stool watching, every single day, since this place opened, twenty-one years ago."

"Wow! Two decades well-spent in the betterment of mankind and a lofty life aspiration fulfilled. Yay, you!"

Again, he seemed confused but still intrigued. "You gonna start coming here regular-like?"

"I assure you that I will walk through those doors each and every time that circumstances compel me to do so upon pain of death."

"Wow! Then I look forward to seeing more of you."

"Uh-huh."

"Whatcha drinking?"

"Sweet tea. Iced."

"You're not going to get much of a buzz off that."

She batted her eyelashes and tried to inhale shallowly to avoid smelling his alcohol-saturated breath. She estimated he would blow a 2.8 on Dirk's Breathalyzer.

"I'm getting a buzz just sitting here next to you," she replied, deepening her dimples.

He looked like he might swoon any moment, so she decided the time was right to get down to business.

Pulling her phone from her jacket pocket, she flipped to Brianne's driver's license photo. She shoved it under his nose and said, "This is a friend of mine. Since you notice every attractive lady who comes in here, I'll bet you noticed her."

He squinted, peering at the picture, and nodded vigorously. "Oh, sure I did. She's a pretty one, too. But she had a guy with her already, so I didn't make a move on her."

Savannah nodded and gave him an approving look of deep respect. "Wise. Very wise on your part."

"They sat over there," he said, turning around and, with great effort, focusing on the far side of the room, where some dark, tight booths provided an intimate setting for those who frequented The Fisherman's Lair with more than just booze on their minds.

"Ah," she said. "That was probably her boyfriend."

"I don't think so," he replied, shaking his head. "Or if he's her man, he wasn't acting like it. He didn't lay a hand on her the whole time they were here. Me, I would've been all over her."

"I'll bet you would've."

On a hunch, she flipped through her photos and brought up Nels Farrow's DMV photo.

"Did he look anything like this man?" she asked, showing it to her new best friend.

He nodded vigorously, then closed his eyes for a long time. She figured he was either meditating or giving his eyeballs a chance to adjust to his head's robust movement.

When he finally opened them, he said, "That's him. That's the guy that was with her."

"Are you sure?"

"Of course, I am. I never forget a face. Though I am partial to the pretty ones, like yours and your friend's."

He tapped her phone screen with an overgrown, dirty fingernail. She decided to scrub it with bleach and steel wool as soon as she returned home.

"That guy there, he could use a dose of Viagra—not that I know much about it or need it myself. I got no problems in that department, if you know what I mean."

"I'm afraid I do."

"If I'd been the one sitting back there in that dark corner in a booth with that pretty gal, she'd have known that I was a man, for sure."

The fellow sitting on the other side of her friend snickered, shook his head, and buried his face in his beer mug. Apparently, her buddy's masculine prowess was more joke than legend in his native habitat.

But he didn't seem to notice as he continued his boasting. "Yep, I'd have shown her what it's like to be with a hot-blooded, American male—not that namby-pamby she was with. I sure wouldn't have wasted my time with her, sitting there, talking about Barbies."

"Barbies?" Savannah's brain searched its libraries for any logical explanation for this sharp left turn in the conversation. It found none. Maybe she'd heard wrong. "Did you say they were talking about Barbies? Like the dolls?"

He nodded. "I had to go to the can to take a leak, so I walked right past them. I swear that's what he was talking about to her."

"They were talking about Barbies?"

He gave her a condescending smirk. "Girl, you're pretty and got a great rack, but I'm starting to think you aren't overly smart. . . . A bit on the thick side even for a girl. I done told you twice already."

For half a second she reconsidered her earlier plan of taking the Beretta from her purse and giving him a single shot in the backside. Just a flesh wound. Nothing that some hydrogen peroxide and a couple of drugstore bandages wouldn't take care of.

She summoned her last smidgeon of patience. "Why don't you just tell me *exactly*, word for word, what you heard him say?"

"Oh, okay. I didn't hear a lot of what they were saying, because I was in a rush to get to the can. But I definitely heard him say something about a Ken doll." He paused, thought it over, and added, "That's Barbie's boyfriend, in case you don't know about stuff like that."

Looking a bit embarrassed, he explained, "I only know that kind of thing because I had sisters. And they used to get super pissed off when I'd shave their dolls' heads and then swallow them."

"Swallow . . . *them?*"

"The dolls' heads."

"Oh, of course. Silly me."

"You really do need to have those ears of yours checked, baby. Either they're stopped up with wax, or you don't believe me."

"Surprisingly, I have no trouble believing everything you just told me. I must say, I can't recall when I've met a more uniquely imbecilic and malodorous Philistine in all my born days."

He actually blushed with pleasure at the "compliment." Shrugging, he said, "Ah, hell. Thanks."

Briefly, the image of the morgue receptionist Officer Kenneth Bates intruded on her consciousness, and she was forced to add, "Actually, there's one other dude who's got you beat, but you're a solid second."

"Well, you keep coming in here and hanging out with me. I'll change your pretty little mind. When I get done with you, you'll be happy to bump me up to that number one spot."

She laughed brightly and smacked him on the shoulder, hard enough to knock him sideways onto his next-stool buddy.

"With just a little effort, I reckon you might," she assured him as she grabbed her purse and rose from her stool. "Yes, if anybody could best that other guy in the fine art of contumelious discourse, I do believe it might be you."

She left him a happy man.

Chapter 20

Savannah had no idea how hungry she was, until she arrived at her rendezvous point on the beach, left her car, and got into Dr. Liu's BMW. Once she was settled, a fine china dessert plate was shoved under her nose with an exquisite Napoleon resting on a lace paper doily in its center.

"Oh, mercy me!" she said, grabbing it. "You have no idea how much I need this. I'm plum famished! For the first time in history, I was actually so busy today that I forgot to eat."

Jennifer chuckled. "You told me once you don't believe anyone who says that."

"I used to think they were lying or a severely disturbed individual. I'll be less judgmental next time."

She groaned as she bit into the delicate pastry with its buttery, crispy crust, drizzled with chocolate, filled with a rich vanilla bean cream, and garnished with fresh raspberries.

There was nothing quite like missing a couple of

meals to make even the most bland and mundane food delicious. But this Napoleon, she decided, must have been baked in heaven's ovens by French angels.

Unless the chef was Dr. Liu. Lately, Savannah had discovered that she was a multifaceted lady, to say the least.

"Did you make this?" she asked. "Because, if you did, I have to get the recipe from you."

"I'm excellent at cracking a cranium or sawing a sternum, but I doubt that I could boil an egg that would be fit to eat."

For once, even the mental images of the activities just described, gruesome things Savannah herself had observed in Dr. Liu's autopsy suite, didn't put her off her food.

The gourmet delicacy wasn't long for this world. To her dismay, she finished it in five bites.

"Okay," Jennifer said, "now that I've fed the help, what do you have for me? Did you find out anything new over at the bar?"

Once Savannah had dabbed the crumbs away from her lips with her pinky and returned the dainty plate to her hostess, she focused on the business at hand. "I got something. I'm not sure what it is."

"Tell me. Maybe I can figure it out."

"All right. This may sound strange, but do you recall Brianne having a particular fondness for Barbie dolls?"

Jennifer gave her a searching look, as though trying to decide if she was serious or not. "What the hell do Barbies have to do with anything?"

"I haven't a clue. But Brianne was seen in The

Fisherman's Lair with a man, whom a regular identified as Nels Farrow."

"Okay. That's good to know. Our first real connection between the two of them, other than the poison formula. But what does that have to do with fashion dolls?"

"This frequent-flier at The Lair overheard Nels say something to Brianne about a 'Ken doll.' "

"Those were his precise words?"

"Yes, and the only ones my source remembers hearing."

When Jennifer didn't reply, Savannah added, "The guy who told me was a bit of a flake, to say the least. And I know it's a weird thing, but he swears that's what he overheard, and for what it's worth, I believe him. About that, anyway."

Jennifer leaned forward in the driver's seat, crossed her arms atop the steering wheel, and rested her forehead on them.

Savannah thought she was discouraged, exhausted, possibly at her wits' end.

Then she heard her whispering, "Ken doll, Ken doll, Ken doll, Ken doll."

Suddenly, she jerked upright and gripped the steering wheel. Turning to Savannah, she said, "Kendall!"

Savannah couldn't interpret what she was hearing. "Ken Dahl? What? Is he someone you know?"

"Not a *he*. A *her*. I'll bet Nels was talking about Dr. Earlene Kendall. *K-E-N-D-A-L-L.*"

"Okay. Who is she?"

"She's a specialist in fatal genetic disorders. After Farrow's general practitioner diagnosed him with Halstead's, he referred Farrow to her."

"Do you know her personally?"

"No, but I saw her name in his medical records."

"Is she local?"

"I don't know where she lives. But I think her office is in Santa Barbara."

"Close enough. I have to talk to her. She might be our link between Brianne and Nels."

The two women studied each other, as best they could, in the semi-darkness of the car. Savannah could sense a bit of hope hanging in the air, like a pleasant, floral scent in an otherwise stale, musty room.

"Looks like we have a lead," Jennifer said.

"Yes, indeed. We do. I'll follow up on it tomorrow." She paused for a moment, then added, "I just have to think of some excuse to give my husband and family about why I'm traipsing off to Santa Barbara."

There was a long, awkward pause as Savannah waited for Jennifer's response. Finally, the doctor cleared her throat and said, "That brings me to the reason why I wanted to meet you here tonight. I've come to a decision. An important one."

Waiting at full attention, Savannah said, "Okay. Let's have it."

The doctor looked defeated and sad when she said, "I have no doubt that Brianne and Nels were murdered. Do you agree?"

Before answering, Savannah took a moment to recall her conversation with Nels Farrow's widow, Candy. She remembered what the woman said about how she and Nels sat at the kitchen table the night before his death and worked on their "bucket list" of things they wanted to enjoy together while Nels was still healthy enough to do them.

Savannah thought of Brianne and Paul, planning their wedding and, in spite of the terrible risk, deciding to bring their own child into the world.

"Everything I've seen and heard," Savannah said, "points to the fact that both Brianne and Nels were looking forward to spending the rest of their lives, whatever time they had left, with their spouses. They seemed incredibly brave and positive under horrible circumstances."

"You don't believe they killed themselves or allowed someone else to?"

"No. I don't. I agree with you that they were murdered."

Nodding thoughtfully, Jennifer said, "That's why I've come to this decision. It's a really hard one, but I can't allow someone to get away with one homicide, let alone two. And I certainly can't let a murderer escape justice when they killed the person I loved most in the world. No matter what it costs me personally."

Savannah had a feeling what was coming next, but she waited patiently to hear the doctor say it.

"Even if I lose my career," Jennifer continued. "Even if it costs me my freedom, I have to do everything I can to catch the person who did this. Otherwise, I can't live with myself."

"I understand," Savannah told her. "I think that's very brave and noble of you. I do."

Jennifer turned to her with haunted eyes. "I've been hampering you severely by not letting you engage your team. Who knows the toll that's already taken on the investigation?"

Certainly, it hadn't been easy, Savannah thought. But there was no point in saying so and driving the spearpoint of her friend's guilt even deeper.

Savannah could tell by the wounded look on her face that Dr. Liu was suffering enough already from her heart's own condemnation.

"I want your team to know everything," Jennifer said. "Even Dirk. You won't be compromising him, because I'm going to go to the authorities myself. I'll even request that he be put in charge of the investigation. For all the good that will do. I won't have much clout, since I'll be under arrest and probably locked up the moment I confess."

Savannah wanted to disagree with her, to console her, and suggest that maybe things might not be so dire, after all. But she couldn't bring herself to lie to a woman who knew the justice system as well as she did.

While it was a courageous thing that Jennifer Liu was doing, by stepping forward, she was virtually ending her life as she knew it. Her license would most probably be revoked, and she would very likely spend some time in prison. If she were really unlucky, she might be incarcerated with inmates who'd been sent to prison on the basis of the M.E.'s own investigations and testimonies.

"I want to help you. What can I do?" Savannah asked, feeling helpless, considering the gravity of the situation, and more than a little guilty for not having succeeded in closing the case on her own.

Maybe if she hadn't been so distracted by her

personal problems she could've done better, found a killer, and saved Dr. Liu from taking this drastic step.

"Call a meeting of your Moonlight Magnolia Detective Agency as soon as possible. I want to be there myself."

"Okay. I'll do that first thing tomorrow morning. What else do you want me to do?"

"The one thing that I *don't* want," Jennifer added, "is for you to feel guilty about this. It isn't your fault. Even if you had solved the case and exposed the murderer, I still would have been forced to explain my false rulings."

Savannah felt both relieved and touched by her words, but not entirely exonerated. "How did you know I was feeling guilty? Are you a cranium cracker, a sternum cutter, and a mind reader, too?"

"I know you, Savannah Reid. You're a softhearted person, who thinks she has to take care of the entire world. You're far too maternal for your own good, trying to save everybody around you, even when they caused the trouble they're in."

"Now, now. I don't know about that. Yes, I've been accused of trying to feed everybody within arm's reach. But I've been known to let a few folks stew in the chowder they made. Especially those who seem to want to live their whole lives floundering around in a soup pot."

"But you feel bad about not rescuing me."

Savannah shrugged and grinned. "From what I can tell, this is your first swim in the soup. If we manage to yank you out of this one, and you go diving back in . . ."

"That's a nice thought . . . you and your team saving me. But I don't believe you or anybody else is going to pull me out of this one." She shuddered, crossed her arms over her chest, and hugged herself tightly. "I'm pretty sure this particular soup pot that I'm in now is about one hundred feet deep."

Chapter 21

When Savannah returned home, it was after 11:00 P.M., so she half expected Granny to be asleep in the guest room with little Vanna Rose by her side. Instead, she found her grandmother sitting in Dirk's recliner, wearing her long-sleeved, flannel nightgown with tiny pink rosebuds, and reading her well-worn Bible.

Little Vanna was nowhere in sight.

Savannah sat in her own comfy chair next to her and propped her feet on the ottoman.

Granny peered over the top of her wire-rimmed glasses, surveying Savannah's attire.

Although Savannah had remembered to button her blouse all the way up before entering the house, the tight fit of her jeans and the strappy high-heeled sandals were enough to spark Granny's highly combustible suspicion.

Her bright red toenail polish didn't help.

Granny sniffed the air suspiciously. "Stale beer

and French pastries," she observed. "Now that's an unlikely combination."

"I swear to Moses," Savannah said, "you've been hanging out with that bloodhound of yours too long. You've got a nose as keen as his. By the way, who's tending to Colonel Beauregard while you're over here?"

"A nice lady who moved in two trailers down from mine there at the park. She loves that hound dog to bits, and since she started giving him day-old biscuits dipped in bacon grease, he's taken a likin' to her, too. Her name's Bess." She sighed, then added, "She reminds me of Sister Elsie."

Savannah noticed the brief look of sadness that crossed Granny's face, and her heart ached for her grandmother. Daily chats with Elsie had been one of the treasures that Gran had reluctantly surrendered when moving from Georgia to California.

Elsie and Gran had been close friends most of their lives, and Savannah was sure it hadn't been easy for Granny to leave her behind.

Sunday afternoon phone calls, even hour-long ones, couldn't take the place of a piece of Elsie's famous coconut cake, washed down with Granny's chicory-flavored coffee, shared during a face-to-face gossip session while sitting on the front porch swing.

"I know you miss your Elsie," Savannah said. "I'm sorry."

"I do, but don't go changin' the subject. We were discussin' your Jezebel attire."

Savannah laughed. "That's true. Go ahead and grill me till I'm well charred. Give me your best interrogation."

"Colonel Beauregard is a fine-tuned, smellin' machine. No doubt about it. He's taught me a few things about sniffin' out dicey situations over the years. So, I couldn't help noticin' the way you smell tonight. Then there's your sprayed-on breeches, and them heels that're so danged high no woman should wear 'em unless she was fixin' to spend most of her evenin' on her back with her heels pointed toward the ceilin'.'"

Savannah giggled. Sometimes, her saintly grandmother came up with some rather worldly observations. Gran might have chosen to live a chaste life, but it wasn't because she was ignorant of the world and its goings-on.

"Let's just say you and your nose have nothing to worry about, Gran. I'm not a maiden of ill repute, and I wasn't up to no good," Savannah assured her, coaxing Diamante and Cleopatra onto her lap.

"You just wanted to look like you might be?"

"Exactly. I went someplace looking for information, and let's just say, some fellas are a mite more informative if they're intrigued by your, um, bright red toenail polish."

Granny grinned and cleared her throat. "Did you find out somethin' that was worth you compromisin' your virtue for?"

"*Looking* like I might compromise. Not actually delivering the goods."

"Okay."

"Yes. I did uncover something that made walking in these stupid shoes and getting blisters on my pinky toes well worth the trouble."

"Did your husband know you were out prancin' around with scarlet toenails?"

"No. But I'm going to tell him all about it the first chance I get. The prancing, that is. Not the scarlet polish. I wear that all the time. He's quite partial to it."

"Does this have somethin' to do with the secret that you can't share, 'cause it ain't yours, and you done promised not to?"

"It does."

"All right then. I won't pry."

Savannah snickered. "A bit late for that, Gran. I feel like a can of Spam with an especially stubborn, vacuum-packed lid."

Gran laughed, too. "All right. Point taken. I know you well enough to rest easy that you wouldn't resort to out-and-out debauchery to finagle some information out of a hapless barfly. With female wiles the likes of yours, t'wouldn't be necessary."

"Thank you. I take that as high praise, indeed."

Savannah looked around for the diaper bag and the other customary baby paraphernalia. "Is our fairy princess upstairs asleep?"

"No. Her momma done come and got her."

"Really? Oh. I thought Tammy would be with Waycross, either at home or the hospital."

"No. The doctor at the hospital had her take him over to a special clinic. It's a place that knows how to help people going through what he's sufferin' with right now."

"Hmm. I see."

Savannah wondered if Granny did.

Gran continued. "Those folks at the clinic said she should leave him alone there with them for a week or two, or however long it takes to help him. Waycross insisted on it, too. She was sad about leavin' him behind, and she wanted to have her baby back home with her. She figured it'd be good for the little one and for her to be together there at her house. Quality time, just the two of them, and all that."

"I understand," Savannah said as she tried to read Granny's expressions and tone of voice.

Did she know?

"I know all about it, darlin'," Gran said, her voice soft and a bit tremulous. "Tammy told me everythin'."

"Okay." Savannah held her breath, waiting, wondering what Gran's reaction would be to one of her grandchildren having a drug addiction. After all, she was a woman who disapproved of even having a beer with pizza or one glass of red wine with a five-course, gourmet Italian dinner. "And . . . ?"

Granny closed her Bible and laid it on the end table between them. "My heart pains somethin' fierce for my grandson. He's always been such a sweet, innocent soul. It just goes to show ya that them drugs is a trap that can snare a body, anybody, when they least expect it."

"I'm afraid you're right, Gran," Savannah said. "I've known a lot of people, folks way stronger and brighter than I am, who've been caught in that trap. Some battled their addictions for years and finally found ways to keep them from ruining their lives. Others never found their way out."

"We're gonna pray, day and night, that our Waycross is one of the first kind," Gran said with tears, but also a lot of determination, in her eyes. "We'll shower him with all the love and encouragement we can, but in the end, it's his battle to fight."

"He and I talked about it in the ambulance on the way to the hospital. I think he realizes that."

Granny shook her head sadly. "You know the strange part about it?"

"What's that, Gran?"

"The very medicine that my grandson's addicted to, the one that came near destroyin' his life . . . it's one that I take ever' single day and have for a couple of years now."

"Really?"

"It's the God's honest truth. Remember, right before I moved out here to California, the rheumatiz in my lower back hurt me so bad that I couldn't hardly get around at all?"

"Yes. I do recall that. You were even having trouble walking around the house."

"I was. Dr. Hynson put me on all sorts of pills, and they didn't do me a lick o' good. He even sent me to Atlanta to get some steroid shots there next to my spine. Nothin' helped. Then the doc retired, and I got myself a new one. I told her how bad off I was, and she prescribed a new pill for me. It just did wonders for my pain. I take one a day, and I feel like I did when I was a girl. Gave me a new lease on life!"

"After you took it for a while, it didn't lose its effect on you, the way it did for Waycross?"

"Maybe a bit, but not enough to matter. It still does me a world of good. I don't know what I'd do without it."

"That *is* strange."

"These here bodies of ours are fearfully and wonderfully made, and ever' one of us is different."

Savannah sat for a moment, digesting the irony. "I guess it's true that one man's medicine is another man's poison."

"Yessiree. Goes for us womenfolk, too."

Savannah placed the kitties on the floor, yawned, and said, "I'm going upstairs to take a hot bath. After a day like this, I figure I deserve it."

"You'd probably like to smell like roses, instead of beer, when your man gets home."

Savannah grinned. Gran was way too smart. Many times, her powers of perception were downright inconvenient, to say the least.

"Relaxing *and* smelling better were my primary motives, to be sure," she confessed.

"I hope you don't mind me spending the night with you. I'm a bit tuckered out after watching the baby. Precious as she is, there's a reason why the good Lord don't give infants to women over eighty."

Or some menopausal women in their mid-forties, Savannah thought with a pang of melancholy.

"Plus, I hate to admit it, but"—Gran continued in a tone generally used by hard-core criminals when confessing heinous felonies—"I can't see in the dark as good as I once did. These days, drivin' around after sundown's a bit harder for me than it used to be."

"Don't give it a second thought," Savannah assured her. "You're welcome to stay here anytime. You know that. We love having you. And if there's ever a time when you need to get from one place to the other, and it's dark outside, you just holler. We'll fight over who gets to take you."

Granny smiled. "What would I do without you, Savannah girl?"

Recalling her husband's recent reassurances and how much they meant to her, Savannah said, "Don't you worry about it. I'm here for you, and I always will be."

"And I will be for you, too. Whether it's on this side of heaven or over there, walkin' them golden streets, I'll do everything in my power to make your life better and safer and happier."

"I know you will, Gran, and that gives me more comfort than you could imagine."

Savannah leaned down and placed a kiss on the top of her grandmother's glorious, silver hair. Then she headed up the stairs, intent on relaxing in her Victorian-style, clawfoot bathtub filled with rose-scented bubbles.

With any luck, she could wash away the cares of the day . . . not to mention the smell of Kenny Bates's doppelgänger.

Two Kennys in this world, she told herself, a few minutes later, as she added a few drops of rose essential oil to the already fragrant, bubble-sparkly bath. *Now, there's a scary thought. Heaven help us.*

As usual, Savannah's biological clock kicked in around midnight, causing her eyelids to grow heavy as the weariness of the day overtook her.

Sometime later, she woke with a start and realized she had fallen asleep in her bath. Though it hadn't been for long, as the water was still pleasantly warm and there were still some bubbles afloat.

She was also aware that she was no longer alone.

Standing next to the tub was her husband, wearing nothing but his boxers and a grin.

She looked around the room and saw that he had turned off the overhead light and lit several pink votive candles that were flickering on the windowsill and vanity.

In his hand, he held a single red rose. She recognized it as one she had picked from her garden and placed in a bud vase beside their bed the day before.

"Hi," she said, returning his smile.

"Hi yourself, gorgeous." He reached down and slowly trailed the rose's soft, fragrant petals over her cheek, then down her neck, and across her chest. "Would you like some company?"

She pointed to the water. "In here?"

"Sure. Why not? There's room for two . . . if we, you know . . . double up."

She lifted one eyebrow and said with her best Mae West impersonation, "Climb on in, big boy. It'll be a tight squeeze. But whatever you've got, I'll try to find a place to put it."

Chapter 22

As Savannah set a platter heaped with her famous mandarin orange pancakes, a dish of vanilla-flavored butter, and a jug of hot maple syrup on the table, then took a seat among the members of her Moonlight Magnolia agency, it occurred to her that she might have seen them this intrigued about a case. But it had been a long time.

A call to each member, telling them that Dr. Jennifer Liu was in desperate need of their help, was all it took for them to come running the next morning. The M.E. had long been a favorite of the team, not only because of her expertise in solving crimes, but also because she had a sassy personality that they enjoyed and a mysterious air that piqued their curiosity.

The moment Ryan and John had received their phone call, they had cancelled their plans for the morning, left the restaurant in their chef's capable hands, and arrived at Savannah's front door, a bottle of Jennifer's favorite cognac in hand.

Dirk was equally eager to assist. After their bath the night before, Savannah had fully briefed Dirk on the situation. Upon awaking the next morning, he had called the station house and informed them that he would be taking a personal day. In an act that surprised Savannah, considering his rocky relationship with the medical examiner, he had also assured Savannah that he would be happy to take even more days off, if necessary, to investigate Dr. Liu's situation.

Granny hadn't been surprised to hear that her suspicions about Savannah's troubled mystery friend were correct, and it was Dr. Liu who was in trouble. But, as always, she was excited and honored to be included in the summons to action.

Just as dedicated as Granny, though not as cheerful as usual, Tammy appeared with little Vanna Rose in tow. To Dirk's delight, Tammy quickly handed the baby to him.

Savannah was sorry to see the usually effervescent, California golden girl less than her vibrant self. She had dark circles under her eyes, and her walk lacked its customary bounce.

The absence of Waycross was painfully evident to all.

"Where's your husband this morning, Tammy?" Ryan asked, when she joined them at the table.

Savannah jumped in, hoping to rescue the awkward moment. "As it turns out, my brother is—"

"Unable to join us," Tammy interjected. "He has some personal issues to deal with today. He asked me to give you his apologies and to assure you that he'll be back on the job just as soon as he can manage it."

Jennifer gave Savannah a worried look. "I thought his accident was a minor one," she said. "Are there complications?"

"His *accident?*" John asked. "Our lad had a car crash?"

Tammy hesitated, then nodded. "Yes. But he wasn't seriously hurt, and his 'complications' aren't related to his wreck. He said for me to assure you that he'll fill everyone in on the details, once he has things sorted out a bit better."

Ryan and John looked at Savannah and Dirk. Savannah did her best to give the appearance of an unconcerned sister. She knew her performance was less than convincing.

Dirk busied himself with entertaining the baby, putting a napkin on top of her head, then pulling it off, reducing her to fits of giggles.

John turned to Tammy and with his soft, soothing, British accent said, "That's fine, love. Send your man our best wishes. Whatever it is, I'm sure everything will work out fine."

"Amen to that," Granny said. "All will be well in the end."

Tammy gave her a somewhat doubtful look.

Gran added, "If it ain't all well . . . then it ain't the end."

"Tammy," Jennifer said, "if there's anything that anyone here can do—including me—just ask. Tell him we're here for him. And for you, too."

Tammy bit her lower lip and nodded. "I appreciate you saying that, Doctor, and I'm sure Waycross knows you're all here for him. But I'll tell him anyway, and he'll appreciate your concern."

Savannah picked up the coffeepot and passed it to her right. "Dig in, everybody," she said. "Those pancakes won't stay hot forever. Be generous with the syrup and butter, too. We're going to need some fuel for the work we've got ahead of us."

It took about fifteen minutes for Savannah and Jennifer to inform the team of what had happened to Brianne and Nels.

Unfortunately, it took less time to explain what they had uncovered so far in their investigation.

"I hate to say it," Dirk announced, "but you haven't got a heckuva lot so far."

"For a guy who hated to say it," Savannah grumbled, "you sure didn't seem to have any trouble speaking your mind there. Thanks for pointing out the obvious."

"I didn't say it was your fault," he added. "I doubt I could've done much better."

"I guarantee you couldn't have," Jennifer mumbled under her breath.

Granny stepped in to make peace. "Some of these here cases are easier to solve than others. I reckon this 'un's harder than most, or you two ladies woulda wrapped it up in no time."

"It *is* a tough one. That's why Jennifer asked me to include the rest of you," Savannah said. "We have to find our killer, or Jennifer's sacrifice in coming forward will be for nothing."

Tammy spoke up. "Not to mention the fact that we need to get justice for Brianne's fiancé and Nels's widow. They may not know what happened to their loved ones yet, but once they find out, they'll want the killer prosecuted even more than we do."

"There's another reason this perpetrator has to be caught," Ryan said. "Anyone who would kill two people so cold-bloodedly may have killed before and most likely will again. We have an opportunity to save lives here."

"Then what's next? Let's get on with it," Dirk said.

"Yeah. Let's get 'er done." Granny reached for another pancake. "Start divvyin' up them chores."

Jennifer squared her shoulders and said, "As soon as I leave here, I have an appointment with my attorney. Depending on what she says, we'll probably be heading to the district attorney's office, where I'll make my statement. After that, who knows? I'll probably be behind bars."

"Surely not, Doctor." John reached across the table to cover her hand with his. "If you have any problem posting bail, you let us know right away."

"Yes, please do," Ryan assured her. "We don't want you spending one minute behind bars, if it can be prevented. Let's just say, we know people who know people who . . . You know what I mean."

"I do." Jennifer gave him a grateful smile. "Needless to say, I'd rather be walking the streets free than sitting in jail—at least until I have to be."

"Don't say that." Tammy's voice trembled when she added, "I can't bear to think of you locked up. You're not tried and convicted yet."

"There isn't going to be a trial," Jennifer said

softly. "I intend to plead guilty. I am. There's no point in fighting it."

"Well, I believe in our American justice system," Granny said. "I know it ain't always perfect, 'cause it's made up of people, and we all know how flawed we human beings are. But in my heart, I do believe they get it right most of the time. I have to."

Gran took a sip of her coffee, then continued. "You did tell some falsehoods when you made out them reports, Dr. Jen, and that was wrong. But I reckon the reason why somebody does what they do is just as important as the action itself. And the reason behind your action was love. You were just trying to help a friend who meant the world to you. Pure and simple. For the justice system to be fair in your case, they'll have to take that into consideration. We're gonna hope and believe that they will."

As Savannah listened, she wished that she could be as optimistic as Granny. But she had seen and heard too many court decisions that, at least in her opinion, were less than perfectly just. Try as she might, she couldn't summon the degree of faith that her grandmother usually could in difficult circumstances like these.

Long ago, Savannah had decided that faith as pure and strong as Granny's was surely some kind of spiritual gift. Few mere mortals could find it in their fearful hearts to believe that, come what may, in the end all would be well. Perhaps in the years ahead she could grow and become more like her grandmother, but for now, she was still a work-in-progress.

Savannah picked up her pencil and started to scribble on a yellow legal pad. "All right, assignments. . . . Dr. Jen, you're off to your attorney and then maybe the D.A. That's enough on your plate for the moment."

"I'll research and see what else I can uncover about Brianne's brother and sister-in-law," Tammy offered. "At the moment, it seems like they would have the strongest motive for killing Brianne."

"Yes," Savannah agreed. "The chance of inheriting an estate the size of hers would be a powerful incentive for the wrong person."

"But whoever killed Brianne must've murdered Nels, too," Dirk said. "We don't know if Henry or Darlene had anything against him. Or if they even knew him."

"We can check into Dr. Kendall for you," Ryan offered. "She seems the most likely link you have between the victims."

"Yeah, that couldn't hurt," Dirk mumbled.

Savannah couldn't help noticing his usual reluctance to admit that Ryan and John might be his equals when it came to investigating. It was hard enough for Dirk to accept that they both had full, lush manes of hair. Then there was the "problem" of women throwing themselves at the attractive couple everywhere they went, ignoring the fact they were in a long-term, committed relationship of their own.

But worst of all, at least on Dirk's jealousy-meter, they owned a five-star restaurant, and therefore had constant and unlimited access to a cornucopia of gourmet food.

Savannah knew that Dirk could get over the hair and the women . . . but free, delicious food?

No. Every guy had his limits.

"What can I do?" Granny asked. "I gotta have some sorta job besides just sittin' around here with my teeth in my mouth, lookin' pretty. This gal ain't just for adornment, you know."

"We could sure use a coordinator," Savannah suggested. "Someone to take phone calls and keep track of who's doing what, where, who's found out what, and figuring out what it might mean. I know it'd be complicated, but does that sound like something you could do, Gran?"

"With my hands tied behind my back, my mouth duct-taped, and wearin' a blindfold. Don't forget, I used to live in an itty-bitty town, where ever'body knew the color of everybody else's underdrawers and when they'd last changed 'em. And they all registered an opinion about it, too."

"That's a sterling resume if ever I heard one," John said, giving her a flirty smirk. "'Twill be a pleasure reporting to you."

Dirk rolled his eyes and said, "If we're all done smooching up, let's get down to business."

Savannah told him, "Once we know that Dr. Liu has talked to her attorney and the DA, I'm thinking maybe you should go on to work. Being senior investigator, you might get first crack at this, once it crosses the captain's desk. It'd be good if you and not McMurtry or some other dimwit was in charge."

"Naw. Captain's not gonna hand me no plum

cases. He's still hung up on the Rhinestone Gladiator Sandal Scandal. If he gets the idea I want the assignment, he'll give it to the dogcatcher before me."

"Then hightail it over to the station house and tell him you desperately need two weeks off, because we bought tickets for a ten-day cruise to the Caribbean."

"Good idea. Then he'll stick me with it for sure."

"As for me," Savannah said, "once I find out where Dr. Earlene Kendall's office is, I'm heading up to Santa Barbara to have a talk with her. The sooner we can figure out the connection between Brianne and Nels, the better."

In seconds, Tammy had pulled her electronic tablet from Vanna Rose's diaper bag and found the information. "Dr. Earlene Kendall has two offices. One is on Dora Drive in Montecito. The second is at the northeast corner of State Street and Selena Drive. Today, she's at the second one."

"Hmm. Both of those places are high-end real estate," Savannah observed. "Her practice must be thriving. I wouldn't think there'd be that much of a demand, considering how rare Halstead's is."

"I did a bit more research on Dr. Kendall last night," Jennifer said. "She's quite an accomplished woman, prominent in her field. She's written numerous books on genetic disorders of all kinds. Not just Halstead's. Also, she lectures worldwide, trying to educate the public, as well as researchers, about these horrible diseases. I wish I had the opportunity to get to know her myself." She shrugged. "But it seems I'm going to be a bit busy. . . ."

"We all are," Savannah said as she scribbled the last bit of information on the legal pad and handed it to her grandmother. "There you go, Gran. Who's doing what, where, and why. Let's get to it. Daylight's burning."

Chapter 23

When Savannah walked into Dr. Earlene Kendall's office on State Street in Santa Barbara, she wasn't sure exactly what she was expecting. But after hearing the physician's credentials from Dr. Liu and having passed the luxury stores in the neighborhood that featured high-end, designer attire on her way to meet her, Savannah had conjured an image of a somewhat stuffy, professional woman.

She imagined the office to be minimalistic and the doctor wearing an expensive, traditional suit, modest but quality jewelry, and a classic businesswoman's haircut.

But not so.

Savannah did a double check to make certain she had the right building. It looked more like a posh, outdoor mini-mall than a medical center.

After walking through an outside passageway lined with greenery and passing numerous intriguing boutiques, a used book store, a handmade candle shop, and a yoga studio, she finally found a door with the doctor's name on it.

She went inside, expecting the routine layout of a reception area and check-in desk. To her surprise, she found that she had stepped inside what looked more like a Moroccan tearoom than a physician's office.

The walls of the large room had been painted a warm, vibrant shade of tangerine and covered with framed, intricate, mosaic murals. Turquoise and purple lengths of embroidered silk draped the windows, tinting the sunlight streaming through.

The furniture consisted of a large, L-shaped sofa upholstered in a patchwork of colorful prints and covered with silk pillows in various sizes, shapes, and hues. In front of the sofa was a large, round table with short legs and a beautiful mandala painted on its center. On the floor, an equally brilliant rug added its own busy patterns to the already dizzying array.

At least half a dozen bronze lanterns with stained-glass panels lent their brilliance to the room.

Savannah felt like she was inside a giant kaleidoscope.

She would have enjoyed standing there, soaking it in for the rest of the day, but she heard a movement behind her. Turning, she saw that she was no longer alone in this exotic, if somewhat unusual, room.

A woman as unique as her surroundings stood, quietly studying her. She was dressed, not in the expected Chanel suit, but in bohemian attire as colorful and flamboyant as her surroundings.

At first glance, Savannah thought she looked like a retro hippy who had aged gracefully. But a closer look told her that no hippy-chick from Haight-Ashbury could have afforded the glorious burnout velvet kimono she was wearing. The delicate garment sparkled with tiny crystals that accented its paisley designs in earthen tones. The sheer cloth flowed gracefully from her shoulders to the floor and accented her movements as she walked forward, hand out, to greet Savannah.

Beneath the kimono, Dr. Kendall wore a simple black tank top and slacks that showed off a figure that was lithe and youthful, considering the fact that she must have been in her late fifties or early sixties. Her silver hair spilled over her shoulders in gentle waves.

Savannah looked into the woman's pale, gray eyes and decided, then and there, that Dr. Kendall was strikingly beautiful in her own unique way. She seemed to have a style all her own, and Savannah both appreciated and admired that.

She had always thought that conformity to someone else's idea of "fashion" was highly overrated.

"I'm Earlene Kendall," the doctor said, shaking Savannah's hand. "Did you have any problem finding me?"

"Not really," Savannah said, noticing the silver rings on the hand in hers. There was one for each finger and even her thumb. Each was set with tiny beads and inlays of turquoise and coral.

Glancing down at her left hand, Savannah saw that all of those fingers were similarly adorned, except her ring finger, which was bare. Savannah wondered if the absence had anything to do with a former marriage or relationship.

"I was a bit surprised to see that your office is surrounded by wonderful places to shop, rather than dentists, gynecologists, and psychologists," Savannah said. "But I applaud your individuality. The unexpected is delightful," she added, waving a hand to indicate the room's décor."

Earlene chuckled and walked over to the sofa. She took a seat and patted the cushion next to her, inviting Savannah to join her. "Any professional can do the gray and burgundy thing in their office. But a lot of sad people come through my door. They're weighed down with burdens that most of us can only imagine. I like to give them a warm, soft, cheerful place to be, even if it's only for a little while, before they have to return to the cold, hard, colorless world."

Savannah settled onto the sofa, melting into the pillows. "I can see why someone might want to spend a lot of time here. It's like . . . a fantasy. Only real."

"Thank you. That's what I was going for."

Dr. Kendall gave her a smile, but Savannah could tell she was looking her over, evaluating, even as she had taken inventory of her. Savannah glanced down at her own simple white blouse, linen slacks, and loafers. Her only adornment was her wedding ring and a simple pair of gold hoop earrings.

She felt dull by comparison. But she strongly suspected that the doctor's appraisal of her had more to do with Earlene's curiosity about this meeting than interest in Savannah's fashion sense . . . or lack thereof.

Earlene reached for a tall, silver teapot on the table and said, "I brewed some Moroccan mint tea for your visit. Would you like to try it?"

"How nice of you. I'd love to."

As Earlene poured the golden tea from the pot into a beautiful red glass decorated with swirls of hand-painted, gold accents, she said, "I heard your Southern accent on the phone, so I made it extra sweet."

"I appreciate that." Savannah took the lovely glass, admiring its beauty. "I'm afraid we do like our tea well sugared down in Dixie."

Earlene shrugged. "Everybody needs a vice or two."

Once they had both settled back on the sofa, their drinks in hand, Savannah said, "I appreciate you seeing me on such short notice, clearing your schedule like this."

"I will admit, it wasn't easy. But you said it was extremely important, so. . . ."

The doctor's gray eyes searched hers so intently that Savannah felt a bit uncomfortable, as though she were the one being interviewed, rather than the other way around.

Savannah took a sip of the tea, savored its unique, sweet, smoky flavor while choosing her next words carefully.

At least, thanks to Dr. Liu's self-sacrifice, she could be open about her purpose.

"As I told you on the phone," she said, "I'm a private investigator. I'm looking into the circumstances surrounding the death of a couple of people I think you might know."

She looked startled and asked, "Who?"

"Brianne Marston and Nels Farrow."

Earlene gasped and nearly dropped her glass of tea. "Nels? Nels is gone, too? Oh, no. Poor Candy. She must be devastated."

Savannah thought of the young widow obsessively tending her dead husband's rose garden. "Yes. She is."

"But Nels should've had more time. He was doing so well. What happened?"

"We don't know for sure. That's why I'm investigating."

"Good. We need to know." With a shaking hand, Dr. Kendall set her glass on the silver tray. Then, abruptly, she turned to Savannah and said, "Please, don't tell me that he was a suicide, like Brianne."

Rather than answer her, Savannah said, "Then you knew Brianne, as well as Nels?"

"Of course. I knew them both. They were members of my group."

"Your . . . group?"

"My support group that meets here once a week. They'd been coming for a while, and I'd come to know and love them both. I thought they were coping well, so I was shocked to hear that Brianne had ended her life. But now Nels, too?"

Her eyes searched Savannah's. "Is that what you're telling me? That Nels did the same?"

"It appears that he died in the same manner as Brianne."

Earlene grabbed one of the cushions from the sofa and hugged it tightly to her chest. She rocked back and forth, as though trying to comfort herself.

"I'm so sorry for your loss," Savannah said,

touched that a physician would have such an emotional reaction to the death of her patients. Especially a doctor who, because of her field of practice, would lose so many.

No wonder Dr. Kendall was so highly regarded in her field and well loved by those she treated.

"Brianne was planning her wedding," Earlene said, her voice choking. "And Nels and Candy wanted to go to Alaska—a cruise and then a train trip through Denali. This is most unexpected and distressing."

"I understand. I'm so sorry."

"How did Nels . . . how did he do it?"

"The same way as Brianne."

"A drug cocktail?"

"Yes. The exact combination Brianne used." Savannah opened her purse and took out the list that Jennifer had given her. She handed it to Earlene. "This is a breakdown of the drugs that were found in both of their systems during their autopsies."

Earlene studied the paper for a long time, then said, "I've never seen this particular combination before. But I must admit, it's a very good one. It would be most effective in delivering a quick and relatively gentle passing."

Handing the paper back to Savannah, she added, "I wonder where Brianne and Nels found that formula. It's quite sophisticated."

"As in . . . only someone in the medical field could come up with it?"

"I should think so. Or, at the very least, someone with an advanced knowledge of pharmaceuticals."

"But neither of them had any sort of training in those areas," Savannah reminded her.

"Then it would seem that someone assisted them."

"Assisted them . . . *if* they asked for assistance."

"What are you saying?"

Savannah hesitated, waiting for the doctor to come to her own terrible conclusion.

Suddenly, Earlene caught her breath and crossed her arms tightly over her chest, as though protecting her heart. "No," she whispered. "No, no. You aren't saying that someone *murdered* them. That's not what you're saying, right?"

"After investigating their attitudes and circumstances, right before their passing, some people observed, just as you did, that both Brianne and Nels had positive attitudes and a lot to look forward to. It's also been suggested that both died before they or their primary physicians expected them to."

"But murder? Really? I can't imagine why anyone would do such a thing. They were such nice people. Even here in the group, they were very popular, an inspiration to everyone."

"The people in your group . . . are they all your patients?"

"No. Very few are. Most were referred to me from various genetic disorder clinics in the Los Angeles area. They have their own general practitioners and specialists. We only offer support."

"How many people attend your meetings and how often?"

"Once a week. Between twelve and twenty, depending on what sort of week they've had, and if they're able to get here."

"Twelve? Twenty? There are that many people with Halstead's?"

"No. Halstead's is rare, even in the rare genetic disease community. Most have Huntington's, sickle cell anemia, cystic fibrosis, or hemochromatosis."

Savannah thought for a moment, picturing the attendees sitting in this room, drinking in the colors, the vibrancy, and possibly Earlene's tasty Moroccan mint tea. "It must help them to be here."

"I hope so. I believe it does. A little anyway."

"It must be horrible, living with a death sentence hanging over you the way they do."

"It is," she agreed sadly. "But their courage is motivating. It inspires us all to live each day to the fullest and count even the smallest of blessings."

"I'm sure that you and this amazing place strengthen and encourage them."

"Many days they help me more than I do them. Everyone in the group does their best to uplift the others. There are so many levels of suffering they endure. From the physical pain to the emotional. Then there are the mental battles as they make difficult decisions, terrible choices."

"Such as . . . ?"

"How to plan for their future, while not knowing what it will bring in the way of challenges. Which life goals they should continue to pursue and which to abandon. Simple things that everyone else takes for granted—completing an education, buying a home, getting married, bringing children into the world, while knowing that they may pass along their conditions to their offspring."

"And they might not be there to help their kids deal with the condition they gave them," Savannah said, as her heart broke for these strangers.

"That's right. Then there's the ultimate choice that at least some of them wrestle with," Earlene said. "Whether to let nature take its course, or to end it before the worst comes, while they're still themselves with the mental capabilities to make that decision."

"I can't imagine."

"No one can unless they've been through it."

"But you encourage them. You must get a lot of satisfaction from your work."

"Mostly, I try to inform them. I make sure they have the facts about their diseases. As much as possible, I try to illuminate the dark path in front of them, to let them know what they can expect and when."

She closed her eyes, and Savannah could tell she was fighting with her emotions. "That's why I feel so bad about Brianne. I misinformed them. I told them both that they had time."

"It isn't your fault. You were probably right. They did have time. But someone stole it from them. That's why I'm investigating these cases. We can't let whoever did this get away with it."

"I agree." Earlene squared her shoulders. "How can I help you?"

"Tell me if there was anyone here that disliked either Brianne or Nels. You said they were popular with the group, but did you ever sense any negative feelings or see any conflicts between them and anyone else here?"

Earlene thought for a moment, then a look of

horror came over her face. "Oh, no!" she whispered.

"Who?" Savannah asked "Who are you thinking of?"

"It couldn't be. He's a jerk, but . . ."

"Tell me anyway."

"I don't want to cast suspicion on someone who's innocent."

"If he's innocent, he has nothing to worry about. Let me know who he is so that, if nothing else, we can rule him out."

"Andy. His name is Andrew Ullman."

Savannah took out her notebook, asked the doctor how to spell it, then wrote it down. "He had a problem with Brianne and Nels?"

"Not with Nels. Just Brianne."

"What happened?"

"He liked her. At first, anyway. That was understandable. She was a pretty lady and very kind. She had a soft, gentle way about her that you might not expect from an attorney."

Savannah smiled. "'Soft' and 'gentle' aren't exactly job requirements for that particular occupation."

"True. I think Andy misconstrued the kindness she showed him as interest. It took him about ten minutes to fall for her. I could see it happening and knew it wasn't going to end well."

"What did you observe?"

"Him making goo-goo eyes at her. Her deliberately looking the other way."

"Hmm. That's never a good sign."

"No. And he didn't take the hint. He kept pursuing her. She even told me that he was continually bringing up the topic of suicide and that made her uncomfortable."

"I can imagine it did."

"I spoke to him and told him that his behavior toward her was inappropriate. He promised to stop."

"And did he?"

"For a couple of weeks. But after the last meeting that she attended, two days before her death, he came on to her, hot and heavy, back there by the refreshments."

She pointed to a table in the corner that held a larger tea service, more of the lovely, jewel-toned glasses, and some empty platters.

"I saw what he was doing, so I walked over there to intervene. But I didn't have to. She took care of it herself. She told him that she was engaged, was in the middle of planning her wedding. She even showed him her ring. Then she marched out the door. I never saw her again."

The sadness on the doctor's face went straight to Savannah's heart. "I'm sorry," she said. "It must be hard, losing a patient."

"It is. It's always difficult. But losing someone as special as Brianne . . . that's particularly painful. I had a bad feeling, when I heard she'd died. Believe it or not, I even thought of Andy, and I wondered if he had anything to do with her passing. But a couple of days later, I heard on the news it was natural causes, and I was relieved. Now you're telling me that maybe he . . ."

She didn't finish the statement.

Savannah sat quietly with her for a while, then she asked, "What does Mr. Ullman do for a living?"

Earlene gave her a look that chilled her. "He's the owner of a compounding pharmacy."

"A compounding pharmacy? Like, one of those places that mixes medicines for customers who—?"

"Who want something customized to their specific needs? Yes. And he's the only pharmacist in his store."

Savannah felt her pulse rate go up and her face flush. "Dr. Kendall, could you please give me Andrew Ullman's phone number and address?"

"I'll do better than that. Come back here tonight at seven-thirty. We're having our weekly meeting. I don't like to do this sort of thing, but under the circumstances, I'll introduce you with any name you like, and you have Halstead's and are having a tough time dealing with the fact that your symptoms are getting worse."

"Ullman will be here?"

"He never misses a meeting. I'll introduce you to him." She looked Savannah up and down and gave her a sardonic smile. "I hate to say it, but I think you'll be just his type."

Chapter 24

A few hours later, as Savannah drove along the Pacific Coast Highway on her way back to Santa Barbara and the meeting at Dr. Kendall's office, she was happy to have her husband along for company.

Upon reporting for work earlier in the day, Dirk had announced his fake travel plans to his captain and had immediately been assigned the double murder case.

He sat in the Mustang's passenger seat, a moderately grumpy look on his face. She wasn't impressed. It was the scowl he wore any time he wasn't behind the wheel.

"One of these days," he said, "you're going to have to let me start driving the pony."

"Not gonna happen," she replied.

"You still don't trust me. You hold it against me, because I wrecked my Buick."

"That accident wasn't your fault. I know. I was there, remember?"

"Then why won't you let me drive your car? I mean, for heaven's sake, it's just a car."

"*Just a car?* That right there is why I won't let you drive her. She's my best friend."

"I thought *I* was your best friend."

"I've known her longer. Why don't you buy a new car?"

"Too expensive. Besides, nothing could ever replace my Skylark. I bought that car the day after I graduated, with money I earned mowing lawns every weekend that I was in high school."

"Then you should understand Automobile Sentimentality. It's a powerful force of nature, surpassing puny Human Affection."

"Apparently so."

They rode along in silence for a while, appreciating the beauty of the road. To their right stood the line of foothills that hugged the coastline in that region. The farther north they traveled, the larger those hills became. Finally, as they approached the outskirts of Santa Barbara, they grew into mountains, rising blue-gray in the distance, framing the historic, Spanish-style city and preventing it from spreading east.

To their left, the sparkling Pacific Ocean did the same, limiting the town's growth, and that was just the way the people of Santa Barbara liked it. Gracious, elegant, and exclusive, the city would have been ruined by urban sprawl long ago, had nature not kept her growth in check.

When Savannah had first moved to the area, she'd wanted to settle in Santa Barbara, but property expenses and her limited budget had stymied her plans, and San Carmelita was a lovely second choice.

"Are you mad at me?" Dirk asked her, pulling her out of her reverie.

She gave him a quick, concerned look. "No. Why would I be?"

"Because I didn't tell you about your brother."

"Oh. Okay . . . I do wish you'd told me earlier about what was going on with him. After all, he's my flesh and blood. But he asked you not to. I have to respect that."

"Then you aren't mad at me?"

"No. I understand. I had the same problem with Dr. Liu. She made me promise not to tell you, and I didn't want to put you in a bad spot, legally speaking, so I didn't. But I want you to know, I didn't feel good about it. It felt like lying."

He nodded. "That's exactly how I felt, not telling you about Waycross. I wished I'd never promised him that I'd keep his secret. Especially from my wife. Me and you, we don't tell each other lies and stuff like that. We keep things clean between us."

"That's right. And this felt kind of dirty. Like when we were in the bathtub and you asked me if I'd had a nice evening at home. I told you I had. But I'd been hanging out at The Fisherman's Lair, breathing a Kenny Bates-wannabe's beer breath. I know it was a little white lie, told for somebody else's benefit, but I still didn't like it."

"I hear ya. It's okay. But I've been thinking, maybe we should make some sort of pact not to do that anymore."

"I was considering that myself," she replied.

"If somebody has a secret to tell us, but wants us not to tell anybody, we could promise not to tell anybody, except maybe our spouses. If they're okay with that, fine. And if they're not, then maybe they should tell somebody else."

"But what would we do, if somebody we really care about came to us with an important secret and asks us not to share it with *anyone?* Even each other? Sometimes people have problems they need to talk about, and I would hate it if somebody I loved felt they couldn't share it with me because I wouldn't be discreet."

"That's what makes it hard, huh? Maybe it depends on the secret and who it is."

"And whether it affects either you and me personally."

"Eh, this crap's complicated. I hate complicated crap."

Dirk received a text. He read it and said, "This discussion is gonna have to wait. Ryan says that him and John are parked about a block away from the doctor's office. They want to know where you think they should set up shop?"

"I scouted the area before I left this morning," she said. "There's a restaurant behind Kendall's mini-mall. A gourmet sushi place. Their parking lot is right next to the mall's, and it didn't look crowded. If they park the van there, they should be able to get a signal. It's not that far away and there's no building to obstruct."

He gave her a long deadpan stare, saying nothing.

"What?" she asked. "It's not that complicated."

"You expect me to *text* all *that*? I told you, I think I'm starting to get some arthritis in my right thumb joint."

She rolled her eyes. "Then send smoke signals, or a carrier pigeon, or get a couple of oatmeal boxes and put a string between—"

"That's enough outta you, Miss Smart Mouth."

"Or you could just phone them, you know, the old-fashioned way."

"Good idea."

Halfway through the meeting of Dr. Kendall's support group, Savannah was either the most depressed or the most inspired she had ever been in her life. She couldn't decide which, so she decided it was both.

To witness such brave people in such dire circumstances was difficult, but it certainly caused her to count the many blessings that her normal life afforded her each and every day.

In years ahead, she vowed that if she felt discontented with her lot in life, she would remind herself of Jeannie who had cystic fibrosis and a bright smile that lit the room. Or quiet, gentle Maria who was fighting Marfan, the same disease that some historians believed would have taken Abraham Lincoln's life, had he not been assassinated. Or young Terrance who managed to laugh and tell jokes, knowing that his sickle cell anemia could reach a crisis point at any time, ending his life.

Remembering them, she would put her own petty problems into perspective. She had no doubt that most of the people in that colorful room, sitting on Earlene Kendall's bright, silk cushions, were living their lives—as long or short as they might be—to the fullest.

Then there was Andrew Ullman.

Savannah wouldn't have needed for Earlene to pull her aside and discreetly point him out. She'd have guessed within minutes who he was.

He was nothing like the others.

As a police officer, Savannah had seen more than her share of ghouls, those who lingered at auto accidents and house fires, absorbing and savoring every bit of human drama they could garner from other people's tragedies.

The moment she laid eyes on Andrew Ullman, she knew he was one of those whom she had told so many times, "Move along! Move along! Nothing to see here!"

However, as she watched his wide-eyed interest, bordering on glee, as the attendees shared their various trials, her instinct told her that his curiosity had crossed the line from distasteful intrusiveness to sick obsession.

No sooner had the meeting ended than she realized that she was yet another object of his fascination. He wasted no time at all in rushing across the room to her, practically tripping over some of the other guests, who hadn't yet risen from their seats on the floor.

"Hi. You're new," he said, grabbing her hand and giving it a far too enthusiastic shake. His eyes were a strange shade of amber, the same as his shaggy, overlong hair. "I'm Andrew, a Marfan," he said. "You're a Halstead's. That's a toughie."

"Yes, it is," she replied, trying to mask her contempt with a sorghum sweet smile. She reminded herself that she wouldn't get very far with her undercover investigation of the guy if she punched him in the mouth five seconds after meeting him. "As I shared earlier, I'm having a hard time dealing with it. That's why I came here tonight."

He gave a quick glance around the room. "They're pretty nice here," he said. "But nothing really helps when you've got something like Halstead's. As genetic disorders go, that's one of the worst. Ugly end. Yuck."

"What do you do when you aren't here?" she asked. "Motivational speaker? Crisis counselor perhaps?"

The jab was lost on him. He didn't look the least bit insulted, only confused.

"No. I'm a compounding chemist. I own a pharmacy."

"That sounds complicated."

"Yeah. Most people can't do it. You have to be really smart."

Is it necessary to be a narcissist, too? Savannah wondered.

She kept that one to herself, figuring he might get it.

"You wanna go get some sushi?" he asked. "There's a good place right across the parking lot in the back."

Weighing the logistics—the location of the restaurant and the proximity of her support team—Savannah decided that if she needed assistance, or if he were to say anything incriminating, they would be near enough.

"I'd love to," she said. "Let's go get some sushi."

*   *   *

"California rolls aren't real sushi," Andrew said, staring down at her choice with a look of disdain. "If this place was really gourmet, like they claim, they'd offer Yin Yang Fish."

Considering the glow in his strange, gold eyes that made her think of movies she'd seen involving demon possession, she was afraid to ask. But she could tell it meant a lot to him.

"What's Yin Yang Fish?"

He seemed surprised at her ignorance. "It's an amazing dish served in more . . . shall we say . . . adventurous parts of the world. It means 'dead alive' fish. They deep-fry the back half, keeping the front of the fish alive, so that you can eat it while it's still—"

"Okay, okay. Stop right there, before I lose what I've eaten of my California roll."

He grinned, obviously quite pleased with himself. Then he poured a generous amount of saké and bolted it. "Did I gross you out?" he asked.

"Yeah," she admitted. "I happen to be an animal lover."

"Me, too. I've got a boa constrictor that I'm crazy about."

"Which you probably feed with live mice."

"Sure. The snake likes it better."

Something told Savannah it was Andrew who enjoyed the experience, probably even more than the hungry snake, who was just interested in having dinner and staying alive.

"See . . ." he continued, "I don't get all hung up on the difference between life and death."

"Oh?"

"Yeah. It's all the same house. Just moving from one room into another."

"That's one way to look at it."

"It's the right way. The only way."

"Okay."

Long ago, Savannah had discovered that it was a waste of breath to argue with someone so opinionated. They saw the world through the narrow toilet roll tube of their own limited perceptions. Facts, figures, or other people's opinions be damned.

"Then I suppose," she said, "the people there in the group, they're just all sitting around, waiting to stroll into another room."

"Yes, and they're scared to death of it. That makes them stupid and cowards."

"I don't think they're either. They struck me as extremely brave and wise enough to have found some peace in their lives, in spite of their circumstances. That's more than most so-called 'healthy' folks can say. I think they're awesome."

"Maybe. But not very many of them had the chestnuts to walk through that door one minute early, before all the suffering and indignities set in. You know, the way Brianne and Nels did."

She tried to sound casual when she asked, "You think Brianne and Nels did the right thing?"

"Sure they did. They're an inspiration to us all."

"Did you know them well?"

"Of course. This is a close-knit group. Everyone knows everyone. Although I was particularly close to Brianne. If you know what I mean."

He waggled one eyebrow in a suggestive way that made Savannah want to stick her chopsticks up his nostrils and stomp out the door.

Like poor Brianne would have done the caribou crawl with a sicko like you, she thought. But she kept her opinions and, more importantly, her chopsticks to herself.

"The only thing I'm disappointed about," he was saying, swigging more saké, "is that she didn't wait for me. We were supposed to be partners."

Instantly, Savannah's interest piqued. "Partners . . . in . . . ?"

"Walking into the next room. Together."

"I see."

He studied her in a way that made her feel like one of the mice waiting to be devoured by his snake. "You do?" he asked.

"I think so." She swallowed and forced a smile that wouldn't bare her teeth. "I mean, I can imagine that something like that would be a lot easier, if you had someone to do it with."

"Really?" He seemed both surprised and pleased, as though he couldn't quite believe his good luck. "You get it?"

She nodded and tried to look convincing. "Sure. I mean, who wouldn't prefer not to do something like that alone? It's so scary."

"It doesn't have to be," he assured her, reaching across the table for her hand and squeezing it. "If you know how, it can be easy, just like going to sleep."

"Really?" She widened her eyes, hoping to portray the epitome of innocence and naivete. "I wish that was true, because sometimes it just gets to be too, too much. You know what I mean?"

"I sure do."

"I don't want to wind up like my dad was there at the end. But I don't want to, you know, do it. I'm not brave when it comes to pain."

"It doesn't have to be painful. I can show you how."

"Really? And we'd do it together?"

He glanced away, cleared his throat, and said, "Not like, in the same room. That's hard to arrange, logistically. But we can both film ourselves and watch and hear each other. We could time it so that we'd be, you know, arriving at the same time."

She batted her lashes at him. "Would you be willing to do something like that for me, *with* me? Really?"

He did a poor job of hiding his gleeful smile, when he shrugged his shoulders and said, "If that's what you want, yeah, okay. I guess I would."

"Wow," she said, "you must really like me a lot."

"Oh, I do. I really, really do!" His eyes glowed with a light that she had seen before—in the eyes of a man who had just fallen deeply, hopelessly in love.

She had also seen narrowed, intense, golden eyes like that on a nature channel documentary about a pack of wolves in Yellowstone . . . who had just caught a whiff of prey.

Chapter 25

Sometimes when Savannah worked on a case with her team late into the evening, it occurred to her that she should have named her company the *Midnight* Magnolia Detective Agency.

Long ago, they had decided it was more productive and emotionally satisfying to discuss the case together, while gathered around her kitchen table or sprawled on her sofa and comfy chairs, than tossing and turning in bed, watching the hours on the clock click by.

That evening was no exception as they sat around her living room, discussing the meeting that Savannah had attended, as well as the information the others had uncovered since their morning gathering.

Savannah sat nearby in her customary chair with a sleeping Vanna Rose in her arms. She and Dirk had flipped a coin for who got to hold the baby, and for once, she had won.

Since he had graciously offered his recliner to Granny, he lay on his side on the floor in front of the television, a less-than-cheerful look on his face.

Knowing her husband all too well, Savannah had no doubt that his bad mood had to do with not getting to hold the baby, rather than the loss of his favorite seat.

She decided to hand Vanna over to him the next time she got up to replenish the cookie platter. No doubt, it wouldn't be long, considering how quickly the gang could mow through a plate of freshly-baked Black-Eyed Susans.

But until then, she hugged the baby a bit closer, relishing every sweet moment.

Glancing over at her grandmother, Savannah studied the large black foam core board Granny was balancing on her lap. Granny had written the names of the victims, along with everyone else connected to the case, on colored sticky notes and applied them to the board in an arrangement that, apparently, meant something to her.

At the bottom, she had even added notes indicating who on their team was working on what.

Studying the notes, Granny asked in a most officious tone, "Ryan, did you or John find out anything new about Dr. Kendall?"

"Not much, I'm afraid," Ryan said from his seat on the sofa, between Tammy and John. "We were busy surveilling Savannah this evening in Santa Barbara, but we did come up with a few things in the afternoon."

"Indeed, we did," John added. "Dr. Kendall is

quite a lady, born into old money that was made in the citrus industry here in Southern California back in the late eighteen hundreds. Her parents left her extremely well off, but other than a lovely home in Montecito, you wouldn't know it. She drives an old Volvo. Lives simply, for an heiress."

"She dressed expensively," Savannah said. "Those were high-grade Austrian crystals I saw on the silk kimono she was wearing this morning, and even more on the fancy duster she had on at the meeting. Many hours of labor must've gone into making them. They wouldn't have come cheap."

Ryan chuckled. "You may be surprised to find out *she* actually makes those garments herself. On her social media pages, she posts about sewing them and gluing on the rhinestones."

"Oh. Okay. I stand corrected. But don't tell me she makes the turquoise jewelry she wears, too. She's got a ring on every finger, except one, and even her thumbs. The stones are small but high quality. I'd say they're from the Sleeping Beauty mine."

"I didn't realize that you're a fan of turquoise," Ryan said.

"I'm not," Savannah said, feeling a pang of sadness mixed with anger. "My mother is."

She glanced over at Granny and saw the same feelings on her grandmother's face.

Both could recall plenty of times when Savannah and her siblings were young, and there had been no food in the refrigerator. But Shirley had always found the money somewhere to buy yet another piece of turquoise jewelry.

With an effort, Savannah allowed the past to slip back into the past, where it belonged.

Someone had talked about that in the support group. An older woman had said, "Unless you're examining your past to learn from it or savoring a lovely memory, let it go."

Tammy handed her tablet to Savannah. She had located one of the doctor's social media pages.

Savannah studied the posted photos of Earlene Kendall applying a blowtorch to a piece of silver jewelry. She saw yet another picture of her heat-gluing rhinestones to a piece of silk.

"Wow! She's a woman of many talents," Savannah conceded.

"She's also generous," Ryan said. "She donates much of her time and money to benefit those with serious genetic disorders, especially children. Other than her artwork, it seems that's all she lives for."

"I heard some of what she was saying tonight through your mic," Dirk said. "Stuff about how those sick people found out something that the rest of us oughta learn. . . . To live every day like it's our last, 'cause, for all we know, it might be."

Tammy nodded, and Savannah saw a sadness in her eyes when she said, "That's for sure. You never know what a day will bring."

Savannah couldn't help wondering if Tammy had any updates on Waycross. But she decided to ask later, privately.

"Miss Tammy," Gran said, tapping her finger on one of the notes at the bottom of her board. "I know you've been awful busy today. But did you dig up anything else for us on Brianne's brother or sister-in-law?"

Tammy took her tablet back from Savannah, scrolled over the screen, and said, "As a matter of fact, I did. From what I gather, Henry and his sister had grown closer in the months before her death. Or at least, he and his wife, Darlene, wanted it to appear that way. They chatted on various forums quite a bit about how his sister had Halstead's and how they were trying to find ways to support her."

"How?" Savannah asked.

"Like researching the best foods for her to eat and beverages for her to drink. What sorts of nutrients she needed most and whether it was good for her to drink strong coffee and teas. They said they were making food for her and taking it to her house."

"That was nice of them," Savannah said. "Paul didn't mention that they'd helped him. To hear him tell it, he was her sole caregiver."

"Apparently, that's the way he wanted it," Tammy said. "On one of the forums, Henry mentioned that Paul was trying to keep them away from Brianne. So, Henry was consulting with an attorney on how to assume power of attorney over his sister's affairs."

"I don't like the sound of that," Dirk said. "Figure the brother and his wife might have been spicing up that nutritious food with a little poison?"

Savannah rose and placed the baby into his arms, causing him to brighten instantly. "Poisons similar to a suicide compound?" she said.

"That sounds more like the lad you shared sushi

with this evening," John said. "Yin Yang Fish, indeed. I saw that served in a restaurant in Taiwan. Truly one of the most revolting things I've ever witnessed."

"He's certainly obsessed with death and suicide," Ryan observed. "That's all he wanted to talk about with you there at the end of the meal. I thought he was going to pull out a suicide pact contract and have you sign it in blood before you'd finished eating."

"That guy's a major sicko," Dirk said. "I wanted to walk in there and punch him out when I heard him pressuring you like that."

Savannah picked up the empty cookie plate from the coffee table. "You should've seen the gleam in his eyes when he told me exactly how to do it. In his not-so-humble opinion, anyway."

"What bothered me most," Ryan said, "was how insistent he was on you broadcasting the whole thing when you did it. Supposedly, so he could follow along, doing the same thing with you."

"That *should* bother you. A lot." Once again, Tammy worked her magic on her tablet. "I couldn't help checking old Andrew out, too. Wait until you hear this. . . ."

Halfway to the kitchen with the empty cookie plate, Savannah paused and said, "Go on. Let's have it, darlin'."

"His name isn't Andrew Ullman. It's Alfred Underhill. He's wanted in two other states for manslaughter. Twice, he not only encouraged depressed, vulnerable individuals to commit suicide, but he coached them on how to do it, and got them to broadcast it to him when they did, just like he was encouraging you to do."

"Like those perverts you were telling me about when we were researching the pro-suicide websites before?" Savannah asked. "Andrew Ullman is one of those guys?"

"Exactly like that." Tammy glanced over at her innocent daughter, who was awake and trying to pull the wedding band off Dirk's finger. She lowered her voice. "Without going into details, the law-enforcement officials who investigated him in both of those states said he played the videos of their, uh, passings, over and over again."

"These crimes are sex-based for him," Ryan said.

Tammy nodded. "They most certainly are."

Granny *tsk-tsk*ed her disgust. "Manslaughter? As far as I'm concerned, he ain't but one notch above an ol'-fashioned serial killer."

"If that," Savannah said as she put the empty plate back on the coffee table. Something told her that after hearing this new bit of news, not to mention the talk about Yin Yang Fish, the crowd wouldn't have much of an appetite. Not even for her cookies.

"At least I can arrest his"—Dirk looked at the baby in his lap, who had given up on the wedding ring and was trying to pick the faded Harley-Davidson logo off the front of his T-shirt—"his mange-infested hindquarters for those outstanding warrants. That'll be fun. I'm sure those other jurisdictions will be interested in the tapes we recorded tonight. Especially the conversation at the sushi joint."

"I'll make you some copies." Ryan gave Dirk a smirk. "Under one condition."

"What's that?"

"That you wear a body cam so we can all see you arrest his . . . 'mange-infested hindquarters.' "

"You got it."

Chapter 26

The next morning, as Savannah parked the Mustang in the Marstons' driveway, Dirk surveyed the home that, according to Tammy, they had bought for seven million dollars. "You couldn't give me this stupid place," he stated. "It looks like a giant, white, plastic, butt-wipe box."

"What an articulate, well-considered review," she replied with a sniff. "If you ever get tired of being a cop, you could write for *Architectural Digest*."

"Don't tell me you like this place."

She gave the home little more than a passing glance. It was too early in the morning, and she hadn't consumed nearly enough coffee to argue the fine points of contemporary architecture.

Besides, he was right. It looked exactly like an oversized "butt-wipe box." However, she had enough caffeine coursing through her bloodstream to warn her of the folly of telling Dirk he was right about something.

Experience had taught her that he would latch on to such an admission, like a determined miniature schnauzer with a dog chew, and never let it go. At the first sign of any future disagreement, he would dredge up the three measly incidents where she had been foolish enough to admit he was right and wave them in her face like red capes in front of a snorting, pawing bull.

With the same results.

No. She wasn't in the mood to hear, once again, how desperately wrong she had been, all those years ago, about Steppenwolf recording "In a Gadda Da Vida."

"*You* wanted to go see Paul and Dee first today," she stated, as they walked up the cement sidewalk with "flower beds" on either side filled with white stone and the occasional, lonely succulent.

She figured she might as well remind him of their most recent squabble . . . which *she* had won.

"Yeah, and it would've been okay," he replied with a slightly pouty tone.

"Except that, if we're looking for information about Andrew Ullman, neither Paul nor Dee would have anything to offer. They didn't even know about the meetings."

"Okay, okay. But you're not right all the time. You didn't even know that Iron Butterfly recorded 'In a Gadda Da Vida,' so—"

"Ugggh!"

He grinned and knocked on the door. A few moments later, it was answered by a tiny, slightly disheveled woman wearing a stained T-shirt and jeans with wet knees.

Savannah surmised on the spot that she was the overworked and probably underpaid housekeeper.

Dirk shoved his badge under her nose and said, "I'm Detective Sergeant Dirk Coulter with the San Carmelita Police Department. This is Savannah Reid. We gotta talk to Darlene and Henry Marston."

"Oh. Okay. Come in."

The woman looked ill at ease as she ushered them inside the house, causing Savannah to wonder if she had something to hide. But then Savannah reminded herself that most people looked that way around her husband.

He had many good points to recommend him, as a husband, friend, champion protector of infants, kitties, puppies, and grannies, and certainly as a police officer.

But when it came to your average, run-of-the-mill social graces . . . not so much.

However, Savannah was proud of her husband a few minutes later as she watched and listened to him explain to a distraught Henry and Darlene Marston that Brianne's death was not being considered a suicide.

Henry, in particular, appeared to be taking it very hard.

They sat on a comfortable, horseshoe-shaped sofa in the outdoor living room that overlooked a peaceful valley planted with avocado trees. Although the setting was serene enough, the mood was anything but tranquil.

"What do you mean 'murdered'?" Darlene demanded, her small, heart-shaped face nearly as red as her fuchsia hair.

Her husband was slumped against her, sobbing on her shoulder. The little man with spiky blond hair and a ready smile who had greeted them most amiably when first introduced was now a picture of uncontrollable grief.

Savannah watched and evaluated his every movement, feeling his sorrow in her own heart, while maintaining the necessary degree of skepticism that the job required.

She had been fooled before.

Every investigator was, once in a while.

Unfortunately, people who lied every day of their lives often became quite good at it.

Wrapping her arms around her weeping husband, Darlene said, "But we thought it was all settled. Her death was ruled to be from natural causes. The medical examiner was Brianne's best friend, and they assured us that she's very good at her job."

Dirk shot Savannah a quick, uneasy glance. Both of them were reluctant to reveal Jennifer's culpability unless they absolutely had to.

"Dr. Liu *is* an excellent M.E.," Savannah quickly assured her. "But since her ruling, other information has come to light that has caused her, and us, to reconsider the facts of the case."

"Yes, that's right," Dirk agreed, giving Savannah a grateful nod. He reached into the pocket of his bomber jacket and pulled out a couple of photos that Tammy had downloaded and printed from Earlene's and Andrew's social media pages.

He leaned over and handed them to Darlene.

"Could you please look at these pictures and tell me if you recognize either of these people?"

he asked. "You, too, Mr. Marston, if you can. I'm
sorry to have to question you at a time like this,
but . . ."

With what appeared to be quite an effort, Henry
Marston gathered his wits, wiped his face with the
hem of his T-shirt, and looked at the photos his
wife was holding.

After considering them for quite some time,
both shook their heads.

"No," Darlene said. "They don't look familiar to
me either. Who are they?"

Henry said nothing.

"The woman runs a support group for people
with have fatal genetic diseases," Dirk replied.
"The guy attends those meetings. They both knew
Brianne."

"Did she tell either of you that she attended support group meetings?" Savannah asked.

Darlene glanced away, and Henry cleared his
throat, also avoiding Savannah's eyes.

Savannah took that as a "Yes."

"You knew she was going then?" she prompted.

Darlene nodded. "She told us, but she asked us
not to tell anybody. She didn't want word to get
back to Paul about it."

"Why?" Dirk asked.

Henry finally joined the conversation. "We don't
know for sure," he said. "But Paul's a super jealous
guy. He could hardly stand it when Bri was out of his
sight. He was so sure she'd hook up with some other
man. But she wouldn't have. She wasn't the type."

"Either that," Darlene added, "or maybe she
didn't want Paul to know because he's the sort of
person who can't be bothered with the negative

things in life. He wanted to pretend that Brianne wasn't sick and everything was going to be just fine. He wouldn't have wanted her to go to a support group and talk about what might happen, you know, further down the line."

"Forgive me for saying so, but it doesn't sound like you two like Paul very much," Savannah said.

"There's not much to like," Henry replied. "He wasn't that good to my sister, and after she got so sick, he wouldn't let her friends come around to comfort her."

"We were having to take legal action to even see her ourselves," Darlene added. "The last time we tried to take her some nutritious snacks and protein drinks that we'd made just for her, he wouldn't let us through the door."

Dirk took the pictures back and replaced them in his pocket. "Do the names Earlene Kendall or Andrew Ullman mean anything to you? Did Brianne ever mention them?"

"She talked about a Dr. Kendall quite a bit," Darlene replied. "I don't think I ever heard the doctor's first name. She led the group. Brianne thought the world of her. Said she was kind and knowledgeable and very good at what she did."

Darlene smiled, then added, "A bit eccentric about her clothing and her office furnishings, but other than that . . ."

"But she never mentioned this Andrew or Andy, huh?" Dirk asked rather gruffly.

Savannah could always tell he was tiring of the small talk that was getting them nowhere. Patience did not number among his many virtues.

"No. Nothing." Henry suddenly looked suspicious. "Why? Do you think he might have done something to my sister?"

"We're pursuing all possible avenues of investigation," Savannah interjected. It was a pat response that usually worked.

But not this time.

"If you're asking about him, then he must be some sort of suspect," Henry said, his former grief turning to anger. "Tell me the truth! Do you think he killed Bri?"

"I don't think nothin'," Dirk snapped back. "It's way too early to be thinkin'. I'm just askin'."

Chapter 27

When Dirk knocked on the door of Brianne's house, Savannah was surprised to see Dee answer it. After all the negative things the groom had said about Paul Oxley during their previous conversation, Savannah figured she would want to stay as far away from the main house as possible.

As Dee invited them inside and seated them in the barn-house's massive living room, Savannah decided to file that fact away for future consideration, should she need it.

Perhaps Dee and Paul weren't as antagonistic as they had initially appeared.

At Dirk's request, Dee summoned Paul from the back of the house, where his studio was located.

When he joined them, Savannah looked him over and briefly wondered if he was ever without smudges of paint all over his clothing, face, hands, and arms.

Once the introductions had been made, Paul

offered them coffee. With a twang of disappointment, Savannah passed on the treat. They had more important things to discuss.

After they told Paul why they were there, she doubted that he would be interested in serving them anything at all.

"I have something to tell you," Dirk began. "I'm afraid it isn't—"

"I already know," Paul snapped.

Savannah was surprised. "You do?"

"Yes. I've been informed." He turned to Dirk. "Brianne's worthless brother called a few minutes ago and told me you cops believe she was murdered. I think he honestly enjoyed telling me something as awful as that. He even accused me of harming her, threatened to kill me if I did. Like I would have ever done anything to hurt the woman I loved."

"I'm sorry you had to find out that way," Savannah said gently.

"Sounds like you and Henry hate each other's guts," Dirk remarked, far less gently.

"Nobody gets along with Henry. Not even his own wife." Paul ran his fingers through his blond hair, an act that left some green paint behind. "Brianne couldn't stand him. She knew what he was after."

"What was that?" Dirk asked.

"Her estate. He'd already run through what their dad gave him. He needed her money to keep them afloat a while longer. He and Darlene spent his inheritance like it was nothing. Now they're broke, and they're looking to Brianne's estate to bail them out." He stopped to catch his breath, then added, "If Brianne was murdered, you'd better take a hard look at the two of them. They're the ones with the most to gain from her dying *before her wedding*, rather than after she had a husband."

Savannah watched Dirk as he carefully considered his response to Paul's outburst. Because she knew him so well, she could practically see his mental cogs spinning, but he appeared calm and unmoved by what he had just heard.

"Thank you, Mr. Oxley," he replied evenly. "I'll take everything you just said into consideration."

Savannah couldn't help noticing that the formerly talkative groom had nothing to say. Dee was just sitting on the fireplace hearth, listening attentively to all that was being said.

Try as she might, Savannah couldn't read her enigmatic expression.

She turned her attention back to Paul and said, "Henry and Darlene mentioned that you refused to let them visit Brianne . . . there at the end."

"I most certainly did!"

Savannah watched Paul's face grow redder by the moment as he said, "They kept showing up, day and night, unannounced, and neither Brianne nor I appreciated it. I had my hands full nursing her, and she didn't want to see them. She knew why they were here. They weren't coming by because they were so concerned about a beloved sister. They hadn't bothered to visit her once in the year before. Not even holidays. They just wanted to make sure they were on her good side in case she passed before the wedding."

"What sort of food did they bring?" Savannah asked.

"Stuff they made themselves. Supposedly healthy junk to build up her system or whatever."

Dee cleared her throat and joined the conversation. "I tasted one of those concoctions," she said. "I think it was some sort of protein drink meant to enrich her blood. It tasted horrible."

"Did Brianne drink it?" Dirk wanted to know.

"She took one sip of it and spit it out," Paul said. "It was disgusting. All she ever wanted to drink there at the end was the coffee I made for her."

For a moment, the angry version of Paul disappeared and a sweet sadness filled his eyes, reminding Savannah of her first talk with him, when he had impressed her with his love for his fiancée.

"I'm not surprised that Brianne asked for your coffee," she told him. "That blend of yours is some of the best I've ever had."

He smiled, but said, "Oh, it wasn't my blend that she asked for. She wanted the special mix that her friend gave her. That's all she wanted . . . there at the end."

Savannah resisted the urge to shoot a glance at Dirk, but in her peripheral vision, she saw him sit up straighter and lean forward.

"What mix?" he asked. "What friend?"

"It was some sort of special dark roast," Paul told him. "She said it was an old childhood friend of hers who was keeping her supplied."

"A childhood friend?" Savannah felt her knees go weak. "Did she mention this friend's name?"

"Yeah. Jennifer Liu. She's the county medical examiner. The one who did Brianne's autopsy."

Savannah's hand was shaking when she reached into her purse and took out her phone.

Dirk saw what she was doing. He drew their attention away from her by asking Paul a barrage of questions.

"Did you ever actually see Dr. Liu give her this coffee?"

"Um. No. I've never met the woman."

"Then how do you know it was from the doctor and not someone else?"

"She went out one evening, then brought home a bright red tin and said she'd just been with her friend Jennifer Liu, and she'd given it to her."

As fast as her thumbs could type, Savannah sent off a text to Jennifer: **"Did U give Brianne red tin of coffee?"**

As she waited, she prayed the doctor had been released on bail and had access to her phone.

"Then you don't actually know for sure that it came from Jennifer Liu," Dirk was saying.

"Well, no. I'm just going by what she told me. Brianne wouldn't have lied to me. Why would she have to—?"

"She lied to you all the time!" Dee said.

Startled by the outburst, Savannah looked up from her phone and saw that the woman's eyes were bright with anger.

Paul and even Dirk were taken aback.

"Wh-what?" Paul sputtered.

"Brianne lied to you constantly, because she *had*

to," Dee shot back at him. "She couldn't do a damned thing—even the most normal, innocent chores, like going to the grocery store—without you interrogating her when she got back. You'd want to know everywhere she went, everyone she spoke to. If she stopped somewhere for a bathroom break, you'd want to know every detail. She told you white lies morning, noon, and night, just so she could have some peace!"

Savannah felt her phone vibrate. She looked down to see that, thankfully, Jennifer had replied: **"No why"**

Savannah answered: **"Thx Later"**

Dirk dug into his pocket and pulled out the photos of Dr. Kendall and Andrew Ullman that he had shown earlier to Henry and Darlene.

He held them out to Paul. "Have you ever seen either of these people?"

Paul looked them over, concentrating on the one of Andrew. Then he handed them back and said. "No. Why? Who's the guy? Did he know Brianne? Why are you asking about him? Was she up to something with him?"

"See?" Dee threw up her hands. "That's exactly what I mean. You're shown a picture, and you automatically jump to a conclusion like that? She loved you, was far too good for you, but you never gave her a break!"

Dee stood and walked over to Dirk. Holding out her hand, she said, "Let me see those."

He handed the pictures to her, then looked over at Savannah and down at her phone.

She showed him the screen, just enough for

him to see that she'd received a reply. Then she shook her head no.

"Where's the coffee tin now?" Dirk asked.

"Still in the kitchen," Paul replied. "Why?"

"Show it to me."

Dirk stood. Paul did the same, then led him across the great room to the kitchen.

Savannah started to follow, but then she noticed Dee carefully studying the picture of Andrew.

"Do you recognize him?" Savannah asked.

"I don't think so. Just want to be sure," Dee replied.

"Good. Thanks."

Savannah saw Paul opening the kitchen cupboard over the coffee station. When he started to reach inside, Dirk said, "Don't touch it. Just point to it."

She walked up behind them just as Dirk pulled a pair of surgical gloves from his pocket and tugged them on.

"Who else has touched this tin?" Dirk asked Paul.

"Me mostly. Brianne a couple of times, when she felt up to making her own coffee. Why?"

"Anybody else?"

"Not that I know of."

Savannah felt Dee brush past her on the way to the back door.

"Don't leave yet. Wait for me," Dee told her, as she went outside. "I'll be right back."

Savannah watched as Dirk pulled a bright red tin from the cupboard and set it on the counter.

He opened the container, then asked Paul, "How much was in here the last time you made coffee?"

"Oh, I don't know. It was about half full, I'd say."

"When was that?"

"The day before . . ." Paul choked on his words, then continued. "The day before she passed."

"I assume Brianne didn't make any coffee on that last day."

"Of course not. She was too weak to move. Why are you asking me all this?"

Dirk held up the tin so that both Paul and Savannah could see inside. "It's empty. Not just empty, it's been cleaned. Looks like there's never been anything at all inside it."

Savannah moved closer to get a better look. He was absolutely right. Without a doubt, someone had cleaned it quite meticulously. It was spotless. The metal interior gleamed like the finest, freshly-polished silver service.

One look at the astonishment registered on Paul's face, and she believed he was as surprised as she was.

"Do you have a housekeeping service?" she asked him. "Or any sort of help with Brianne, anyone who might have cleaned that and put it back?"

"No. We liked our privacy. I did the cleaning myself, while Brianne was at work. After she got sick, too."

Savannah heard the back door open and close again. She turned to see Dee holding a small, brown paper bag.

"What do you have there?" Savannah asked her.

"Goat manure" was the unexpected answer.

"Um. Okay." Savannah couldn't imagine what purpose goat manure might have at that moment, but . . .

Without further explanation, Dee marched to a cupboard on the other side of the kitchen, pulled out a white plate, and placed it on the marble counter. Then she handed Savannah the two photos that Dirk had given her.

"I thought I recognized someone or rather, something, in that picture," she said as she proceeded to open the paper bag, then hold it over the plate.

"Hey!" Paul exclaimed. "What are you doing? You said that's goat droppings in there. You're not going to—?"

"Yes, I am," Dee replied, emptying the bag onto the plate.

"You recognized something? What do you mean? What? Which picture?" Savannah asked, completely bumfuzzled.

"Come here, and I'll show you."

Having shaken the last bit of the bag's contents onto the plate, Dee moved aside for the others to see. Then she slid the plate across the counter, closer to Savannah.

As the groom had said, it was goat manure. There wasn't a lot, but enough for Savannah to know what it was. It was a plateful of dark brown pellets that looked like shiny beans, not unlike what Savannah had seen in abundance inside the goat pen when she had visited the mini-herd before. She had also seen a lot of it as a child in McGill, where gardeners used it to fertilize their blue-ribbon winning flowers.

"Last week, when I was mucking out the goats' pen, I picked up a shovelful and saw this," Dee said, pointing to the manure. "You can imagine my surprise! I was wondering what the heck the goats had eaten."

Dee reached over and tapped one of the pictures in Savannah's hand.

"See what that woman's wearing there?" Dee asked her. "That fancy top with all the sparklies?"

"Yes. They're crystal rhinestones that she—"

"I know. And that's what's in the crap."

Savannah leaned over the plate, peered at the droppings, and instantly saw what Dee meant.

There, mixed in with the dark brown pellets, were bits of blue fabric that had, no doubt, been fine silk in a previous life. And scattered among the manure were tiny blue, purple, and iridescent rhinestones.

It was, without a doubt, the most elegant poop Savannah had ever seen.

She felt someone brush the back of her arm, and she realized that Dirk was right behind her, also looking at the plate and then the picture in her hand.

While the digested remnants of finery didn't appear to be from the garment that Dr. Kendall was wearing in the picture, the rhinestones were the same size and the fabric the exact style and texture.

"Has this woman ever been on this property?" Dirk asked. "Think about it. Be sure."

"Not that I know of," Paul replied.

"Me either," said Dee, "and one of us is always here. With the goats and the horses, we don't like to leave the place unattended for long."

"Except for when we went to Brianne's funeral," Paul said.

"True." Dee nodded thoughtfully. "We were gone for a couple of hours that afternoon. And as I recall, it was a day or two after that when I found the fancy manure. I thought it was weird, rather funny actually, and I remembered where I'd dumped it . . . in the back corner of the compost bin."

"Could someone have gotten into the house that day, when you were gone to the funeral?" Dirk asked.

"Sure," Paul said. "I only lock the doors at night, and not even every night. This is a very safe area. We've never felt afraid out here."

Savannah wasn't concentrating on what they were saying. She had spotted something else on the plate. Something tiny, but colorful, embedded in one of the soft pellets.

"Somebody hand me a knife, please," she said.

"What?" Paul looked disgusted at the thought of what she might want it for.

But before he could object further, Dee had opened a drawer, taken out a table knife, and given it to Savannah. "What is it?" she asked.

"I want to see what this is. It doesn't look like something that was in the goats' feed, if you know what I mean."

She used the tip of the knife to remove what looked like a tiny coral-colored bead. "Do you have a little plastic zip baggy?" she asked.

This time it was Paul who supplied what she needed.

"Gimme a bigger one of those bags," Dirk said. "And a fresh, unused paper bag if you've got one.

Chapter 28

As Savannah walked out of the house with Dirk and his bags of new evidence, her heart was heavy.

"There has to be some sort of explanation," she told him when they got back into the Mustang. "I'm telling you, if it's Dr. Kendall who did this, I'm the worst judge of character ever. I thought she was awesome."

Dirk placed his bags carefully on the back seat, then said, "You only spent a few hours with her. What's that saying that Granny's always telling us about personality and character?"

"Someone's personality is obvious within the first ten seconds after you meet them. But it takes years to learn their character."

"True. But I just can't believe it. I'd have to have more than an empty coffee tin and some sparkly goat crap to convince me."

She started the car and headed down the canyon.

As she approached the main road, she heard a pleasant little chime from her car phone system.

"Tammy," she said. "What's going on, sugar?"

"I've got some news for you."

"About Waycross?" she asked hopefully.

"No. He's about the same" was the sad response. "It's about the case, and it's kinda sad, too."

"Uh-oh."

Dirk said, "Give us whatcha got, kiddo."

"I've been digging into Dr. Kendall's personal history, and I found something. I don't know if you've heard it or not, Savannah, but I got the idea it isn't public knowledge."

"What's that?" Savannah asked.

"She's never been married, but when she was young, she had a child. The little girl's name was Allison. She would have been about forty now, if she'd lived."

Savannah was afraid to ask, but she had to. "What did she die of?"

"Novak's disease," Tammy replied. "It causes problems with the lungs, sort of like cystic fibrosis, but you can inherit it from only one parent. And that parent doesn't always manifest the disease themselves."

"How old was Allison when she died?" Savannah asked.

"Six."

"Damn," Dirk said. "That's young. Poor kid."

"I know." They heard Tammy sniff. "It's a really awful illness, too. I couldn't stop crying when I read the list of symptoms. I think of Vanna Rose and . . . I can't stand to think of a child going through all of that."

"I know, honey. Fortunately, it's a rare disorder, but I've heard of it," Savannah said. "I wonder if the girl got it from Dr. Kendall or her father."

"I don't know who the father was. He was listed as 'Unknown' on the birth certificate. It appears Dr. Kendall was a bit of a free spirit back then."

"That doesn't surprise me."

"But I did a search of her family, and she had a brother who died of Novak's."

"Before or after her own kid was born?" Dirk asked.

"Long before. He was an older brother. He passed at the age of nine. Earlene was seven."

"Then she knew it ran in the family," Savannah said. "But she chose to have a child anyway."

"Maybe she didn't realize that what her brother had was hereditary," Tammy suggested, "or the pregnancy was unplanned, and she didn't feel it was right to have an abortion."

"That's all possible." Savannah couldn't help feeling sorry for Earlene Kendall, whatever her circumstances had been forty years ago. "But it must have been devastating to watch your child suffer like that, knowing they would die early from a disease you had passed to them. You would never, ever get over something like that."

"That's for sure." Dirk reached into the glove compartment, took out his stash of cinnamon sticks, and stuck one in his mouth. "It would mess you up, somehow, some way."

"There's something else," Tammy continued. "I managed to find some email addresses and screen names that she obviously intended to be anonymous on various social networks and forums. When she's not officially speaking as herself, she's extremely outspoken about people with fatal genetic disorders not bringing children into the world."

"That's understandable, I guess, considering her personal history."

"No, I mean *rabid*. She never mentions her own daughter, but she attacks other people with genetic disorders who've either chosen to have kids or are considering it. She's accused them so viciously that she's been kicked off a number of websites for being abusive."

"Wow, that's a long way from the woman I met," Savannah said as she pulled onto the Pacific Coast Highway and headed toward Santa Barbara. Turning to Dirk, she said, "You and Gran are right. It takes a long time to get to know a person's true character."

To Tammy, she said, "Thank you, darlin'. I can't say I'm happy about what you uncovered, but we needed to hear it. Now, if you aren't busy, could you call Ryan and John?"

"Sure. And tell them what?"

"Ask them to meet us in that parking lot behind Dr. Kendall's Santa Barbara office. Make sure they bring the van and recording equipment. We're on our way there now. I'm going to have another talk with Dr. Earlene. And I want to be wearing a wire."

After the phone conversation was completed, Savannah turned to Dirk. "You don't mind if I interview her first, do you? I think I might be able to get her to talk. She and I sort of, well, bonded. At least I thought we did."

"I don't mind at all. I agree you'd probably get farther with her than I would."

"Thanks."

He gave her a sad, soft smile. "I'm sorry, babe. I know you're bummed about hearing all that stuff. You said there had to be some sort of explanation."

"Yeah, and it turns out there is. I just wasn't expecting something like that."

Chapter 29

A little over an hour later, a "wired-up" Savannah walked into Earlene Kendall's office and was relieved to find the doctor there and alone.

Unfortunately, the vibrant colors and furnishings of the room did little to cheer her, as before. This time, they seemed false somehow, like a fanciful façade that overlaid a much darker, more sinister, structure.

As before, Earlene was wearing one of her signature garments of flowing silk, brightly patterned and embellished with crystals.

She jumped up from her seat on the sofa, tossed the book she had been reading onto the mandala table, and hurried toward Savannah, a smile on her face.

To Savannah, the smile seemed as false as the room's bright colors and patterns.

"Savannah! How nice to see you again!"

"You, too," she lied. "I hope you don't mind me dropping in unannounced like this."

"Not at all. Please have a seat."

Savannah sat on the sofa and placed her purse close to her thigh. It held her Beretta, and as benign and charming as her hostess appeared to be, she couldn't forget that Earlene Kendall was a murder suspect.

Savannah didn't want her weapon too far away.

"Shall I make us some tea?" Earlene asked.

Savannah couldn't help noticing that, although the woman's mouth was smiling, her eyes were bright with something that looked like suspicion mixed with anger.

"No, but thanks," Savannah replied. "I just thought I'd stop for a few minutes."

Earlene settled onto the sofa a few feet away and began toying with the rings on her fingers in a way that Savannah hadn't seen her do before.

"I'm glad you came by," Earlene said. "I saw you and Andrew leave together last night, and I've been a little worried about you. You know, after all we talked about before. How did it go?"

"We went out for sushi. He drank far more saké than he should have and tried to convince me that I should commit suicide with him."

"Seriously? On the first date? Boy, he moves fast."

"I know, huh? He was telling me the easiest ways to do it and—"

"There are no easy ways. Even when the mind is ready to go, the body doesn't give up all that quickly."

"He also pressed me to film my death and broadcast it to him. Supposedly, so that he could do the same thing at the same time, and we would 'walk into the next room' together."

Earlene gasped. "I can't believe this. I've been harboring a wolf in sheep's clothing. Do you think he did the same to Brianne and Nels?"

"We're considering all possibilities," Savannah replied evenly.

She could tell that her noncommittal answer hadn't pleased Earlene, and she wasn't sure how to read that.

If she was innocent of the murders, she'd want her friends' killer to be uncovered and brought to justice. If she was guilty, she would, no doubt, prefer that Savannah accuse someone else.

"Whether he hurt Brianne or Nels remains to be seen," Savannah said. "But Andrew Ullman isn't his real name, and he's wanted in two other states for manslaughter. He encouraged and advised some depressed people to end their lives in places where that's a serious crime. He'll be arrested and extradited very soon."

"Thank goodness. Or, I should say, 'Thank you!' Otherwise, I'd be looking over my shoulder every minute, wondering when he was going to show up here and worrying what he might say and do to my group members."

"You're welcome."

"But you don't think he was the one who was behind Brianne's death and Nels's?"

"I thought he might be, so I went out to Brianne's house to see if Paul could identify a picture of him."

Savannah watched for it and saw a slight narrowing of the eyes, a wee furrowing of the brows.

No, Earlene didn't like the sound of that.

"It's such a beautiful estate," Savannah continued,

forcing a light, happy tone. "Lots of land, a beautiful post-and-beam, barn-shaped house, horses, and the cutest little goats you've ever seen. Have you been there?"

"No" was the quick answer. "Brianne and I only knew each other through the group here. We never met outside of the meetings."

"Too bad. Those goats are just adorable. Though you have to watch out for them. What they say about them chewing on everything is true. One of them nearly ruined the cuff of my best basic white blouse."

Glancing down at the doctor's ring finger on her left hand, Savannah saw that it was no longer bare. Like the others, that finger was also adorned with a silver ring. This one was studded with small, turquoise and coral beads.

Savannah reached into her purse and pulled out the plastic sandwich bag. "I found something while I was up there. It reminded me of you."

Earlene stared at the bag. "Really? What was that?"

Savannah leaned toward her and took hold of her left hand.

For a second, she thought Earlene would snatch it back, but she didn't. She submitted as Savannah held the bag next to her ring finger.

That was when Savannah noticed something else. A small injury, hardly more than a superficial scrape, on that finger. There was another even smaller one on the pinky next to it.

"Ouch," Savannah said. "You hurt your hand."

"No big deal. I was cutting a sheet of metal and I scraped it with a dull saw blade."

"Hmm. Looks more like a bite to me."

Earlene didn't reply, but Savannah felt her hand flinch ever so slightly.

"You weren't wearing this ring the last time I saw you," Savannah told her. "Was it out for repairs? Oh, that's right . . . 'cutting a sheet of metal.' You make your own jewelry. You probably fixed it yourself."

"I do all of my own jewelry repairs."

Savannah slowly twisted the ring around, studying all sides of it, until she found one small stone that was far paler than the others. "Too bad you couldn't replace that missing coral bead with one that matched the others better."

"It's hard to match coral," Earlene snapped. "It comes in so many different shades."

"Really? I have one here that looks like a perfect match to the others. What do you think?"

Savannah let go of her hand and lifted the baggie to her eye level, where she could see the tiny bead more clearly.

"How lucky for you! I found your missing bead!" Savannah exclaimed cheerfully, as though informing her best friend that she was a lottery winner. "And you'll never guess where. Not in a million years."

Earlene gulped. "Where?"

Savannah put the baggie with the bead back into her purse and pulled out the even larger bag—the one containing the manure.

She dangled the clear bag in front of the woman's eyes. "It was here in this goat poop."

Turning the bag back and forth, she let the doctor get a good look . . . at the manure . . . at the sodden fabric . . . at the glistening rhinestones.

"Now, ain't that about the fanciest doody you've ever seen in your life?" she said. "Laced with China silk and spangled with fine Austrian crystal. . . . Like the silk and rhinestones you're wearing." She leaned forward and pretended to study the doctor's kimono more carefully. "Hey, *exactly* like what you're wearing."

Savannah waited for Earlene to reply. But she just ducked her head and sat quietly as tears began to fill her eyes.

"This was found on Brianne's property. My husband, who's the police detective assigned to Brianne's and Nels's case, found something else there. In her kitchen. An empty coffee tin."

Once again, Earlene said nothing. She didn't even ask the simplest questions that an innocent person would. Like, "What's important about an empty coffee tin?"

She just sat there, her head bowed as the tears began to roll down her cheeks.

"At one time, it contained coffee that Brianne's 'friend' gave her. Coffee that she drank and drank as she got sicker and sicker. Now it's empty, and whoever got rid of the leftover coffee washed the tin thoroughly. Just in case we got that far with our investigation and decided to test it . . . as in, test it for a rare but highly effective cocktail of drugs that, when ingested, would bring on symptoms similar to Halstead's."

Earlene began to cry in earnest as she twirled the newly-repaired ring on her left hand so hard and so fast that it tore open the small bite. The wound began to bleed.

"My partner had another detective go to the Farrows' residence a while ago and guess what? There was a similar tin there, too. Candy had thrown it away, but he found it in the trash. Thoroughly washed. Spotless. He asked Candy if it was possible for someone to get into her home undetected, like when she was away at her husband's funeral. Turns out, like a lot of trusting people who don't know better, she leaves a spare key under the mat."

When, once again, Earlene said nothing, Savannah started to be concerned. She had to get some sort of confession out of her. So far, the recording that the guys in the van were getting would be worthless. Savannah knew she'd need a lot more than just herself making barely-veiled accusations and Earlene weeping.

"What I don't understand, Earlene, is why you didn't just take the tins with you. Why did you stay and risk getting caught while you cleaned them?"

No reply.

"My guess is . . . you thought that finding empty tins would be less suspicious than someone discovering that they were missing altogether."

Earlene shot her an ugly, angry look that gave Savannah instant access into the other side of the woman.

That one glance said it all.

Dr. Earlene Kendall wasn't just a kaleidoscope of color and light. Not by a long shot. She had a lot of pain and its resulting anger stored inside. As a result, she was a highly dangerous person.

Savannah thought of all that Tammy had just told her on the phone. The excruciating secrets this successful, prestigious physician was hiding from the world.

Normally, Savannah wasn't cruel enough to drive a knife into the wound created by someone's worst life experience. She knew people who gave themselves permission to do that, but she refused to.

Usually.

But this was a special circumstance.

She decided, to protect society from this dangerous woman, to get her off the streets and behind bars, she needed more than the flimsy, circumstantial evidence they had.

It was enough to point a finger at Kendall, but it wasn't nearly enough to convict her in court. Savannah knew she had to get that confession.

"This is about Allison, isn't it?" she asked gently.

"Shut up! You shut up!"

Earlene screamed it so loudly that Savannah jumped and reached for her purse.

Her heart was pounding as she pushed her hand inside and grabbed her Beretta. But she left both her hand and the weapon inside.

That certainly got a reaction, she told herself. *Might as well keep it going.*

"Both Brianne and Nels had just come to the decision that, since they weren't manifesting any symptoms, they would risk having children," Savannah said. "They probably shared that here in the group, didn't they?"

"Yes, they did!" Earlene literally spat the words. Savannah could feel the droplets of saliva hit her face. "They announced it like they were *proud* of themselves. They went on and on about how they'd found the courage to live their lives to the fullest. Like it takes courage to gamble with someone else's life. What about their children's lives, huh? What about the innocent, unborn kids who'd have to pay the price if their gamble didn't pay off?"

Savannah sat a moment, digesting what she had just heard. Deciding what it would take to get the killer to actually admit her guilt.

Hammer her with accusations?

Or appeal to her lacerated mother's heart?

"Is that what you did, Earlene?" she asked, her tone soft, her Georgia accent pronounced. "Did you find the courage to take a chance and watch your child suffer when it turned out badly?"

"We are not going to talk about my daughter! You don't have a clue what she was about or what happened back then. Don't you dare give me your opinion of what I should or shouldn't have done!"

"I'm not going to. You did what you felt was right for you, for your life, for your child. I've never been in your place. I wouldn't dare pass judgment on you. My grandmother always says, 'It's easy to know where you stand on life's biggest decisions . . . until it's you who's gotta make them.' "

Earlene's rage seemed to subside a bit as she considered those words. "Your grandmother's a wise woman."

"She is."

"No one can know what I experienced. No one understands what the people who come here feel, how hard their lives are. Their families', too. It's hell. And believe it or not, but the judgment, the harsh words they have leveled at them . . . sometimes that can be worse than the pain from their disease itself."

"I believe that." Savannah drew a deep breath. "So, why would you judge Brianne and Nels for their decisions? Why would you appoint yourself their judge, jury, and executioner?"

Again, rage contorted the doctor's face, as she shouted, "Because, unlike *you,* *I* know what I'm talking about! *I* can make a judgment because no one knows better than *I* do what their children would have to suffer."

"I see."

"Yeah, you better see! It's not like I didn't try to talk to them. I pleaded with them. But their minds were made up. They were determined to do what they wanted to!"

"We human beings are like that," Savannah replied, as calmly as the other woman was agitated. "We insist on making the big decisions ourselves. And that's what they did. They rejected your advice and—"

"Not *advice!* My *warnings* ... based on painful life experiences."

"They ignored your warnings, and you had to save them from themselves."

"No! You don't get it! I had to save *their children!* It was all about the kids ... and *their* kids ... and *their* kids ... generation after generation suffering because their parents insisted on having everything that everybody else has. Well, we aren't like everybody else!"

"So, you killed them. Because you felt you had to ... ?" Savannah coaxed.

"Yes, I did what I had to. What no one else had

the strength to do. And I'd do it again in a heart-beat."

Savannah felt a wash of relief go through her body and spirit. "Okay. That's it," she said, speaking the code words to bring Dirk inside to make the arrest.

As she waited for her detective husband to come through the door, Savannah knew . . . this was one case, one resolution she wasn't going to look back on with warm feelings of accomplishment.

This one would forever be a source of sadness.

Chapter 30

At twilight, Savannah sat on the patio behind the giant "barn-house" in the canyon, watching her loved ones enjoy the many pleasures the great estate had to offer.

Ryan and John had taken a couple of the horses for a ride along with Dee. Tammy and Waycross were in the deep end of the pool, cuddling and, considering their giggles, doing heaven-only-knew what beneath the surface of the water.

"He's getting better now," Savannah told Gran, who was sitting nearby, her feet stretched out to capture the warmth of the fire pit.

"Took long enough" was Granny's reply. "Who woulda thought it'd be a solid three months to get over the effects of that drug?"

"He's one of the lucky ones," Savannah replied. "Some take a lot longer. Are you still taking it?"

"I am, and as long as it helps me, I'm gonna keep on. My doctor says I'm doin' okay with it. I told him about Waycross, and he said some folks do fine, others not."

"Everybody's different, I guess."

"Reckon so." Gran pulled her feet back under her and scooted her chair a bit closer to the pit. She picked up a stick that someone had left propped near the flame, dug into a bag of marsh-mallows, and speared one.

"That's somethin' else about Dr. Liu, huh?" Savannah said. "Talk about a change in life circumstances. She goes from being the county's first female medical examiner to . . . well . . . where she is now."

"No kidding. When I heard about it, my head plum near spun right off."

"What's this?" Jennifer Liu said as she exited the back door of the mansion, a lemonade pitcher in her hand. "I believe I heard my name mentioned."

Savannah laughed. "You'd best get used to it."

"That's for sure," Granny said. "Folks are gonna be talkin' 'bout you so much your nose'll be itchin' and your ears burnin' day and night."

Jennifer refilled their glasses, then set the pitcher on a nearby table and took a chair next to Savannah's. She was dressed in a halter midi-blouse, three-inch high mules, and cuffed short-shorts that showed off her long legs to perfection.

"Some people have already told me to my face that I got off easy," she said.

"Don't pay buttinskies like that no nevermind." Granny held her marshmallows over the flame. "Some folks ain't satisfied with anythin' less than a tarrin' and a featherin' and a ride outta town on a pole."

"A couple of months in jail and a year's suspension of your license, those aren't exactly a slap on the wrist," Savannah said.

"I think my critics could have handled the fact that I didn't get the needle a bit better if it hadn't been for my unexpected windfall." She waved a hand, indicating the house and surrounding land.

Savannah chuckled. "That's so true. I couldn't help noticing that most of the complaints popped up *after* Brianne's will was read."

"I, for one, am tickled pink for you," Granny said, sampling her toasted-black marshmallow. "You put yourself in the hot seat in order to catch a killer, and that makes you all right in my book. Nobody deserves this place more'n you."

"I don't know about that." Jennifer looked around her newly-acquired domain. "It never occurred to me that Brianne would make me her heir, over her fiancé and her brother."

Savannah shrugged. "She was about to dump ol' Paul, and from what I heard, she'd already decided that her brother was more interested in her money than having a relationship with her."

"I'm afraid that's true."

Granny added, "Besides, her brother would have squandered it like he did his own. You'll use this place for good in her memory."

"I'm sure going to try." Jennifer looked up the hill to the goat pen, where Dirk was introducing Vanna Rose to the miniature crime solvers. "I've offered to hold Dr. Kendall's meetings here, now that she's, um, otherwise occupied for the next fifty years. One of the women in the group has volunteered to lead the meetings. Afterward, everybody, especially the kids, can go up the hill and pet the goats or ride the horses. Dee wants to stay on and be involved in all of it." She paused, swallowed, and added tearfully, "I think Brianne would like that."

"I know she would love it," Savannah assured her. "No doubt that's why she left this place to you. She knew you'd use it to help others. Besides, she knew that it would remind you of all the good times the two of you shared . . . as it did her."

Jennifer just sniffed and nodded.

Savannah heard some splashing and saw that Tammy and her brother were getting out of the pool.

"He's looking good," Jennifer remarked as they watched Waycross stride over to them, limp-free, his arm tight around his wife's waist.

"He *is* good," Savannah said. "He's great."

When the young couple joined them, Waycross plopped himself down on a chaise and pulled Tammy onto his lap. "When's our birthday boy gonna come down from that goat pen? I'm gettin' hungry for that cake!"

"Your daughter's done waylaid 'im," Granny said. "It does my heart good to see how much them two enjoy each other's company."

"Who would've thought?" Jennifer added dryly.

"Me," Savannah told her. "He's not as bad as you think."

"Hey, I know. I know." She held up both hands in surrender. "I have to treat him with love and respect."

"Well, *respect* anyway."

"If it weren't for each and every one of you, I'd probably be in jail right now."

Waycross turned and saw Dee, Ryan, and John galloping up the road and turning toward the barn. He pinched Tammy's rear and said, "Whaddaya think, sugar? Is it time yet? I don't reckon I can wait much longer. I'm fixin' to bust."

"I never heard you so eager to dig into a piece of birthday cake," Savannah said.

"Oh, it's not just the cake that he's looking forward to. It's his big secret," Tammy said.

"Secret?" Savannah asked. "Why, Waycross Reid. You've got a secret, and you didn't tell your big sister about it?"

"I couldn't," he replied with a big grin. "You and Dirk made me swear I'd never tell either of y'all a secret I couldn't tell you both. And this is one you couldn't tell him."

"Um. Okay. I guess. What is it?"

Tammy stood and pulled Waycross to his feet. "Everybody's here now. Let's show them."

Savannah watched as Tammy and her brother headed in the direction of the animal enclosures. She turned to Jennifer and Granny. "I guess we better go see what it is."

"Wild horses couldn't stop me," Granny said as she abandoned her marshmallows and stick and started up the hill.

Savannah caught up with her and took her arm, while Jennifer followed them.

"Come on over here, Dirk-o," Tammy shouted as she and Waycross headed for the barn.

Dee, Ryan, and John released the horses into

the corral, then joined them, wearing broad smiles on their faces.

"Somethin' tells me them three are in on it," Granny said. "Unlike you and me."

"Or at least they know what it is." Savannah saw Waycross opening the barn door. "Oh, Lord, please don't let it be a horse. He needs a horse like he needs a sixth piece of birthday cake."

"It ain't a horse," Waycross said, having overheard his sister. "I think you'll approve."

As Dirk approached the barn, Tammy took Vanna from his arms and waved him toward Waycross. "Go on," she said. "This is just between you guys. I've had nothing at all to do with it."

"O-o-o-kay." Dirk gave her a suspicious look then walked over to Waycross.

Savannah watched, her heart full and warm, as her brother draped his long, skinny arm over her husband's broad shoulders.

"I wanted to do something sorta special for you this year," Waycross said, "but not just on account of what you did for me a few months back. Truth be told, I'd done started this before that. But once I got out of that clinic and pulled myself together a bit, I thought about where I'd be without my brother-in-law, and I set my mind to get this done for you."

"O-o-o-kay," Dirk repeated, giving his brother-in-law an even more wary look.

Opening the barn door wider, Waycross said, "Go on in there, big boy, and tell me if I done good."

Dirk turned and gave Savannah a questioning, helpless look.

She laughed and waved him on. "I can't help you, darlin'. I have no idea what it is. Go in and find out."

"Yes," Granny said. "The suspense is fixin' to kill me."

Dirk walked inside with Waycross beside him, Savannah behind him, and the rest bringing up the rear.

The first thing Savannah saw was a powder blue fender, glistening in the light of the setting sun. Then, as Ryan and John pulled both of the barn doors completely open, letting in even more light, the 1962 Buick Skylark was fully revealed in all its exquisitely restored grandeur.

Savannah couldn't recall ever seeing a more beautiful vehicle.

Except, of course, her own Mustang.

She heard her husband gasp in a way that she had only heard come out of boxers who had caught a direct blow to the solar plexus.

"Well? Do you like it?" Waycross asked him, giggling.

"Like . . . it . . . do I . . . do I . . . like it?" Dirk reached out and touched the side panel with one finger, as though to convince himself it was real. "It looks . . . looks just like my old car!"

"That's because it *is* your old car," Waycross said, patting Dirk on the back.

"It can't be! After the wreck, the junkyard told me they were gonna smash it. 'Flat as a Frisbee,' they said."

"Yeah, I know." Waycross laughed. "I told 'em to say that. I bought it off 'em for fifty bucks."

"But . . . but it was *totaled!*"

"Eh, one man's 'totaled' is another guy's 'restorable.' "

Dirk turned to Savannah. "You told me to move on, give it up, put a period to my grief. You told me that my Buick had gone to Automobile Heaven, where all good cars go."

Savannah was as flabbergasted as Dirk. "I really thought it had! I swear, I had no idea about any of this."

She walked up to the car and looked thorough the windshield at the interior that was impeccably restored. She had never seen the car looking so pristine—or even basically tidy, for that matter—before the terrible wreck they'd suffered inside it.

She grabbed her brother and enfolded him in a bear hug that took his breath away. "I can't believe this, sugar! I can't even imagine all the work you had to do to . . . oh, Waycross!"

The others were crowding around the car and were adding their praises to the cacophony.

"Splendid job, lad!" John exclaimed. "Can't say as I've ever seen its match!"

"Really," Ryan said. "You outdid yourself, Waycross. Fantastic!"

"I'm mighty proud of you, grandson," Granny said. "I declare, when you set your mind to somethin', you keep at 'er till she's done!"

She pushed Savannah away so that she could hug him even harder.

He blushed, turning bright red under the praise. Or from his grandmother's embrace. It was hard to tell. "Shucks. I didn't work that hard. It ain't work if you're enjoyin' it."

He walked over to Dirk and opened the driver's door. "Hop in. Try it on for size."

Dirk started to get in, then bent over and looked at something under the dash. "Holy cow," he whispered. "This really *is* my old car." He turned to Waycross. "This is like a miracle. Man, I'm gonna owe you forever!"

"Aw, you don't own me nothin', brother." Waycross laughed heartily, the laugh of a man with his debts paid and his conscience clean. "I reckon I might've," he said, "but I don't now, huh?"

"That's for sure." Dirk got into the driver's seat, reached across, and opened the passenger door. He waved to Savannah. "Come on, Van. Let's take her for a spin!"

Feeling like a sixteen-year-old going on her first date, Savannah climbed inside. Moments later, Dirk was driving it carefully out of the barn.

"See ya in a few!" he shouted out the window as they took off.

"Seriously, did you know about this?" Dirk asked her the moment they reached the road.

"Nope. Nothin'. Nada. Zippo. Remember, we tell each other everything now."

Dirk revved the old muscle car up as they sped through the canyon. "She runs like new. Better than she ever did!"

"That's because Waycross Reid tuned her up. He's famous for that back home. They say you can lay your hand on the hood of a car he's tuned and not even feel a vibration."

Her curiosity getting the better of her, Savannah leaned down and tried to see beneath the dash. "What was it you were looking at?" she asked.

"Huh?"

"Before you got in, you looked under here some-where and said, 'Holy cow, this really is my old car.' How did you know for sure?"

"Nothin'. Just somethin' I sorta scratched under there one time. No big deal."

"Yeah, well, I know you pretty well, and from the embarrassed look on your face, I'd say it *is* a big deal. Or, at least, a medium deal."

She leaned down farther and searched again. "You say it's scratches that I'm supposed to be looking for?"

"No. You're *not* supposed to be lookin' for nothin'. You should just mind your own business."

"I can't imagine that my little brother would go to all the trouble to restore this car and leave some scratches behind."

"He probably figured I wouldn't want them pol-ished out or painted over or whatever."

She leaned down a bit farther and saw them . . . two letters that looked like they had been hastily scratched into the finish with a crude tool, like a key.

She sat back up, fluffed her hair, and straight-ened her shirt. "So . . . when did you scratch my initials under your dash, darlin'?" she asked.

"The day I met you."

"Really?"

"Yeah. Really."

"Why?"

"Because I knew, right then and there, that I wanted you with me, everywhere I went, from that day on."

"Oh." Tears welled up in her eyes. "That's, just . . . oh, darlin', that's just so, so sweet."

He growled. "Yeah, yeah. Just what every manly man wants to hear. That he's 'sweet.' "

She leaned over and rested her head on his shoulder. "How about if, instead, I tell you . . . 'Those initials, and the fact that you scratched them there the day you met me, has earned you the hottest, steam-shootin'-outta-your-ears birthday night in the history of manly men'?"

He growled again. Much deeper than before. "*Now* you're talkin'!"

Author's Note

Dear Readers,

As I began the research necessary to write this book, I became aware of a group of people whom, I'm ashamed to say, I knew little about. I'd heard of Huntington's, cystic fibrosis, and some other fatal genetic diseases. But I had no idea how many of these disorders there are in the world, or how many people suffer from them.

We, who haven't faced the terrible challenges these individuals and their families deal with on a daily basis, have no concept of what they're going through. How could we? Life's worst horrors must be lived to be fully understood.

But, even if we'll never know what they experience, we can at least be more knowledgeable about them and what they face. By learning about them, we may shed some tears, but we will be richer for it. Not only will we appreciate many of the things we now take for granted, but we can open our hearts to the inspiration they offer with their stories of courage, determination, love, and their fierce desire to live each day to the most and leave this world a better place than they found it.

Whether you are basically unaware of their struggles, or someone living in the fear that you may have inherited one of these disorders, or a person who is in the throes of their illness, or someone whose loved one is . . . please take the time to click on the links below and read some of the articles. If you need help, encouragement, or simply information, you may discover what you're looking for there. These sites can assist you in finding a local support group, where (unlike the poor characters in this story) you'll receive encouragement from people who know exactly what you're going through, because your trials are theirs.

Not only will you be given practical help at a support group, but you'll have the opportunity to share, inform, and uplift others in a way that most other people can't, because they don't have the hard-earned knowledge that you have. You know, even better than their physicians, what they're going through and how to deal with day-to-day problems. You may be forced to walk this difficult road, but you don't have to walk it alone.

May you find the answers you need, as well as peace and comfort. And may we all find a true purpose for this life we've been given. Whatever its length.

Sincerely,

Sonja Massie (G. A. McKevett)

National Institutes of Health
https://rarediseases.info.nih.gov
Phone: 1-888-205-2311
Guides for Patients and Families
https://rarediseases.info.nih.gov/guides/pages/96/patients-families-and-friends